Pilgrims of Valdeor

Book 3 in the Valdeor Chronicles

Sandralena Hanley

The Valdeor Chronicles

Book One
Champion of Valdeor

Book Two
Waykeepers of Valdeor

Book Three
Pilgrims of Valdeor

Editing by Jacinta Patterson
Cover by Emily Anne Hickman
Interior Formatting by Michelle M. Bruhn

ISBN: 978-1-7377398-2-1

Dedicated to my fans
especially Leo, Perpetua, Danny, and Carl

Table of Contents

CANTEOR

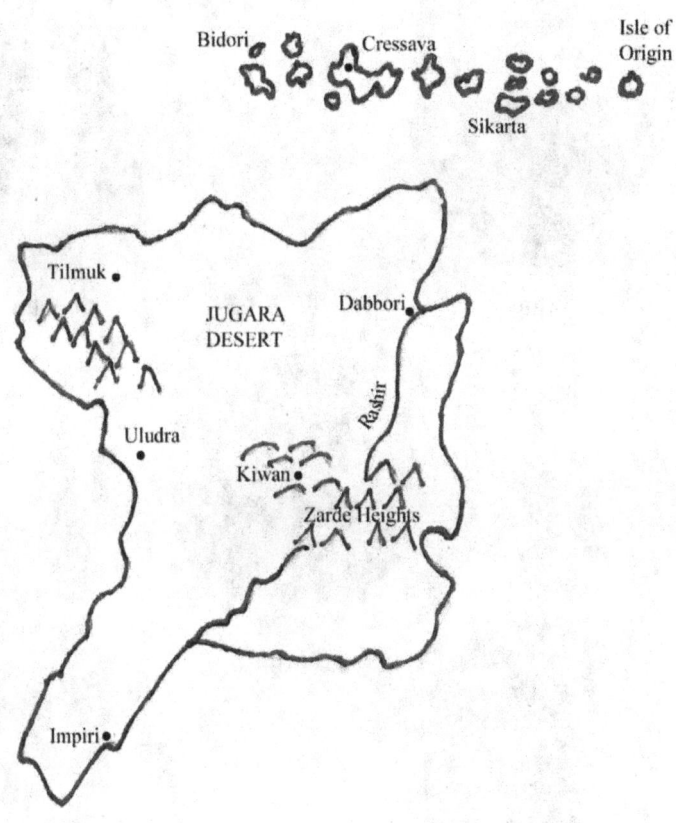

Bidori Cressava Isle of Origin

Sikarta

Tilmuk

JUGARA
DESERT

Dabbori

Uludra

Rashir

Kiwan

Zarde Heights

Impiri

Guy

Donella

Barbu

Gensard

Jiana

Andro

Sefira

Lauressa

Alloyrn

*All the paths of the Lord are
mercy and truth to those who
observe His covenant and
precepts.*
Psalm 24:10

1 Mission to Canteor

*G*uy stood disoriented in the night. Dark clouds scudded across the half moon. The cold breeze penetrated his cloak and tunic, right into his bones. Fear beat a drum in his gut.

Figures moved in the black and white world. Dark shapes against a crack of light.

He must stop them!

He couldn't remember why, but his brain screamed for him to move. His feet couldn't make headway. It was as if he were slogging through molasses.

Mist swirled around the base of the crack of light. A portal! An image of the palace of Mintala, its tower of twinkling stones, appeared in the center of the mist.

No! Guy reached out to close the portal and save the Reina.

Suddenly, two dark figures materialized beside him. They were dressed all in black, cloaks waving in the wind. The moon peeked out, illuminating their hoods. Where their faces should be, only black holes existed.

Guy sprang back, but not before he felt their blades enter his side and shoulder. He cried out with the pain.

Something tangled around him, pinning him in place. Guy fought back. He sat up and found himself in his bed, the blanket wound about him. He let out a breath.

Another nightmare.

He had dreamed of the day he closed the portal against the assassins sent to kill Reina Lauressa.

Reina Lauressa was fine, probably asleep in her wing of the palace. He and his waykeeper friends had alerted her and her husband, Prince Alloryn, of the Canteor invasion in time for them to stop it.

An image of the Guardian of Valdeor, the winged being of light, flashed in Guy's memory. "The portal is not meant for war," he warned Guy, after Guy had used the portal to funnel troops to different ports as the Canteor fleet attacked.

Guy absently rubbed his shoulder, more out of a desire to make sure it was not injured. But it had finally healed. An occasional ache was all that was left.

Light streamed from a crack in the curtains of his room in the palace. From experience, he knew he wouldn't be able to fall asleep after a nightmare.

Pushing aside the bedclothes, he stumbled to the ewer of water, poured it into the matching bowl, and splashed his face with cool water. He hurriedly ran a brush through his straw-colored hair. Nothing he did made it lie flat, so he didn't even try. More awake, with the dream fading, he sought the dining hall and some breakfast.

The closer he got, the stronger the smell of bacon and eggs wafted down the hall, drawing Guy in. His stomach grumbled.

Donella was there before him, her dark ringlets flowing down her back. Not surprising since she was an early riser.

She was a few months younger than his seventeen years.

She looked up from buttering her toasted bread. "You're up early." She smiled, then as she studied him, her expression changed.

No doubt she saw his tired eyes. After months of living at the palace, they knew each other very well. Unlike him, she was very observant of the people around her.

"Is your shoulder bothering you? I have some salve."

She made her own herbal medicines or knew where to get them. She was adept at procuring the right potion to help, although they tended to smell awful.

"No, my shoulder is fine."

"Good to hear it." Her pearly white teeth bit into her food.

Guy helped himself to the warm eggs and topped them with several slices of bacon. He dug in with a good appetite.

Donella smeared a blob of butter on a second piece of bread. "So, what's bothering you?"

He should have known she wouldn't drop the subject. He shrugged one shoulder. "I didn't sleep well." And as she opened her mouth, he continued, "And no, I don't need a sleeping potion." At the hurt look on her face, he tempered it with, "It leaves me groggy in the morning."

She narrowed her eyes. "Nightmares?" She must have seen the truth in his face. "Oh, Guy that happened months ago. You saved the Reina by banishing those men." She reached for the teapot and poured a cup, which she pushed toward him. "You have to let go of your guilt."

Easy for her to say. Guy looked at the interlocking symbols on the back of his left hand. He was the strongest waykeeper in generations. Maybe ever. He had wrested the portal control from the three invaders as they stepped through and sent them into a whirlwind in a distant land. He had probably killed them. No matter that he still bore the scars from that encounter.

He shook off his gloomy thoughts. "Are you ready for your language lessons?" He hoped to divert her thoughts.

She washed her fingers in the bowl of water provided for that and wiped them on a napkin. "Oh, yes! What are we practicing today?"

"I thought we'd run down to the market by the river. Hiram, my friend, is in town. He knows the Canteor language better than I. I thought we could both use some time with him. He learned the language as a child. He far surpasses my ability after one month aboard the Canteor pirate ship."

"The fisherman's son, right? He's the one who helped you escape the pirate ship, isn't he?" Donella sipped and put down her teacup. She pushed away from the table and followed Guy from the table.

"Yes. If it weren't for his friendship, I think the pirates would have thrown me overboard to the sea monsters. Hiram taught me to climb the mast and watch for storms and land."

"I don't know what I would have done with my time all these months without your language lessons and Odem's defense lessons." Donella twisted a strand of her hair around her finger.

Guy knew the feeling. He was grateful that the Reina housed them, letting them continue learning their craft as waykeepers from her extensive library, while Valdeor prepped for war. Their unique ability to travel across vast distances through the portals made them powerful yet vulnerable. But the Guardian of Valdeor's quest, telling Guy to find the shrine on the Isle of Origin, was like an itch under his skin these many months. Only the fact that his shoulder and side needed healing kept him from seeking it out before now.

The throne room in the Mintala palace was circular in shape and two stories high. Six giant gems, in the colors of the rainbow, representing the virtues of courage, justice, moderation, wisdom, faith and hope, sparkled from evenly spaced embrasures. The stones shone on the center of the room where a small pedestal stood before the throne. The seventh jewel, a diamond representing charity, twinkled there in the reflected light.

A beautiful woman sat upon the throne. She wore a white lace gown that shimmered with the gems' colors as she shifted. Her chestnut hair encircled with a pearl tiara was swept up from her face.

Guy felt abashed as he gazed at Reina Lauressa, ruler of Valdeor. She had called him for a private audience. Her garb and the place she chose to speak with him let him know that she met with him as his sovereign.

"You have proven yourself a powerful waykeeper. I have a new mission for you, Gyfar. I need agents on the ground in Canteor. I want to know the numbers and strength of the army and navy. I want to know everything about Prince Pashmi. I want to know why he fights this war with Valdeor. And is he open to negotiation with me?"

Guy grew more and more uncomfortable as the Reina spoke. She only used his full name at her most serious. Like when she had a mission for him. He fought the urge to squirm.

"I am not a spy, your majesty. I'm a simple farm boy." He rubbed his sweaty palms on his trousers.

Lauressa tilted her head. "The mark on your hand says otherwise," she said, gently. "The One Who Fashioned All Things gave you that symbol and the power to wield it for a purpose."

Reina Lauressa's words echoed others who told him the same thing, including Donella the first day she met him. Even the winged Guardian of Valdeor had said something similar.

Guy dropped his eyes from her knowing gaze and contemplated the floor in front of him, rubbing his earlobe. He thought back to the previous fall. The last time he said yes to her, he had been stabbed in the shoulder and rib cage while blocking conspirators from invading this palace. Hence the nightmares.

And the winged Guardian of Valdeor had also given him a quest. *Find the Isle of Origin.*

Guy raised his eyes and locked with Lauressa's green glance.

"I will ferry others to Canteor if I can figure out how. But I have been tasked by the One Who Fashioned All to find His lost shrine."

Lauressa's eyes widened. "Gyfar, why didn't you tell me? When did this happen?"

"I saw the Guardian of Valdeor when I was traveling between places. I thought the sun was rising through the portal, but a being of light materialized before me." Guy paused.

"I have seen him myself a couple of times." Her expression was solemn. Her eyes distant, as if reliving it.

Guy gasped with astonishment. He had heard the story of how she was hidden for a century and found by her champion. The fact that the winged Guardian had something to do with it was not so surprising once he thought about it.

He swallowed and went on. "He said the portals are not for war."

Putting her chin in her hand, Lauressa leaned an arm on the chair, a crease between her brows. "I see. I hadn't considered that their use might be restricted. Go on."

"Well, later when I stopped the Canteorans all over Valdeor from using portals to attack here—"

"What? I thought they were only coming from Prince Alloryn's camp." She straightened.

"No, Your Majesty. I entered the portal when I summoned the storm. That's when I felt multiple invasion points. I blocked them all, except for Donella sending Prince Gensard to your rescue."

"I'm thankful for that." She rested her hand on her enlarged belly. "He saved not only my life, but that of my child."

"Then while I lay wounded, after the Canteor assassins attacked me as I held the gate against them, the Guardian told me I was the Gifted One. He said I was meant to find and reopen the great shrine to the One Who Fashioned All. The pilgrims used the portals in ancient times to visit it and worship Him. If I do not, Valdeor will lose the faith."

Guy bit his lip. He didn't know where to start to fulfill his quest. He wasn't sure he could find the lost Isle of Origin where the shrine was located. And, if he did, how did he bring the pilgrims to it?

"I see. Your mission is as great as mine." Lauressa tapped her fingers on her chair arm. "But I must defend Valdeor from the pagans who would decimate her. I think that if you do not send troops through this time, we would not be disobeying his command. What if you send Prince Gensard and Commander Odem to Canteor as my spies? I think the Guardian would accept that. Then you are free to pursue your quest."

Guy scratched his cheek. "I think I can do that. Thank you, Your Majesty."

"I'll see you in the morning." Lauressa dismissed him.

Guy bowed and left the throne room.

He entered the grand hall. Mirrors reflected the candles lighting the way, giving a larger feel to the place, and making him think a thousand eyes winked at him.

He ran into Donella as she entered from one of the many doors that led into it.

"Would you come with me on the Reina's errand?" Guy blurted out before he lost courage. He matched his steps to her smaller ones as they traversed the corridor.

"Go where with you?" Donella sounded distracted as she studied her myriad reflections.

"To Canteor. Then to find the Isle of Origin." Guy huffed when she stopped walking and he plowed into her.

"You want me to come with you?" He heard the surprise in her voice. "Really?" Her eyes opened wide, and she grinned at him.

"That is what I just said." Guy looked away from her face and at his toe scraping along the floor. "I might be able to get us there, but I am not cut out to be a spy. I know the language, but you are better at playing a part."

"Oh, so I lie easier than you do, is that what you are saying?"

Guy looked up horrified. "No, no, that is not what I meant. You are just so—" he struggled for the right words, "—so good with people. You know just how to come across. I am only good at sticking my foot in my mouth." He lifted a shoulder, looking at her hopefully.

"Well, you got that right. I am a good spy." Her lips twisted in a wry grin. "And sometimes I can lie. Always in a good cause, of course." Her eyes twinkled.

"Then you'll come?"

"You couldn't stop me."

Guy's candle guttered down, and still he lay awake.

Why did everyone expect so much of him because of a birthmark? Reina Lauressa could easily command Commander Odem, who wore a waykeeper's ring, to open the portal and travel through it with Prince Gensard.

Prince High and Mighty would be more than happy to take on the entire invader's army to prove himself the best swordsman in Valdeor. Maybe even the best swordsman in all of history itself, so proud was he.

Guy was no spy.

His gift lay in the ability to travel through the portals to anywhere, even places he had not seen. Which was unique among the order of waykeepers he belonged to.

Which was of course why the Reina asked him and not Commander Odem to open the portal to Canteor.

He understood the danger Canteor represented—a pagan people bent on conquering Valdeor. Reina Lauressa had only taken the crown five years previously, after a century of civil war and depraved rulership by warlords.

The peace she brought was still fragile, the treaties with the princes of the realm untested.

The Reina was worried and so she asked him to use his power, But the Guardian had a different path for him. Maybe his purpose would negate the need for war.

Guy determined he would do as the Reina asked as soon as he could. She was guided by the heartstones of virtue, after all. But then he would immediately leave Odem and Gensard to their task and turn his attention to seeking out the shrine.

Guy's thoughts strayed to the pretty, dark-haired girl. At least Donella would join Guy on his mission. He would have liked to have Usher, his mentor, along, but he understood the older waykeeper would not be up to the demands of a long, dangerous journey into foreign lands.

Guy was not sure he was up to it either.

Could he open a doorway to another land across the sea? Guy's mind boggled at crossing such distances with a single leap.

He remembered his dream of the maze. *Many specks of light twinkled below me, as if on a map, while I floated above the world. I saw Valdeor from the air. Hadn't I seen the brightest light a long distance from the others beyond the continent? Did the message of the dream vision mean I could reach that far?*

Guy longed to wake Usher and ask the questions churning in his brain. He toyed with the thought of going into the archives and asking the archivists his questions. Would they be able to answer them?

His thoughts were going round in circles. Maybe tomorrow would show the way. Guy reached over and blew out the candle.

The next morning, Guy and Donella gathered with Odem and Usher in the throne room. Reina Lauressa sat erect on her throne, her baby bump very prominent. She wore an elaborate crown, and the medallion of her office was prominently displayed on her chest. There was no softness in her eyes today. She seemed regal and unapproachable.

Prince Gensard strolled in as if he owned the palace.

The Reina announced her plan for Guy to use a waypost to jump them over the seas to the land of the invaders. Guy fidgeted. He might succeed or he might fail.

"But is that even possible?" Usher glanced from her to Guy.

A stone settled in Guy's stomach. Usher's words disheartened him. If the head of the waykeeper order doubted his ability, could he possibly succeed? And, yet what choice did they have?

As Reina Lauressa pointed out, she could not summon a fleet out of desire. "It has been half a year since the assault on the palace. Even though we have started to establish a fleet, it takes time to build ships and train sailors."

"The next invasion will come again by sea," Odem muttered.

"I suppose reaching Canteor might be accomplished by jumping through a portal." Usher rubbed his bald head. "I would think the closer to Canteor you start from, Guy, the better the chances of success. I only wish I were going with you. But I have determined that I can best serve by training more waykeepers."

Considering there were only six waykeepers, the need had become more apparent when they served as couriers during the multi-point invasion last autumn.

Usher advised the Reina against having them start from the waypost within the palace compound.

"I agree. The portal is only to be used in emergencies," Lauressa pronounced.

"I believe the longer a waypost is not activated, the less likely it'll be found by a new user, namely the enemy. I feared it was my use of the waypost that alerted the enemy to its location." Usher shrunk in on himself. "Which ultimately led to the attack on the palace."

Guy was thankful not to be put on the spot before the palace staff again, like when he opened two portals to let the troops go to two locations simultaneously.

Lauressa gripped her hands on her throne. "I sent my husband, Prince Alloryn, to inspect the shipyards in Tulken Harbor and Laketown. He is also mustering forces from the Domadaria, Samarantha, and Winterhome provinces. They haven't fought as one since the provinces faced Warlord Feornson and his army of mercenaries. But my cause united them to put me on the throne. And they rallied against the recent Canteor invasion. Now that all Valdeor is threatened, I hope they come together again and face it, putting aside petty bickering."

Guy hoped the prince had success. He had been gone for weeks.

"Which is why Prince Alloryn is not going with you. But I will send Prince Gensard in his place."

Gensard smirked.

Guy groaned inwardly. *Prince Gensard? Who betrayed them once, seeking to impress everyone and leaving Guy, Odem and Donella to face wolves?*

Donella piped up, "I'm traveling with them, too." She lifted her chin at the frowns sent her way.

"I do not think that is wise. I can use your listening skills—," Lauressa began.

"Then you will have to lock me in the dungeon," Donella interrupted, crossing her arms. "I can be more valuable helping Guy on his mission."

"We don't need children along. It's bad enough the farm boy needs open the way. Odem and I can handle it ourselves."

Donella ignored Prince Gensard's words, but she bristled with suppressed anger. "I was thinking on it last night. We can disguise ourselves as merchants. I know the best rug dealer in

Valdeor. I can persuade him to give us carpets for our merchandise."

"Her idea has merit." Odem stood up for her.

"I want her to come," Guy added his voice.

Lauressa's expression softened slightly. She was silent, considering Donella's plea. "Very well. But—"

Donella did a happy step.

"—on the condition that you learn the language and how to defend yourself."

"I've already started, Your Majesty." She grinned. "In the months since the assault, Guy gave me speech lessons and Commander Odem taught me to how to defend myself with a dagger."

Guy had learned the Canteor language while captive aboard the pirate ship. He found Donella a fast study.

Guy's heart stuttered at the thought of her in danger. And yet she belonged to their band. She would never consider staying behind.

Keeping the mission a secret, the group set off on horseback without any fanfare just before dawn the following week. It had rained the previous evening, making the air crisp and leaving the grass sparkling with drops. The earth smelled fresh.

Spring had finally come out of hibernation.

They rode toward the southeastern seaboard. Guy rode Seeker, accompanied by Donella and Odem riding on either side. Prince Gensard rode his stallion in the rear leading a pack horse with rugs for their cover story. Donella had acquired them from her friend the rug merchant.

At least Odem oversaw this mission, not the prince.

The fields of newly planted wheat surrounded them as they left Mintala, the capital, behind. Guy idly wondered how his stepmother was managing on the farm. Planting season had arrived. He visualized the garden and fields, and all the work to be done, before the rainy season that preceded summer.

By late afternoon, the riders had journeyed past the fields and rode into the rolling hills surrounding the city.

As they struck camp that evening, Prince Gensard kept to himself. He seemed to expect the others to gather wood and make the fire, and to cook a meal. The only thing he looked after, besides himself, was his horse, Fiery.

He had traveled home to Samarantha after rescuing the Reina. When he returned a month ago, he rode his personal stallion.

"I'm amazed that Prince Gensard cares for anything other than himself," Guy told Donella, when he brought pails of water from the nearby spring.

"They make a good pair." She dumped a load of brush down to start the fire and tossed her hair from her eyes. "Both are stubborn with a temper."

Guy snorted in agreement.

The prince was out of hearing range, wiping his stallion down after the ride.

Odem busied himself with the stewpot, raising an eyebrow at their words, but he didn't reprimand them.

"Why must he come along? Why not Prince Alloryn?" Donella grumbled. She had changed her allegiance from one prince to another, not that Guy blamed her. Prince Gensard had astounded them with his sword fighting prowess upon their first meeting. And Guy had to admit, Gensard was extremely handsome with his devil may care attitude and thick, curly, dirty blond hair.

Guy's own hair was like wheat—that color and annoyingly unruly. He was lean, but no one would call him handsome. Boyish, maybe.

Whereas Prince Alloryn, the Reina's husband, was everything

a boy dreamed of growing up to be—handsome, muscular, confident, yet not condescending. A true warrior. A champion.

"We've already gone over this," Odem chided her. "Prince Alloryn is raising an army to repel the invaders. Do you want to find yourself amongst the enemy with only my sword to protect you?" He squatted beside the fire, adding ingredients to the pot.

Donella pouted, gathering sweet grass for the horses in great clumps. "I'll admit, he is the best swordsman I've ever seen. He turned the tide when I sent him to Reina Lauressa's aid." She glanced over to where Gensard was checking the stallion's hooves for pebbles.

"The prince has potential. No one is all bad."

Both Guy and Donella stopped what they did and frowned at Odem.

"What? Are you always perfect?" Odem looked sternly from one to the other. "Donella, you can act rashly and not think things through."

Donella bit her lip. Guy nodded in agreement.

"And you, Guy," Odem pinned him with a stare, "you hold back from acting, out of fear of the consequences."

Guy wriggled and looked away from Donella's knowing glance. Odem touched a raw point.

"Even I tend to overthink things." Odem paused in his work. Stirring the stew, he spoke seriously, "The One Who Fashioned All brought us together for this mission. We each have a role to play. Our individual weaknesses are less than our combined strengths. Gensard is part of His divine plan, too." He gestured at them with his ladle. "Let us see how things play out. Be patient with the prince."

"I'll try." Donella sighed.

By nightfall of the next day, they were in the hills that eventually led to the Blue Range, several days away. The foothills were visible in the distance but sank from view as their path followed alongside the Windmyr River through lush green valleys. Towns nestled among orchards of cherry and apple trees.

The pink blossoms fluttered in the breeze.

Guy urged his horse to ride beside Donella. "A copper for your thoughts."

Dimples peeked out as she smiled. She wore a faded cherry-red cloak over a plain brown wool dress. The splash of color brought out the roses in her cheeks.

"Do you know exactly where Odem is leading us? You showed us a map of the wayposts from the archives, but how do you know which portal to use? Any one on the coast facing Canteor?" She tilted her head.

"In my vision, I saw at least three wayposts that shone brighter than the rest. I'm not sure what that meant, but one of them is at the southeast tip of Valdeor. That's where we're heading. I won't know if I can send us across the seas until we get there."

"But has anyone jumped that far before? Not that I'm getting cold feet."

Guy rubbed the tip of his nose. "I'm not certain, but Usher thinks it can be done. He found references in the archives. After all, the portals were built to ferry pilgrims from the Valdeor mainland to the Isle of Origin, wherever that is."

"You'll find the strength when we face the obstacle. You always have. Remember, you are the Gifted One." Donella's belief in him echoed in her voice.

They rode on in silence.

2 Bottoms Up Tavern

*T*he foursome continued along the Windmyr's banks. At the end of a week, fog-filled valleys replaced the orchards as they rode into the lowlands. Lone dwellings sat amongst the encroaching reeds as the land turned into marshes. Sickly smelling vapors rose in the air. Strange slurping sounds broke the silence interspersed with sad, crying bird calls. It was a land of mud and water and reeds.

Donella preferred the orchards they had recently passed through. The gloom depressed her naturally high spirits.

"Stay on the road. The quicksand can pull your horse into the mud. Reptiles with enormous snouts full of teeth float in the waters. They can easily kill a horse," Odem warned them.

"And they will eat a man as well." Riding beside Donella, Prince Gensard laid his scimitar across his legs. "If you encounter a lagator, stab at its eyes. The skin is tough, turning all but the sharpest sword away. Boots made from their hide are highly prized among my people."

Donella shuddered. She put her hand on the dagger Odem had given her to reassure herself it was still there. "Ugh! Will making noise keep them away?"

Odem shook his head no. "They generally avoid people, but be careful not to rouse one."

The road narrowed into a path that two horses couldn't ride side-by-side, so they rode singly. Odem took the lead, followed by Prince Gensard, Donella, then Guy following her as the flank guard, leading the pack horse.

Donella's eyes darted back and forth as she saw flickers of movement in the gloom. A reed waved in the air. A duck floated on the brackish water. A startled bird took wing, making her heart nearly leap out of her chest. She spotted a rough log floating a dozen feet away. With a start, she realized two bumps on it were eyes.

"On the left! Reptile!" Her heart beat against her ribcage.

Metal scraped as Odem drew his sword. The paddling duck drifted closer to the beast. With a quicksilver movement, the giant lizard leapt at the fowl, exposing huge rows of teeth, before it clenched the duck and dove under the water with it.

"Ride!" Odem commanded, and they all kicked their skittery horses into motion.

Donella's horse didn't need much encouragement to get away, as it nickered in fear. Mud from Gensard's steed, Fiery, splattered her as she kept her mare on his heels.

After fifteen minutes, they slowed their horses back to a walk. Before them was a narrow wooden bridge spanning a murky, sluggish stream. A smell of rotten eggs permeated the air.

"I will cross first. I think it best that we ford it singly. The wood seems rotted in some areas." Odem urged his gelding onto the bridge with no rails. The animal strode confidently across.

Prince Gensard followed. His stallion tossed his mane and backed up before Gensard got him under control. Donella was amazed to see him calm the steed with soft words instead of the whip she expected him to pull out. The horse cautiously trod the wooden planks and made it to the other side.

Her own mare gave her no trouble starting across but stopped halfway. She flattened her ears and swung her head side to side refusing to budge. Donella spoke soothingly. When that didn't work, she kicked her heels. The horse moved a few steps and stopped. Donella felt the mare tremble.

Maybe it wasn't the click of the shod hooves on the wooden planks that spooked her animal.

Donella scanned the area, searching for the source of the horse's fear. She spotted a lagator floating fifty feet away.

"Donella! On your right!" Guy cried.

"I see it!" Donella's heartbeat accelerated and her hands shook on the reins. Not enough room to dismount. The mare refused to move even as Donella kicked her harder.

The lagator swam closer.

Thwack! An arrow pierced through the lagator's right eye. The arrow must've entered the brain because the beast stopped.

Donella glanced behind her. Guy lowered his crossbow.

The marsh grasses exploded. A frenzy of reptiles swarmed their dead comrade's corpse.

Donella's horse leapt across the rest of the bridge, Seeker burst after her, carrying Guy, the pack horse on his heels. Back on solid land, the group galloped far away from the prehistoric monsters.

Donella gulped in air as reaction set in. She fought back tears as she realized how close she had come to being attacked by the lagator. What other dangers were in store for their band?

They left the marsh behind. In the following days, they journeyed out of the dank valley into the foothills of the southern end of Blue Range. The air changed to clear and sweet. From the bare foothills, they moved into a forest heavy with the scent of cedar wood. Thick, dark woods eventually gave over to open meadows and sweeping views of the delta spreading wide below them. The fresh scent of heather was churned up by the horses' hooves.

By the end of the second week, Donella could smell and taste salt in the air. An occasional sea gull flew overhead. The sea was near.

Odem and Gensard trotted ahead. Guy's horse trailed behind Donella, so she slowed down and came even with him.

She gave an enormous yawn.

"You seem tired lately." Guy frowned at her. "Do you feel well?"

"I've had nightmares of a reptile chasing at my heels. I wake many nights in a sweat. I never properly thanked you for saving my life that day."

"You're welcome. That lagator was nasty." He grew silent. Donella noticed he frequently seemed lost in his thoughts.

"You're awful quiet the closer we get to our destination. What's on your mind?" She cocked her head and gazed at him earnestly.

Guy glanced at her. He chewed on his lip. "I'm afraid of letting everyone down. It's so far to jump!" He sounded worried. "And the Guardian of Valdeor said the portals were not created for war. Will I be able to open it?"

"Well, you're not sending troops through, like you did last time. We're going to spy on the enemy, not fight him. Not quite the same." Donella was unsure if the difference was quibbling, and Guy didn't look convinced. Not having met the Guardian, she couldn't judge how he'd react.

"What was he like? The Guardian." She was slightly envious of his encounter with the supernatural.

Guy stared into the distance, a faraway look in his eyes. "A man made of light, streaming from him. He was slightly taller than me. Stern-faced. Power emanated from him. I felt he could see into my very soul."

"I wouldn't want to cross him." Donella shuddered.

Guy's eyes sought hers. "He wasn't terrifying." He rubbed the back of his neck. "Just very intense."

As the horses crested the next hill, the sea came into view. Without a word, they all stopped and stared. The blueness spread from horizon to horizon. The water sparkled in the clear sunshine, making Donella shade her eyes. Gulls cried overhead. A strong breeze blew off the water causing loose strands of her hair to swirl around her face. She brushed it back.

Guy scanned the crossroads before them. "I sense a waypost a week's ride east from here." He urged his horse forward and took the lead.

Donella stretched with her mind but couldn't sense anything. She was halfway across Valdeor, far away from her home and the wayposts she knew. It must be a part of Guy's gift and the mark on his hand. She needed to leave a token at every waypost in order to find it again.

When they first met, she had been envious of Guy's powers. She had overcome her jealousy. He was the Gifted One, not her, and she was alright with that.

A week on the coastal road brought them to a large town, the southernmost port city in Valdeor. Where the Glame River met the sea, Tulken Harbor's whitewashed houses shone with their green roofs. On a headland jutting into the water, a great cathedral with its emerald, green dome seemed to watch over the town. The harbor was deep enough for a ship to anchor, and many vessels bobbed in the swells—merchant ships, fishing boats, and a few new warships. On this side of the harbor was a shipyard busy with construction of Valdeor's fleet.

They rode up to a city gate, a watchtower looming over it. Entering through it, the main street opened wide before them.

Odem suggested they spend an evening at an inn. He wanted to hear the latest gossip. He chose Bottoms Up Tavern.

Donella was excited to revisit the bar where she had been a singer and a barmaid for several weeks the previous year. So much had happened since she and Guy had set up as spies in the town.

The place hadn't changed in the months since she worked there. The wooden bar, the cheerful fireplace, the tobacco smoke swirling overhead were all the same. The fat owner, Tolly, made them welcome. Cassie and Bess, the barmaids, whispered for her to visit them in their old attic room when the place shut down for the night.

She and Guy split from the men, sat at a table and ordered dinner.

Donella sighed. "I feel a sense of homecoming."

Guy sat across from her, near the window. He hunched his shoulders. "Not me. It's just down the road from here where the pirates pressed me into serving aboard their ship."

A pang of regret hit her as she thought how selfish she was, not realizing Guy would not feel the same about returning here.

"Those months of separation were hard." She swallowed.

She took a deep whiff of the lamb roast garnished with rosemary and the buttery potatoes on her plate when Bess brought it over. She savored the first bite. "Mm, delicious. I'm so tired of fish."

They ate in companionable silence.

Odem stood talking with the patrons at the bar, while Prince Gensard nursed an ale near the fireplace.

"I, for one, cannot wait to soak in a warm bath." Donella pronounced when she finished.

"And I'm looking forward to laying myself down in a real bed." Guy pushed away his empty plate.

As tired as she was, Donella waited until the tavern closed for the night before heading upstairs. She went past the floor with her room, climbing to the attic level. Entering her old bedroom, she looked around. The streaked mirror still stood on the washstand, warping her reflection.

The door opened behind her, and the girls entered.

Bess gave her a quick hug. "Fancy you here as a guest."

"And who's the cute guy you were sitting with?" Cassie giggled.

Donella blushed.

She had decided to tell them part of the truth. As much as Donella trusted the girls, loose lips endangered everyone in Valdeor. "A friend of mine. We're on a mission from the Reina."

The girls' eyes grew big. "You're joshing." Cassie raised her brows, but her voice held a question.

"No. Did you see the soldiers come through the wayposts?"

Cassie leaned forward, her right hand rubbing her plump left arm. "You mean the doorways between places?"

"Yes, we are mapping their locations so the Reina can protect against the Canteor raiders in the future." Technically, it wasn't a lie. They were searching for new portals that would get mapped.

"Have you seen any more foreigners since Prince Alloryn pushed them back to sea?"

"Well, there was a man with a limp a few weeks back." Bess' voice pitched up. She pushed her unruly red curls back from her thin face.

Cassie pursed her lips. "I didn't see anything different about him. He just didn't tip you."

Bess pouted, removing her apron and hanging it up on one of the clothing hooks by the fireside. "There was something sinister about him."

Donella pushed for details. "A pearl earring? An embroidered vest? A foreign accent?" Bess shook her head, no, at each one.

An image inserted itself in Donella's mind of the spy she had caught and the goat head amulet he wore.

"Did he wear any jewelry or tattoos?"

Bess' brow cleared. "That's it. He wore a medallion around

his neck with an animal's head on it. I only glimpsed it for a second when he bent down." Bess' eyes went from Donella's face to her friend. "See. She thinks he's one of them."

Wishing the girls a good night, Donella sought her room. She'd tell the others about the new conspirator in the morning. Right now, all she wanted was to fall into a soft bed and get a good night's sleep.

As the next day dawned, Donella strolled with the others in the market. Her empty satchel slapped her back, ready to fill with supplies for the coming journey. Sellers were setting out their wares. Horses stood with drooping heads while farmers touted their produce. Dogs sniffed around the butcher's table as he threatened them with his knife. A rheumy-eyed woman pushed fine cloth at Donella, naming an exorbitant price. Donella shook her head and caught up with Odem.

"I have some possible news."

Odem glanced down at her, raising an eyebrow. "Of course, you do. Eleven hours in Tulken Harbor and you know everyone's secrets." His voice was teasing.

Donella ignored his gibe. "My sources say they saw a man with a limp who wears a goat god medallion."

"Impressive." Odem's expression sobered. "Good to know."

Donella joined Guy in a line for hot baked bread. The aroma made her mouth water. She hid a smile as his stomach growled.

"Adventures always make me hungry," Guy complained, his brown eyes embarrassed.

They bought hot buns to eat, as well as hard biscuits, which they stashed in their satchels. They sought out Gensard and Odem.

As they broke their fast, Guy seemed nervous. He looked up as he wiped the last crumbs on his trousers. "The waypost we need is on the headland outside of town."

Odem nodded. "I'll send the Reina a message that we found the closest portal. She can have someone retrieve the horses."

When they finished gathering food and supplies for their journey, the four strolled back to the stable for hire and retrieved their horses.

Odem negotiated with the stable owner to hold the horses until a courier came for them. He paid a stable boy to ride with them and return the horses.

Donella's palms began to sweat as it hit her that where they were going, they could not take the horses. Her pulse quickened at the thought of stepping through the portal onto an alien shore. She looked to the other three. They were the only ones she could rely on in the next weeks or months. Soon she would be surrounded by people who spoke another language and lived in a very different culture. Nothing would be familiar for a long time.

She suddenly felt small and, she hated to admit it, *afraid*. She questioned whether she made the right decision in coming along. *Is this what I'm meant to do?*

Guy took the lead, seemingly confident about where he was headed. Donella contrasted the hesitant farm boy she met nearly a year ago to the boy who opened multiple portals for the army to march through. And who risked his life to hold all the Valdeor portals against the invaders, even though he was bleeding from stab wounds. He had grown and embraced his destiny.

Pride swelled in her heart. She had helped him reach this point, goading him into taking a different path. She took courage from him and pushed away any nagging doubts.

The road wound through the town, up the hill to the cathedral watching over the inhabitants, then along the headland jutting into the sea. They followed the winding trail to the edge of the cliff. Blue waves stretched to the horizon. Gulls cried and circled above.

A stiff sea breeze whipped Donella's hair around. She pushed it back, as a roar filled her ears. Was it the sound of the sea, or her own pulse hammering in her ears?

This was it. A leap into the unknown.

Help me, O One Who Fashioned All. Give me courage. Help me to use my gift as You see fit.

3 Through the Portal

A storm-weathered waypost stood on the rugged, southern-facing headland. Tulken Harbor encircled the bay in the distance. Waves pounded a hundred feet below on the rocks. Sea mist sprayed Guy's face.

Somewhere ahead lay Canteor across the vast ocean.

His friends stood around him, pile of rugs at their feet. The stable boy held the horses' reins in the background.

Guy put his marked hand against the waypost's cool stone. A tingle started in his hand and ran up his arm. Mist swirled around his feet.

Taking a deep breath, he searched for a distant shore. He stretched his mind as far as he could. A coast wavered in the mist, but the image was indistinct.

His focus wavered, then he felt a strong hand on his right shoulder. Odem reinforced him. A slighter hand pressed on his left arm focused the picture further, as Donella added her strength to theirs. Blurred features formed before them in the portal. The fog dimmed a little, but the coastline remained vague.

Without a clear image, it was too dangerous to step forward.

Guy felt frustration build in him and he groaned aloud. The mist dissipated and the image vanished. But before the portal closed, he glimpsed a place similar to where they stood—two waypposts overlooked the surging sea below.

"We almost had it." Donella sighed and turned to him. "You must try harder."

Guy knew what he had to do. "Take my hands." He held them out for Donella and Prince Gensard. Her touch was warm. The prince's grasp was bone crushing. Odem's hand squeezed Guy's right shoulder.

When they grasped him, Guy concentrated on the two waypposts again. They were perhaps two days east of their position. When they coalesced, he stepped forward, taking the others with him. The world went white, and Guy struggled with disorientation, then his feet were back on solid ground.

Gensard and Odem released him.

At first, it seemed they were back where they started. They stared at the sea seething below them.

"We haven't moved at all!" Donella dropped Guy's hand.

"Not so. Look to the left," Odem directed.

Three pairs of eyes swiveled to see an identical waypost about twenty feet away.

"Where are we? We have not even left Valdeor." Prince Gensard flung out an arm. When nobody said anything, he strode away in disgust. "Is this the best you people can do?"

Guy ignored him.

Something about this place felt different. Without a word, Guy walked to the halfway point between the posts. His marked hand tingled with a strong vibration. He knelt. He didn't see anything.

After a moment, Donella joined him, kneeling at his side. "It is not your fault. None of us can conjure up such a distant place." She pulled idly at the grass. "I guess we expected too much from you."

Odem came to stand behind them. "Don't feel guilty. I cannot perform such a feat. But maybe if together we try one more time—"

Guy stopped listening. Maybe something was below the ground. He pushed the grass away and scooped out dirt. Donella leaned in to see what he did. A perfect square emerged from the sea grass. As Guy brushed a stone off, he saw the interlocking ovals symbol etched in its surface. The trinity design!

Donella jumped up and grabbed Odem's arm. "Look what Guy found!" She dragged Odem over.

Guy stood and brushed the grass from his trousers. He faced the others, a giant grin splitting his face. "Can't you see? This is the jumping point to Canteor. It's obvious now that more than one waykeeper is needed to travel such a distance."

He pointed to the right and left wayposts. "I need each of you to stand at one of those. When I begin to open the portal, join hands with me and help me focus."

Gensard wandered over at the commotion, as Donella skipped over to the left waypost and laid her ring hand on it, while Odem took up his position on the right one.

Guy stepped on the rock pedestal at his feet, directly onto the symbol. Tingles ran up his legs. He closed his eyes and took a deep breath. He let it out slowly, and as he did, he emptied his mind. He placed himself in the in-between place of the portals. He waited until he felt the emptiness of space all around him—no up, no down, just tumultuous light and mist. He flung his mind forward with all his strength searching for a distant shore.

He opened his eyes, straining to see Canteor's coastline come into focus in the mist.

"Grab my hands!" he cried and held out his arms. Odem grabbed his right hand and Donella stretched out for his left. Guy could not reach her hand, but suddenly Gensard was between them, bridging the gap.

Vibrations started in Guy's feet and traveled up through his body and into his head with a deep thrum. The energy of the three portals pulsed like an earthquake through him. Guy clenched his teeth as he fought the unnerving feeling.

He heard Donella gasp and Odem grunt.

Guy focused on the emerging shore that grew in detail before him out of the mist. The image coalesced into solid land. When Guy deemed the picture clear enough, he yelled, "Now!" and leapt forward.

For a terrifying moment, the four flew from the eastern cliffs of Valdeor and floated above the roaring sea a hundred feet below. They fell. The jagged rocks reached for their dangling feet. The gaping portal opened wider, and whiteness surrounded them. They were in a tunnel with a pinprick of an exit ahead. Guy's will pulled them forward. With the others' help, the image grew closer and closer until they seemed to hover above a beach's gently lapping waves and sand.

But just before Guy exited the portal, arced lightning flashed around him. Its force ripped his friends' hands from his grasp. Blinded, he called out. He felt himself plummeting.

He splashed into water. He gulped seawater as he sank, then kicked hard for the surface. Gasping for air when he surfaced, he spun in place looking for his friends. Seeing no one, the current causing him to drift away from land, he had no choice but to strike out for the shore. He crawled on the sands of an unknown beach. He collapsed on the sand. He retched as waves of dizziness poured through him. When it finally subsided, Guy lifted his head. He peered all around but saw no signs of Donella, Odem, or Prince Gensard.

His brain struggled with the reality of what happened. He was alone, unsure of where he landed. *Was this Canteor, or somewhere else? Were his friends safe? What had he done wrong?*

Guy took stock of his surroundings. The sandy beach stretched to a bluff on the right. To the left it ended in a peninsula. Palm trees swayed in the gentle breeze. Heady floral scents filled the air. Colorful, exotic birds flitted from tree to tree with harsh calls. The only other sound was the slap of the waves behind him.

Guy stood on unsteady legs. Shading his eyes, he stared at the light-reflecting sea waves, desperately searching for heads bobbing in the water.

He stumbled down the beach, shouting his friends' names.

Where were they?

Getting a grip on his emotions, he scanned the sand for footprints. After a while, he ran back the other way, calling for them.

They had to be here somewhere!

He couldn't go on his quest without their help.

After forty minutes of fruitless searching, he accepted that he was alone.

He hefted his waterproof satchel on his back and headed for the bluff. Nothing guided him but the desire to stand on a high point and get his bearings, and possibly see a sign of his friends. It was his last hope of finding them.

In any other circumstances, he would have enjoyed the stroll. It was a beautiful day with sunny skies. But worry for his friends knotted his stomach. He watched for any trace of them. *Wouldn't they have landed with him?*

He relived over and over their last moments together. Standing on the way stone. Holding hands. Stepping through the portal. A flash of light. And a wrenching force ripping him from the others.

Nothing I could have done. Yet guilt weighed on him anyway.

When he reached the base of the bluff, he saw a trail of sorts leading to the top. Pushing fronds out of his way, he started climbing. The sun beating down caused his shirt to stick to his back. He itched all over from the dried saltwater. He stopped to drink from his waterskin. After another half an hour, he came to a small waterfall feeding a pool. Kneeling, he scooped some water in his hands and splashed it over his face and neck. It felt so cool and refreshing that he stripped down and plunged in the pool, washing off the itchy salt caking his body. He ducked under and bobbed up, shaking his wet head.

He only wished he could shake off the feeling of remorse as easily. He unpacked his cloak from his satchel and used it to dry himself. He spread it over a bush to dry and dressed.

It was then he noticed his birthmark. His heart skipped a beat. It had faded.

His mouth suddenly dry, he turned in place until his left hand was in full sun. The mark was not as pronounced as he remembered. A feeling of foreboding washed over him. He stared at it a long time, unsure what it meant. Was it because he had traveled so far in the between place? Was it a punishment? Had giving in to the Reina's request disobeyed the Guardian of Valdeor's rule after all? Sending spies through the portal was not the same as soldiers . . . or was it? Was his power waning?

Eventually hunger distracted him.

He dug in his satchel and pulled out some dried meat. His supplies would last several days, a week if he were careful. He took a small portion and sat and chewed in the sun's warmth, unable to push away the fear in his heart that something was very wrong.

Feeling drowsy from the food and the exertion, he fought it the only way he could. He regathered his stuff and hit the trail.

Maybe from the high point he would see his way.

After another hour of walking, the trail became nearly vertical. Spending weeks climbing the main mast aboard the pirate ship, *Indomitable*, he was comfortable with heights. Using his hands and feet, he found footholds and clambered up the volcanic rock. His shoulder ached with the exertion, but he pushed through the pain. Climbing twenty minutes brought him to the top of the cliff.

The black, pockmarked land jutted over the jungle below. A crisp breeze cooled Guy. He hiked to the point sticking out above the ocean. Calm blue water sparkled in the daylight. He shaded his eyes and saw a hazy, blue island in the distance and another past it.

He turned and saw the place he stood was also an island. Jungle spread out beneath him. He stood on the highest point except for the volcano on the other end, its black conical shape telling the history of this place.

Nowhere did he see a mark of human habitation. He scoured the inlets for any sign of ships at anchor. Zilch.

He reached out with his senses but could find no waypost. Slowly spinning around, he faced the far islands. He stretched his mind forward, searching for a waypost. Nothing.

How odd. There must be a waypost nearby, or how could the portal have transported him here? Did it have something to do with the faded waykeeper symbol on his hand? It was still there, just less obvious.

And where were his friends?

Since there were no habitations on this isle, he'd head to the next one. Too far to swim, he'd have to make a raft.

But first he had to find a safe place to make camp. Not enough daylight remained to build a makeshift boat and set sail. He'd find a safe place to stay for the night, then he'd gather branches for a fire and a conveyance.

Guy spent the rest of the daylight hours following his plan. He climbed down and made camp near the waterfall. When darkness fell, he had a large pile of branches. He made a bed against the base of a cliff. His fire crackled, deterring animals.

He made a soup of sorts using half a giant nut as a bowl, adding some dried meat to the white liquid inside. He dug into the fire and partly buried the thick-shelled nut in the fiery embers to warm it. It had an odd flavor but tasted better than he expected.

Being early spring, the tropical night was mild. Guy slept fitfully, wrapped in his cloak.

He dreamed of Donella crying out as she was sucked from his side in a black whirlwind. Lightning flashed all around him as he called her name. The storm whipped his words away. Odem fell into deep black water and sank out of Guy's view. Prince Gensard held his sword above the waves crying, "Is this the best you can do?"

Guy woke with a start. He was drenched in sweat.

Putting his head in his hands, Guy cried out in prayer, *Help my friends, You Who Fashioned All. Let them be safe! Let me see them again!*

Silence. Guy drew in a deep breath. He shivered as a breeze cooled his skin. He added a few more sticks to his small fire. As he stared into the flames, his mind circled back to the day's events over and over. Eventually growing drowsy, he drifted off again. But dreams of his companions continued to haunt him.

Even though he woke up feeling drained and tired, Guy spent the next day trimming the branches with his knife. Work kept him from thinking and worrying.

He cut the branches a uniform length. When his stock was gone, he explored the surrounding area and collected more, as well as some sturdy vines. It took all day to make a craft.

Guy stood up and inspected it. Twilight would come soon. He'd have to test his raft tomorrow. He wiped his brow. Thoughts of food crossed his mind.

A rustling came from behind. Spinning, Guy glimpsed the tail of a medium sized animal disappearing into the brush. Knife in his hand he followed it.

He ate a hot meal that night. His hunting had yielded an animal which looked like a cross between a rabbit and a groundhog. He roasted it on a wooden skewer over his fire. When he finished, he buried the carcass so it wouldn't attract predators.

He felt better after his meal and a hard day's work. With luck, he'd find his friends on the nearest island tomorrow. The current could have carried them there.

Maybe it was the day's exertion, or his prayer for his friends' safety before he laid down, but he slept better the second night alone.

4 Slave Trader

*D*onella's heart lodged in her throat as she stepped off the precipice and fell into the portal. For a few long seconds she felt suspended in the air. The waves rose to meet her. She squeezed her eyes shut. No up or down. Her stomach threatened to heave up her last meal. She opened her eyes. Lightning flashed and she felt herself flung around. Prince Gensard's hand clamped tighter around hers, crushing her fingers.

Out of the mist, sea and sand came racing up at her. She hit the ground, the air left her body, and she blacked out.

The next thing Donella was aware of was motion. Bright light assailed her when she opened her eyes. She squinted, the world out of focus. Dizziness and roiling insides made her push herself to kneeling. She emptied the contents of her stomach.

Under her hands was a rough, splintered surface. Vomit and sweat assailed her nose.

A bump and a listing right made her fall on something soft beside her. She leaned against Prince Gensard, who was slumped in a heap. She blinked and gazed around. They were in a wagon with a roof. *And . . . were those bars?*

She gripped the bars beside her. Solid. *What in the world?*

She sat up and scrutinized her surroundings. Two male strangers and a girl sat watching her from the other side of the cage on wheels. *Where were Guy and Odem?*

Panic fluttered in her middle.

She stared back at the other passengers. A giant man had a thick mop of red hair and a scruffy beard. He wore nondescript trousers and a brown vest over his bare, muscled chest. The other man had a scar from his droopy left eyelid to the corner of his lip and sported a ring in one ear. His cinnamon brown hair was pulled back in a ponytail. His sweat-stained shirt was grayish white tucked into his black trousers. The girl had enormous eyes in a pale face. She wore a honey brown robe, and her blond, braided hair hung over her shoulder. She huddled apart from the men.

Leading the ox pulling the wagon was a large, muscular man wearing a brown and green vertically striped robe and a conical hat shading his head. Walking beside him was a female. She wore a gray robe tied at the waist and had dark, braided hair poking out beneath a similar hat.

The wagon rolled over a barely visible road in an otherwise trackless wasteland. Scrub brush, giant boulders, and packed earth met Donella's frightened gaze. Behind them was no sign of the sea. By the length of the shadows, Donella guessed it to be late afternoon.

Her eyes were gritty, and she tasted sand as she wet her lips with her tongue. A sour taste lingered in her mouth. A raging thirst consumed her as the sun beat on her.

"Awake, are you?"

Donella jumped to find the man in the striped robe standing nearby. He was middle-aged and barrel chested. He was bigger than her friend, Rongel, the prize fighter. Removing his hat, he wiped his shaven head, which reminded her of an egg. He had a dark mustache under little pig eyes that looked her up and down.

She realized the wagon had stopped.

Without turning away from her, he called, "Zaniah!"

The woman stepped over. Her face was partly shaded by her

hat, but the light mercilessly picked out a large red birthmark across her right cheek. Her weary eyes under dark brows darted from his face to Donella's. She dropped her gaze and stood with eyes on the ground.

"Who are you? What happened?" Donella demanded.

"I am your new master. You'll bring me a pretty penny at the market. Young. Fire in your eyes." He smirked and turned to the woman. "Make camp."

Donella trembled and clenched her fists. *Almighty One, help us.* They had fallen into the hands of a slave trader!

"Yes, Agomeisa," Zaniah answered. She hurried to obey, taking a basket off the ox's back.

Agomeisa's voice drew Donella's eyes back to him as he towered over her. "You will help the women make camp or you will not eat, and the man you travel with will not get water." He gestured with an arm at the emptiness surrounding them. "Look around. There's nowhere to run. You will die in the desert without water. Only I know where the springs are.

"Do you hear me, girl?"

Donella could only nod.

Agomeisa pulled out a key and fit it into the cage's lock.

The blond girl exited the wagon and joined Zaniah.

Donella glanced at the prince, who stirred and groggily blinked in the light.

She shuffled to the exit. She wanted to run as far as she could from this bully, but the slaver was right. She'd never survive on her own. For now, she would obey, but when they came to the slave market, she would take her chance.

"Out. I will take care of your companion." The slaver's words sounded more like a threat.

Climbing out of the wagon, Donella stretched cramped muscles.

She walked nearby to where the women were clearing the ground. Donella helped the blond-haired girl gather stones and put them in a circle. The girl was shorter than Donella but seemed to be a couple of years older. Her slender, white arms peeked from under her sleeves as she picked up stones. Her face was heart shaped, and her beautiful blue eyes were her finest feature.

"Hello. I'm Donella," she introduced herself as they gathered dry brush and grass. "What's your name?"

The girl glanced quickly at Zaniah, nearby, whose back was turned to them.

"Jiana," she replied softly.

"Are you a captive, too?" Jiana didn't look like Agomeisa or Zaniah, but for all Donella knew, she could be their daughter.

"A slave. My brother sold me." Jiana limped with her sticks to the stone circle. She sharpened a stick and spun it, trying to light the fire.

Donella swallowed, frozen where she stood. She couldn't imagine anyone selling their sibling. What kind of place was this?

Donella made her feet move. She reached for the pouch she kept around her neck, which held her fire starter, among other things. It wasn't there. She glanced down at her hand where she wore her most prized possession—her waykeeper ring. Gone!

The slaver had removed all her valuables. She squirmed at the thought of him groping her as she was unconscious. She hoped that it had been the woman who searched her.

Donella glared at Agomeisa's back as he leaned over a groggy Gensard. She saw the prince's scimitar hanging from Agomeisa's belt. Even if Gensard could fight, and he didn't seem up to it, his weapon was out of his reach.

Donella's spirit plummeted.

"Don't stand there!" The older woman blocked her view of the wagon. She frowned, causing her mark to pucker. She might've been pretty once, with high cheekbones and almond shaped brown eyes, but deep lines of dissatisfaction etched her face. "Fill these water skins."

Donella looked at her blankly.

"The spring under the big rock behind you."

Donella turned. They stood at the base of a twenty-five-foot boulder rising from the desert, offering shade. Moving closer, she saw bubbling water coming from under the rock. It flowed into a little pool, then disappeared back underground.

Kneeling, Donella took a long drink of water and wiped her mouth on her sleeve. Her tongue no longer cleaved to the roof of her mouth. She cupped her hands and washed her face and the back of her neck. Then she filled the three water skins Zaniah gave her. Seeing some melagria tubers growing nearby, she pulled them. She also picked the seeds from the periwinkle spiked balls of the desert chia and filled her pockets.

By the time she returned, Jiana had the fire flickering. Taking the water skin from Donella, she sprinkled some into a bowl of grain. She kneaded the meal into a flat bread. She put it on a flat metal pan and put it over the fire.

"May I help?" Donella's empty stomach ached. Anything to make dinner ready faster. Jiana showed her how to make barley bread. They worked quietly making enough for the group.

"I found some edible bulbs." Donella held them out to Jiana, but Zaniah grabbed them. "Are you sure they are edible?"

"Yes. They need to be boiled."

Zaniah retrieved a pot from the basket of supplies and took care of cooking them herself.

Out of the corner of her eye, Donella watched Agomeisa chain each man's hands and feet, as they exited. He led them behind the standing rock presumably to take care of bodily functions. They then shuffled to the camp where Agomeisa made them sit down. Donella saw how short the chains were between their feet. They would never have a chance to run away.

Zaniah poured a ladle of water from a leather water skin. She let each man have a drink before refilling it for the next.

She snapped her fingers. "Jiana, bring the food."

The girl jumped to obey. She served Agomeisa first. He ate three cakes and the bulbs that Zaniah prepared while they all watched.

Donella's stomach grumbled.

Zaniah handed the male prisoners each a barley cake, which they hungrily ate. Then Zaniah ate hers. Finally, Donella and Jiana got one each.

Donella ate slowly, trying to make it last. She burned inside that the melagria tubers weren't shared. They needed nourishment to survive in this harsh climate. Next time she'd keep the food she found to herself. At least she still had the chia seeds in her pocket.

5 Prince Gensard

*G*ensard's head pounded like he had too much to drink. His right eye felt as if a knife was lodged into his brain. He groaned. Something soft landed on him. The pain made him succumb to the darkness.

When he awoke again as the ground jolted, he forced his eyes open. The bright light stabbed at him. He closed them again. Sweat coated his body. His teeth were covered in grit.

"I'll take care of him," a male voice said.

Scraping sounded nearby. Gensard cracked open his eyes. A large shaven head wavered into view. A big, muscular man clamped chains on his hands and feet. Gensard realized too late what he did. He struggled, but was unsuccessful.

A meaty hand hauled him up. Gensard fought a wave of dizziness. His head ached, but not as much as earlier.

"Yer my prisoner now. No fighting and I won't hurt the lass with you." Little pig eyes stared at him menacingly. "Any trouble and I leave you staked in the desert for the birds and wild dogs to devour." He bared his yellowed teeth in a menacing grin.

Gensard blinked at the cage he was in. The man dragged him out of it. Gensard managed to stay on his feet when they hit the ground.

He straightened up and peered around. He stood beside a

wagon with barred sides pulled by oxen, resting in the shade of a giant standing rock twenty-five feet high. Flat, barren landscape stretched in every direction. Heat beat down in waves in the open.

His captor chained two other fellows. Then he chained the three together. The slaver led the three of them around a boulder to do their business. Gensard's feet were chained so close together that he could barely shuffle with tiny steps. No chance of escaping unless he could remove them.

He eyed the other two, one a giant, the other slender as a rapier. If only they were not shackled together, Gensard was sure the three of them could take the bald man down.

He needed to escape. He'd watch for an opportunity.

Their captor led them to a campfire. Gensard easily squatted, while the tallest prisoner half fell into place with a grunt. The other man gracefully sat.

Gensard was baffled how he came to be in the company of ruffians. The last thing he remembered was stepping off the cliff for Canteor with those wizards. *What went wrong?*

The slaver walked to where three women worked. Gensard recognized Donella's black ringlets. *But where were the other two? Commander Odem and the boy?*

An older woman looked up. "Agomeisa." She held out a water skin to their captor. He drank his fill and handed back the leather bag.

Gensard's tongue felt swollen twice its size. She walked over to Gensard next, pouring water into a ladle. He grasped the handle and gulped the fresh, cool water.

She had an ugly mark over half her face. She took the ladle and repeated the process to the next man.

She called out, "Jiana!" and the third female brought food. She looked to be several years younger than him. Her face was lightly tanned, with startling, light blue eyes when she glanced up. Her hair was the color of golden wheat. He thought at first that her ankles were chained as she limped toward him. But when she knelt in front of the woman, he caught sight of delicate, unfettered legs. Was she injured?

Gensard bit into the cake Jiana gave him. It was plain barley. He wolfed it down, wishing for more. Unabashedly, he licked his fingers, tasting barley and salt.

"Where did you get the tubers? Have you been holding back on me, woman?" Agomeisa's voice boomed.

"No, husband," Zaniah whined. "The new girl found them. I thought to please you."

Agomeisa turned to Donella. She lifted her head and glared back at him. Her boldness in the face of the bully struck Gensard.

"You know how to find edibles in the desert?"

"Yes," her voice squeaked. Not quite as brave as she seemed.

Agomeisa rubbed his head, brow creased. "Then I will let you forage. But," he held up his palm, "if you try to escape, I will beat you. Do you hear?"

Donella looked as if she wished to refuse but nodded instead.

When they finished eating, their captor led the men to the wagon. Once they were inside, Agomeisa locked them in the cage, leaving on their fetters. He proceeded to rummage in a basket and pulled out a rope. He tied one end to Donella's hands, slipped it through the bars of the cage, then tied the other end to Jiana's hands. The girls had just enough slack to lie under the wagon.

Agomeisa and Zaniah lay near the low-banked fire.

When their captors were having a discussion, Gensard whispered, "How did we come to be here, Donella?"

"I don't know. Last thing I remember is stepping toward the seashore," Donella whispered back.

"Agomeisa found you on the shore near the road," Jiana's soft voice floated up from the ground. "You were lying side by side. I thought you had drowned, and the sea had washed you ashore. Once Agomeisa ascertained you lived, he tossed you in the wagon."

"Where is he taking us?" Donella's voice trembled.

A deep voice answered, "To the slave market in Dabbori. The capital city draws the best buyers. I'm Hazibal." His red hair shone like a beacon in the fiery sunset.

Slave market? Gensard furthered his resolve to escape.

"First, we must survive crossing the Jugara Desert. You can call me Sad-alah. And you are?" His droopy eyelid gave him a lazy expression, but his eyes were intense.

"Gensard. And my sister is Donella." The words slipped out without thinking. He thought he heard Donella's intake of breath, but she didn't contradict him. These two characters seemed rough. Best to let them know not to mess with her. The easiest method was to claim a relationship to him.

But he couldn't let himself be slowed down by her. When the opportunity presented, he would finish the mission Lauressa had given him. Compassion didn't figure in his plans.

A warrior ignores his discomfort and keeps his eye on the goal. The words of his brother Leander came unbidden to his mind as Gensard stretched out to sleep. Gensard often found his brother's advice echoing in his head when faced with dire situations. He closed his heart to the ache that always accompanied the thought of his exiled, beloved older brother.

Gensard pushed away a guilty twinge at the thought of leaving his companions behind. His need to prove himself made it possible to suppress that nagging inner voice.

Few knew he was actually the second son of his father, Prince Xander.

In his mind rose a memory of his brother Leander—tall, fair, and beloved of his people. Prince Xander raised Leander to follow in his footsteps, but Leander lacked his father's cunning and ruthlessness. Leander was an impish rogue, full of laughter and pranks. Gensard, much younger, had worshiped Leander, his own serious ways not endearing him to those around him. Looking back, Gensard was surprised that he was never jealous of his brother and his easy ways. Leander knew how to tease anyone out of a bad mood, especially serious Gensard.

But when Leander turned eighteen, and Gensard was only twelve, Warlord Bastil sent his men over the Domadarian Mountains to plunder Samarantha's fertile fields. That year a harsh winter threatened to starve the Domadarians.

Gensard spent many years imploring those who were present to tell him the details of what happened next, to the point that he felt as if he had witnessed it first-hand.

Prince Xander gathered his forces when the raids of the Domadarians continued. Xander's soldiers hid in the Blue Range's foothills, the boundary between the two provinces. When the next raid commenced, Xander surrounded the forest men and began systematically destroying them.

Leander empathized with the hungry invaders' plight and begged his father to show mercy. "The men's real crime is they suffer from hunger. Our bounty is enough to share. Father, please stop this."

"They brought this fight to our land. If Bastil had tried negotiation, I might have considered it." Xander sat astride his horse and watched dispassionately as his men butchered the invaders on the plain below them. "A strong leader must send a strong message to his enemies. Any less, and he will diminish his position."

Leander turned his horse back toward the capitol city. "I will not be a part of this."

"Leave, and you will no longer be my son! I cannot allow you to disgrace me in front of my troops." Xander gave him a look that usually cowed Leander into submission, but the bile rising up his throat at the slaughter before him gave him the will to turn

and ride away.

"So be it," were the last words Leander spoke to his father.

Gensard had not been present, as he was still too young. But he heard the tale as he stood behind the kitchen door, listening to his father's bodyguards tell the servants why his brother did not return with the others.

Still, Gensard refused to believe his elder brother was a coward.

He remembered many pranks that had gotten Leander in trouble with their father in the past. And although his brother stood silently while their father admonished him, even whipped him in front of those he pranked, Leander's eye would catch Gensard's and he'd wink. An upward twist of Leander's lips showed that their father had not broken his brother's will.

Gensard could only wonder if Leander endured the punishment while he planned his next outrageous joke.

So Gensard ran from the kitchens through the palace to confront his father, ignoring the councilors gathered in the throne room. Normally, Gensard would have never been so bold, but his heart threatened to burst from his body at the lies they told about his roguish brother.

"My liege." Gensard reverted to the formal title when his father's hawk eyes landed on him as he burst unbidden into the chamber. Gensard stumbled to a halt, all eyes upon him.

Pushing past his fear of retribution, he gasped out, "Is my brother here?"

His father's frown deepened. Silence greeted Gensard as he looked in turn at the men gathered. None met his gaze, shifting their eyes away from his.

Naively, he pushed for an answer, desiring to hear that his brother was only in disgrace again for some boyish peccadillo. "They are telling lies about him in the servants' hall. Nasty things about my brave Leander . . ."

"Silence!"

Gensard eyed his father with trepidation. Prince Xander's temper was legendary.

A tic in Prince Xander's jaw was an indicator of his anger. "How dare you barge in here spouting that traitor's name!"

Xander rose to his full height and met every eye staring at him with fury and determination. "His name shall be struck from the chronicles." As silence stretched out after his words, he motioned a scribe over. "Make it so."

Gensard stood as if rooted to the spot. *It could not be true! Not Leander!* But he could not oppose his enraged father. Almost as if his tongue cleaved to the roof of his mouth, he could not cry out the denial in his heart.

"But, sire, he is but young and hot-headed. After all, he is your heir." A grizzled councilor spoke the words Gensard could not speak.

"I have no son but Gensard." Xander motioned to his scribe. "So it shall be written."

And from that day to this, no one dared speak Leander's name in Prince Xander's presence. And Gensard strove to prove his worthiness to his father, for several more sons had been born to his father in the meantime. They all vied for their father's favor. Gensard must continually prove to others that he was his father's true heir.

When, for all his good looks and superb swordsmanship, he had failed to wed Reina Lauressa, he disgraced his name. Now he must win her favor by escaping his present situation and gathering the information she needed on Prince Pashmi's fighting force.

So Gensard pushed away his feelings of guilt. He planned to escape, leaving the others behind. For Valdeor's fate and the gratitude of the Reina were paramount, so that his father would continue to acknowledge him as Samarantha's heir apparent.

6 Storm at Sea

*I*n the early morning, birds made a racket in the leafy jungle canopy. Calm waves rippled to shore. The sun shone but clouds gathered in the west. Guy stood on the beach, shading his eyes. The island he hoped to journey to didn't look too far away. Maybe a couple of hours.

At his feet, his satchel held food he had brought from Valdeor, as well as some nuts, berries, and tubers he foraged. Donella had taught him some basic herb lore in exchange for her Canteor language lessons.

He missed her dry wit and company. He prayed that she was safe. Odem and Prince Gensard would take care of her. But what if, like himself, she was flung out of the portal alone?

I can't go there. It's my fault if she is in peril. Please watch over her, One Who Fashioned All.

But would the Almighty listen? Had using the portals for a spy mission angered the Guardian, the being of light sent by the Almighty? Is that what this was about?

A stone lodged in Guy's chest. Whatever his friends suffered was his fault. The Guardian of Valdeor had warned him the portals were made for pilgrims. Guy had let Reina Lauressa convince him to act against his misgivings.

His only hope to make amends was to find and rescue his

friends.

When the tide turned, Guy pushed his raft into the waves. He swam, kicking with all his might and pushing it until he was beyond the breakers. He pulled himself aboard. He used a paddle he had fashioned of wood to steer himself into the current. The raft floated out to sea.

Guy attached his cloak to a pole and the wind filled it.

A seagull landed on the raft, tucking its wings and pecking at the bugs on the vines.

An hour passed, then two. The eastern island Guy headed for still seemed as distant as when he started.

The bird suddenly took flight, screeching and gliding on an air current. Guy felt more alone. Facing the way he had come, the shore he launched from was impossibly far away.

But what grabbed his attention was the dark angry clouds drawing near. Having sailed for a month on a pirate ship as a captive, Guy knew how quickly storms could blow up, and how violent they could be. His shoulders tensed as the wind picked up.

He left his makeshift sail aloft until the winds became too strong. He had a hard time keeping his feet as the raft bounced in the waves. But when he detached his cloak, the gale blew it out of his grasp. He started paddling for the nearest island. After half an hour, his muscles screamed with effort. Still another forty-five minutes to the shore.

But the tempest hit, and the waves tossed the little craft around. It became harder to steer, and he lost all sense of direction.

Lightning flashed. Thunder boomed overhead. Gusts lashed the water. Then giant drops of rain fell. A few at first soon became a downpour. The sea heaved around him. One mighty wave washed over the raft, carrying his satchel away. Guy flung himself flat and grabbed for it. He stretched as far as he dared, but it floated out of his reach.

Water crashed over him, chilling him. He lay drenched on the raft, his fingers clutching the vines which held it together as the craft swung this way and that at the mercy of the sea.

Despair crowded his thoughts. How did he ever believe he could float from island to island? What if he crashed on reefs or hidden shoals? Maybe he should've searched harder for a waypost before embarking on this journey.

Please, please, bring me back on land!

Rational thought wasn't possible. Just pleas for his life.

Hours passed.

Guy came out of his stupor to realize the wind had died down. His hands were stiff from clamping onto the vines. The sun peeked out and his clothes steamed. The waves were still choppy. A landmass was off to his left.

Salt dried on his lips, but licking it only made his extreme thirst worse. He didn't have the strength to jump off and swim to shore. The raft hit a rock, taking the decision from him.

He plunged in the cool water. Lungs bursting, he fought his way to air. Taking a deep breath, he kicked for the nearest board. Clinging to it, he rode the waves to the shore. With his waning strength, he kicked for the rocky beach. Underwater hazards cut his shins. A large wave pushed him right up to the beach. Standing, he fought the undertow and walked out of the water.

The sharp rocks were painful to walk on. Coughing up water, he went further up the sand and then collapsed.

Thank you for my life. He aimed his thoughts at the Creator of All before succumbing to sleep.

Guy lost track of time. Eventually the need for water drove him to sit up and study his surroundings. Out to sea, the storm moved away on the horizon as a black smudge. Rocky shoals protected the area from ships landing. He sat on a narrow beach which stretched out in both directions. A rocky cliff face towered above him.

High tide marks etched in the rock wall let him know he couldn't make camp here.

Guy searched for an easy access point to climb. Finding one, he limped over to the gray rock. His shoes lost in the storm, he found purchase with his toes and hands. The month he spent climbing the mast aboard the *Indomitable* helped. Scaling the wall, he made frequent stops, exhausted as he was from his ordeal. Glancing down, he saw the tide starting to slide in.

Definitely no going back.

Slow and steady he climbed. Halfway up he came across a ledge four feet deep and twelve feet long. Hoisting himself up, he knelt on it. Water from the storm had collected in a depression. Not caring if it was a little muddy, he slurped it up. It tasted like iron. He drank it all.

Propping himself against the cliff wall, he rested. He was banged up, with multiple scratches. But nothing was broken. Food and rest would take care of everything else.

He analyzed his situation. Lost somewhere among the islands between Valdeor and Canteor. Alone without food or water. The sea surging in below him. He hated adventures.

But he was alive.

What of his friends? He put his head in his hands. Guilt washed over him. He relived over and over the last moments together. They had all held hands. The Canteor shore appeared a step away. But a flash of light blinded him. And a wrenching force had ripped Prince Gensard's and Odem's hands from his.

Forgive me!

But he needed to move forward. If he could find a waypost, maybe he could reconnect with Donella and the men.

Another forty-five minutes of climbing and he made the top. He pulled himself over the edge of rough grass and crouched. Before him lay a lush jungle of exotic trees and intertwining vines.

A riot of colorful flowers perfumed the air. A cacophony of birdcalls overwhelmed the sound of waves crashing below him.

This island was shaped like a triangle. Guy stood at the base. About a third of the way to the tip was a cluster of buildings along the southern shore. Fishing boats were tied up along the beach.

He wasn't sure of his reception, but hunger pushed him to make for the village. He reckoned his heading by the sun's position.

He pushed his way through the thick foliage. It would be easy to become lost. The overhead canopy blocked the sun. Fronds slapped him in the face, centipedes moved along the ground. Strange birds cried out and flapped away. Vines tangled his feet.

Guy's legs felt like lead. His arms and face itched from salt spray and scratches. The humid air formed a vapor around him, making it hard to breathe.

Late afternoon, he stood at the end of the jungle, staring at the edge of the village.

Commander Odem had tried to instill into Guy a sense of his surroundings as part of his training for entering foreign territory, so Guy recalled his lessons.

The inhabitants had cleared the land around their homes and stockyards. Crude, single-story huts nestled together against the elements: the sea on one side and the jungle on the other. Poles and log fences kept in goats and chickens.

The strong smell of something rotting filled the air.

Seeing no occupants, Guy walked past the nearest animal pen. The goat in it walked alongside him, complaining loudly.

Entering the village, Guy noticed brown-skinned men up and down the beach using rakes, as if they hoed the sand. Their bare torsos gleamed with sweat. Women and children gathered around a large mound of some sort. As he approached them, the stench grew stronger. The group sorted through a giant pile of clam shells, each collecting some in a basket. A small group of teen boys dug a pit, while teen girls dragged branches and carried seaweed to it.

"Where did you come from?" In his absorption, Guy hadn't noticed several men approaching. So much for Odem's training.

The language wasn't pure Canteor, but a dialect close enough to it that Guy understood.

The man asking the question had geometric tattoos over his dusky brown chest. He wore an olive-colored garment from his waist to his knees. Chocolate brown eyes looked with interest at Guy.

"I was shipwrecked." That was close enough to the truth. "The current dumped me on the far side of your island."

"You search for other white men, no?"

A surge of hope sprung up at the tattooed man's words. His face must have shown his shock.

"This way. I will take you to them." The man gestured for Guy to follow. "I am Nadun of Bidori."

He led Guy past the women toward the men raking. The smell of mud and clams was overwhelming the closer they got.

The clammer's instruments were long-handled wood sticks with a bar at the end. Teeth in the bar dug at the muck, disturbing the clams and bringing them up. The men dressed similarly to Nadun, standing ankle deep in mud. Most had the same dusky brown skin as Nadun. But as they walked closer, Guy noticed two of them had white features, although their tanned skin helped them blend in from a distance.

Both men turned as Nadun and Guy walked up. The taller one was solid like a mighty oak with a scraggly brown beard, the shorter one had the look of a wrestler with his thick arms and neck. A goat amulet hung from a chain around his neck.

Guy's heart plummeted. He had hoped to find Odem and Gensard.

The tall man stared as if in shock. "You!" He hit his companion, getting his attention. "You're the one who sent us here. I'll kill you for that!" He lunged, but the strong, short man held him back.

"Kadar! Are you sure, man?" Both men glared at Guy.

The natives stopped clamming and watched.

Guy blinked. He couldn't remember meeting either man. "You are mistaken. I've never seen you before!" Guy backed up, gut clenching. He hoped the short man could calm Kadar down. Out in the open he saw nowhere to escape.

"I know it's him! He sent us into the storm. Let me go!" Kadar growled.

The three men using the waypost to attack the palace! I sent them into the stormy portal! They landed here.

Frozen, Guy stared at them. "You survived!" *Wait, did I just say that aloud?* Guy readied himself to be torn limb from limb.

7 Jugara Desert

*D*onella blinked. Prince Gensard claimed she was his sister? She puzzled over why he would say such a thing. Not that she wanted to be his girlfriend. Or did she? That led her to thoughts of Guy. She missed him. Closer to her own age, they sparred over everything. Yet he was more than a brother to her. Then she thought of Odem, of course, who was like a father to her. Not that she remembered much about her dad since he died when she was small. And on these thoughts, she drifted off to sleep, even though she lay on the hard ground under the wagon, Jiana's soft breaths nearby.

Donella was awakened by a rude jab in her side. Squinting in the dawn, she saw Agomeisa's foot. She had slept fitfully. Her arm tied to the wagon above her was asleep. Her shoulder ached.

The sky was barely light.

Agomeisa untied her and yanked her up. Donella bit back a cry as he pulled on her sore arm. Jiana stood nearby, untied. Donella better understood the forlorn expression on the girl's face, if this was typical of the life she led.

Agomeisa passed them to Zaniah, who guided them behind the standing boulder to relieve themselves.

Donella couldn't help noticing Jiana's pronounced limp. Jiana caught Donella's questioning gaze, but turned away, her eyes sad.

Recognizing the futility of trying to escape in the barren wilderness, Donella's chest was tight with frustration as they returned to camp.

Agomeisa passed them on the way, leading the chained men behind the rock formation.

When Zaniah poured the waterskin into a ladle, Donella gulped a mouthful gratefully before the woman snatched it away, giving it to Jiana. She passed the ladle to the male prisoners when they joined the women.

"In the wagon with you." Agomeisa unlocked the cage door, motioning them in with a wavy-edged dagger in one hand. Jiana climbed in and sat apart from the men. Donella followed and sat near her.

As the slaver couple climbed on the wagon seat and urged the ox forward, Donella softly asked Jiana, "Are you alright? I couldn't help but notice your limp. I know something about healing."

Jiana's expression remained closed. She looked at her hands clasped in her lap. "There's nothing you can do." Her voice was crisp, dismissive.

Donella glanced at the men. Prince Gensard scowled at Agomeisa's back. Hazibal cracked his knuckles, sitting with his back to Zaniah. Sad-alah sat cross-legged, seemingly at peace, twisting playing cards through his fingers like some magic trick or meditative technique.

To while away the time, and befriend Jiana, Donella shared her memories at random. "I grew up at an inn." Seeing Gensard clench his fist, she remembered his lie. "I—I mean we—had plenty of clients and there were lots of chores. But when I was able, I used to sneak into the stable. I wanted a horse of my own. My mother said we had no need of one beside the draft horse we used to pull the wagon for supplies. But eventually a friend loaned me his horse."

Jiana's posture relaxed. When Donella stopped, she leaned forward slightly. "What was the horse's name?"

"Seeker. He's a big, black stallion. But he doesn't have a mean bone, unlike many stallions. He'll eat carrots out of my hand." Donella sighed. "I had to leave him behind to make this trip."

"You're not from Canteor, are you?" Jiana's eyebrow rose. "You have an accent."

"I'm part of a band of rug merchants now that Mother is gone. With the—my brother." Donella glanced up to see Prince Gensard listening to them. His eyes flitted to Jiana's face and remained there.

Jiana's lips parted slightly. Her shuttered expression had disappeared. "I've never ridden a horse." She smiled shyly.

"There's nothing like it. It's not like this bumpy wagon. Riding Seeker, well, it's as if you are carried on the back of the wind."

"Fiery could beat your horse any day." Prince Gensard scooted closer and joined the conversation.

Jiana's eyes swiveled toward him. Her expression became tinged with apprehension as she stiffened.

Donella hoped Gensard wouldn't cause the timid girl to clam up again.

"My horse is the finest in my father's stable." Gensard grinned at Jiana, waving his hand expansively. "He's very high-spirited. But he obeys my slightest command." He exuded confidence. He cocked his head at Jiana. "If I took you up for a ride with me, you'd feel like you were flying."

Sitting back, Jiana giggled behind her hand.

"I wish we all had wings to fly out of here. What's the use of wishing for the impossible?" Sad-alah sarcastically threw out, crossing his arms.

His words threw a wet blanket over the light banter.

The sun rose higher and beat down on them. Soon the waves

of heat from the road made Donella feel as if she were in an oven. Thirst overshadowed all other desires. Her tongue felt big in her mouth, and it was hard to swallow. The top of her head pounded. She tasted grit on her parched lips.

The others seemed equally miserable, huddled with their own thoughts.

Donella's chest was heavy thinking of the loss of her friends. She wondered how Guy fared. And Odem, whom she had grown to love in their time together. Were they safe? Would she see them again? She regretted the loss of her ring. Without it how would she find the way home? Would she ever see her home again? Misery settled over her like a heavy cloak.

It was sometime past midday when Agomeisa guided the wagon between two canyon walls and stopped. The slaver let the girls out to do their business, while he left the men in the wagon. When they returned, he motioned her and Jiana back into their prison.

This time no spring was nearby, so Donella eagerly sipped the water from the leather skin when it was her turn to drink. Zaniah fetched hard biscuits from the ox's basket and passed them through the bars. The biscuit was especially hard to chew and swallow because of lack of saliva.

Donella idly watched a lizard dart from rock to rock in the sun. Already it seemed a lifetime in this desert.

Jiana felt the pull of friendship for the other girl, Donella, as they broke bread in the shade of the canyon wall. She showed no sign of pity or scorn. Her openness and amiableness were as welcome as water in the heat.

But Donella and her intense brother Gensard just didn't understand. One could tell they had never been slaves. They were too confident. They spoke too much and asked too many questions.

Most slaves hid their feelings and thoughts. It was better not to have them. You couldn't get hurt if you didn't feel.

When Jiana was eight and put on the slave block, she hoped some kindly woman would buy her. A rich lady did buy her to be a helper in the kitchen. Jiana did her best to please. She kept herself neat and spoke politely. She hungered for a kind word. But the woman never noticed her or showed her love. Neither did the cook or housekeeper, although she did her best to please them.

She frequently caught Donella's brother staring at her, which made her uncomfortable. Just as Pim, her last mistress's son, had followed her with his eyes. Returning from years away at a distant school, he took a sudden interest in her. She didn't like the bold way he looked at her. Pim would show up unexpectedly as she worked. Once, he grabbed her and planted hot kisses on her before a disturbance allowed her to escape. She managed not to get caught alone with him after the first time. But finally, a few weeks ago, he did catch up with her and she slapped him. Because of that, her mistress sold Jiana the next day to Agomeisa, blaming Jiana for enticing her son.

Now the slaver was taking them to Dabbori, center of Canteor culture. The capital city had the largest slave market in the land.

Jiana tried not to think of it. She had served in the same house for nine years. Sure, it wasn't a happy time, but she knew the other servants and slaves. They at least tolerated her, and no one whipped her.

But she couldn't depend on mild treatment anymore. She knew some masters were cruel. She prayed fervently that she wouldn't fall into the hands of such a one.

Slaves went about their business not expecting praise. Some were sullen, others resigned, but none were cheerful.

As much as Jiana longed to have Donella as her friend, the

first one she could remember ever having, she feared the day coming soon when they'd be separated. Sold on the slave block. And Jiana would be alone again.

8 Friendship

The next afternoon, Gensard looked for any weapon when the slaver allowed him privacy behind a boulder. Nothing but scrub brush with brittle stalks. A rock wouldn't do much good against a dagger. If only he could get his scimitar away from Agomeisa. But his hands needed to be free.

He scowled. He needed help. He hated depending on others. So many times, they failed to come through. The only way to be sure of the outcome was to rely solely on himself.

He searched for an escape route, knowing he wouldn't find one in the bleak canyon land. Angrily, he shuffled back to the wagon.

Agomeisa forced the prisoners to eat in the wagon. Hard biscuits again. The parsimonious amount of water Zaniah allowed them was not nearly enough to wash the grit down in his throat.

Gensard ground his teeth. How could this happen to him? He was the son of a prince imprisoned amongst slaves, facing the prospect of being sold as a slave himself. Unthinkable. There must be a way out. An opportunity would eventually arise, and he would grab it.

He glanced at Donella and the intriguing slave girl.

Jiana's appeal was not just in her heart-shaped face. Her sad, light-colored eyes pierced his heart like an arrow. Her slender body moved gracefully. His pulse elevated just gazing at her. She was not a beauty as Lauressa was, but her fragility, yet strength to survive, attracted him. And he had seen plenty of beautiful young ladies at functions in the Samarantha palace. Their awareness of their own charms bored him. Jiana seemed unmindful of her allure.

But no, he didn't have time to acquaint himself with her.

He steeled his heart. He would travel faster if he wasn't burdened with the responsibility of taking care of the girls.

He forced his gaze on Agomeisa's back. If he could retrieve his scimitar, he would skewer the slave trader. He indulged in imagining the scene multiple ways. He spent a pleasant half hour of daydreaming.

The slaver and his wife lay down in the deepest shade for a siesta within watching distance of the wagon.

The wagon's roof and canyon walls offered the captives some relief from the baking sun.

As they rested in the heat, he turned his attention to the other men and assessed them. Hazibal seemed a worthy opponent with his muscled arms and barrel chest. He would do well in a street fight. Brute strength. Break a man in two without breaking a sweat.

Now, Sad-alah was another kettle of fish. Wiry. Nimble. Shrewd. Likely to stab you in the back rather than fight fair.

Donella sat across from him. She was covered in dirt and sweat, as they all were. Since the girls were unchained, she was able to braid her dusty hair. Jiana reached over and helped her.

"Where are you from?" Donella smiled kindly at Jiana. She seemed the only one able to get the shy girl to open up.

Sitting near the door, Gensard surreptitiously tested the strength of the bars around him while idly listening to the girls. He was careful not to clink his wrist chains and draw attention to himself. The cage so far had proved solid. Nothing budged. Wait, one was slightly loose. He wiggled it. If only he had a tool.

"Originally, I grew up in Uludra, a town in the hill country. When my parents died in the plague, I went to live with my grandpap in Tilmuk. I helped him in the vineyards."

"What was that like?"

"My grandpap oversaw the workers. I was only five when he took me in. I would give him lengths of string to tie up the vines. At the time, I thought my job was very important." A dimple peeped out as she smiled.

"He told me stories while we worked. I spent a lot of time with my grandpap. The other children wouldn't play with me. They made fun of my limp."

Gensard paused wiggling the loose bar. He had wondered how she became lame. "Did you suffer an accident?"

Her eyes slanted at him, her expression closed. He was afraid she wouldn't answer.

She curled her foot under her. She raised her eyes, hesitant. "I was born with one leg shorter than the other." Her chin jutted in the air, as if she dared them to say something.

"No one seeing your pretty face notices it."

Her eyes opened wide, surprise crossing her features.

"He's right." Donella nodded.

Glancing over at Agomeisa and his wife, then the other two male prisoners, who all slept, Donella removed something from her pocket and passed it to Jiana. When she noticed Gensard eying her, she held out some seeds to him as well. "Desert chia will give you energy."

Gensard took the seeds. He wouldn't turn down anything that would help him keep up his energy and escape. He chewed slowly. He had the feeling that Donella wasn't fond of him. But it didn't stop her from sharing her food with him.

"Thank you," he mumbled. He wasn't in the habit of thanking servants. They lived to serve him. But she was born a free woman, and they were in survival circumstances.

"It's what way—um, wayfarers do." Donella glanced at Jiana sideways. "Show hospitality."

He knew she meant waykeeper. Just as he kept his parentage a secret, she and their original companions had decided to hide their vocation amongst the goat-worshiping peoples of Canteor. Those who served the One Who Fashioned All were considered the enemy.

"How different your customs are." Jiana wiped her hands on her dress. "My people are suspicious of strangers. Many bandits and cutthroats travel the byways. Hospitality is for family and close friends. Panmin discourages kindness to disbelievers."

"Panmin?" Gensard leaned forward. "The goat god?"

"You've heard of him? He's terrible but powerful." Jiana hugged herself. "We shouldn't speak of him."

"I sacrificed my firstborn son to him," Sad-alah opened his eyes from where he relaxed against the headboard and glared at them. "And what good did it do me? I'm not prosperous, as the black priest promised. That's why I don't believe in any god. They're all false."

Repulsion traveled up Gensard's spine. Expressions of horror were mirrored on the girls' faces.

"Not so. Look around you." Donella gestured with her hand. "Where did the land come from? The sky? The water? The tiniest bug to the largest beast? There is one God. Creator of all. Powerful and loving. My people follow Him."

"Can he release us from our bondage?" Sad-alah raised a dark eyebrow at her. When she didn't answer, he smirked. "I didn't think so."

Donella crossed her arms. "His ways are not our ways. He let this happen to us for a reason."

Sad-alah snorted.

Jiana reached out tentatively and touched Donella. She spoke so low that Gensard had to lean forward to hear her. "I would like to believe in a loving God. No one has showed me love since my grandpap died." Her expression turned sorrowful.

"You said you had a brother—," Donella let her voice trail off. She put her hand over the other girl's.

Jiana stiffened. "My older brother. He sold me into slavery when I was eight. When grandpap died there was no money. The vineyard owner threatened to throw us out. My brother begged for mercy and promised to work hard. He was seventeen, strong. The owner agreed to keep him on. But since my brother couldn't feed us both, he took me to the slave market."

Jiana turned her head away, but Gensard saw tears glistening. Her voice was thick. "I don't want to talk about it anymore."

Gensard had seen some cruel things in his life, but selling a child was the worst. Pain stabbed his heart at the thought of the lovely girl sold off like a piece of furniture.

He had never considered how slaves must feel.

Maybe he would free the girls when he escaped. But then they'd be on their own. He couldn't be responsible for them.

Gensard wished for a means to help Jiana. Her limp looked painful. If he could add something to the bottom of her sandal, it could add height to the shorter leg. Although it would present no problem to a cobbler in Samarantha, out here in the wilderness, it would be difficult. But he was not one to give up easily.

First, when they were all resting, he used his hand to measure the size of Jiana's foot.

When he was sitting by the campfire waiting for dinner in the evening, Gensard looked about for a piece of wood. It took several evenings before he found a properly sized piece. Since Agomeisa allowed him no knife, he was at a loss how to whittle the shape. The only thing at hand was a sharp stone. Awkwardly, he used it on the piece of wood, shaving off splinters.

This would take forever. But what else did he have to occupy himself?

Days later, he got it to the size of Jiana's sandal. As he moved around outside the wagon, he searched for a vine or pliable grass stalk that he could use to tie it to the sandal. But his freedom was limited compared to Donella. He decided to enlist her help.

That evening, after Jiana gave him his serving and Donella passed him the waterskin, he motioned her to come closer to him. In an undertone he said, "I could use your help. I am making a platform for Jiana's sandal." He pulled the wood piece from his pocket and showed it to her before slipping it back out of view.

"That's a wonderful idea!" Donella's face lit up with joy, either at his cleverness or for her friend.

"But I have no way to nail it on the bottom of her sandal. I thought I could tie it with some rope or vine or stalk of grass. I need you to keep your eyes open for one of them."

Donella nodded.

Agomeisa bellowed for her. "Hey, girl. Give me that waterskin. The dust on the road makes a man thirsty."

Several days went by before Donella dropped a piece of leather strap, which had a frayed end, in his lap. She was returning from filling the leather waterskin at a waterhole. He wondered if she found it or broke it herself. Gensard tucked it in his pocket.

That night was clear with a full moon. While the others slept, Gensard gently removed Jiana's sandal from her small foot. He laid the piece of wood against the bottom. Tying the leather strap through the sandal, he attached the platform. It was a clumsy fix, but the best he could do with what was at hand. The strap would rub her sole raw. He frowned. Untying it, he worked the leather through the sandal straps, weaving it in before tying. A little better, but still amateurish.

In his privileged palace life, he had taken everything for

granted. He only had to send a servant to the cobbler to fix a shoe or buy a new one. Someone had cleaned, pressed, and mended his clothes. He didn't even know her name. If he ever returned home to Samarantha he promised himself he would learn it and thank her in person.

Jiana was delighted the next morning when he showed her the sandal and told her what he'd done.

Her eyes filled with wonder. Putting it on, she walked about. "My limp is gone! How can I ever thank you, Gensard?" Her smile shone on him like the sun after a storm.

His chest swelled with pride. He realized he couldn't remember offering a girl a gift. And he certainly never made a gift for anyone. He was always on the receiving end. Who knew how good it would feel to give rather than receive? How selfish he had been his whole life. Why had he never realized it until now?

9 Bidori Island

Nadun called out a command and several burly men surrounded the group. "So you know each other? Kadar? Pellas? Bad blood between you and this young man?"

"Not exactly." Guy defended himself.

"Yes!"

Guy glared at Kadar. "You attacked me first! You threatened the sovereign ruler of Valdeor!" Guy appealed to Nadun, "I saved lives."

"He banished us here!" Kadar growled, fighting to free himself from his friend's grasp.

Nadun held up his hand. "I listen to both sides." He motioned to the burly men. "Bring them to the meeting house."

The villagers grabbed them and bound their wrists behind them with strips of rope. Guy twisted his hands and the rough twine bit into his skin.

Nadun clapped his hands, calling the natives to attention. He made a series of clicks and whistles. Guy wondered at the strange language, for that must be what it was. The villagers abandoned their rakes, passing them to the women. They clustered around, whistling and gesturing amongst themselves.

Then the men marched the three after Nadun, who headed into the largest structure. The villagers streamed after them.

The meeting house was twice as large as the huts surrounding it. Sturdy beams of wood supported the entrance. Sea serpents and marine animals were carved all around the beams. The thatched roof was a round conical shape. Inside was cooler and dim. Benches lined the walls around a central platform. On it was a wooden chair which had the same carvings of sea creatures as the outer door.

The captors forced Guy, Kadar, and Pellas to their knees in front of the platform. The village men took their places on the benches.

Guy wondered if this was going to be a trial. He swallowed.

After what felt like a long time, Nadun appeared in a ceremonial headdress studded with shells and topped with feathers. He wore a necklace of large teeth strung together over his bare brown chest. His staff seemed to be made of one swirled horn or seashell.

One of the guards clapped three times and the room went silent. "Chief Nadun judges."

Guy broke out in a sweat. He glanced around the room at the stern faces. His gaze landed back on Nadun. The chief 's serious expression hid the once friendly native.

"Let Kadar speak."

"Great Chief, your men found us half dead on your beaches months ago. Subar, our comrade, drowned. At the time we begged for shelter while we waited for passage on a ship to Canteor. This magician is the one who banished us. He practices the dark arts."

Gasps came from around the room and Nadun's expression darkened.

"No! That's not true!" the words exploded from Guy. Shock reverberated through him. His gut twisted at the lie.

The man guarding Guy shook him. "Quiet!"

As he held up a hand, Nadun's steely glance quelled Guy. "Your turn will come." Turning his head, he nodded to Kadar to continue.

"He used his powers to summon a storm which sucked us up into a giant whirlwind and dropped us on your shore." Kadar bared his teeth triumphantly at Guy. His tale had all the men whispering and glaring at Guy.

"And do you, Pellas, agree with Kadar?" Nadun pursed his lips.

Guy sent a pleading glance Pellas' way.

Pellas shifted as if uncomfortable. "Yes," his voice was subdued. He wouldn't meet Guy's eyes.

Kadar gave Guy an evil grin.

Guy grit his teeth. He lifted his heart to the winged Guardian of Valdeor. *Please help me convince them of my innocence.*

The guard pushed Kadar back to his knees before the assembly.

Nadun tipped his staff and commanded Guy to stand before him. His guard yanked him to his feet.

"What have you to say to these accusations?"

Guy lifted his chin and met Nadun's eyes. "I serve the One Who Fashioned All. He gave me a gift to open portals—doorways—that go from one place to another. I offered my gift to the queen of my country."

"What country is that? Queen Nerea of the Isles never spoke of this."

"Reina Lauressa of Valdeor."

Nadun raised his eyebrows and leaned forward. "I have heard of the wise queen. She was lost for a hundred years." Murmurs went around the room until Nadun's glance silenced them.

"Did you use your magic to find her?" Curiosity replaced his stern expression.

Guy saw a way to justify his "magic" in their eyes. He arranged his thoughts.

"I have met her. I came here under her protection. Let me tell you about her. A winged being of light extended Reina Lauressa's life beyond the normal years. He gave her an old man to hide her and watch over her. Then when the time was right, a young man accepted the quest to find the lost queen. He guarded her and fought for her. They made alliances with all the peoples of Valdeor who helped them overthrow the evil warlord who sat on her throne."

The village men no longer glared as hostilely. Even Pellas and Kadar seemed caught up in the tale.

Guy searched for the right words to continue. "The winged being, who we call the Guardian of Valdeor, appeared when she was crowned and promised her line would prevail for many centuries because she was faithful to her God." Guy modulated his tone to one of confidence. "The Guardian appeared to me a few months ago and gave me a mission to find the shrine of this God, the Creator, the One Who Fashioned All."

A gasp went around the room.

"I bear a birthmark on my left hand. The Creator blessed me with it."

The room erupted with muted chatter and calls of, "Let us see!"

Nadun stood and the villagers quieted. Nadun stepped off the dais. He motioned to the guards to untie Guy.

Guy's arms tingled from the strain of being tied behind him. He flexed his fingers causing pins and needles to shoot up his arms. He held out his left hand toward Nadun. The interlocking ovals, though faded, were still distinguishable.

The Chief paled. "'Tis the ancient symbol of the Unnamed God."

He went down on one knee before Guy. The villagers imitated him.

Guy stared at the sea of bowed heads. This was worse than being on trial. Guy didn't want them to treat him as a god.

"My deepest apologies, my lord. We did not know who you were." Nadun bowed his head. He stood and his subjects took their seats. "Long ago, we of the isles worshiped the Unnamed God. But great sickness came and many of our people died. We lost our way to the shrine you speak of. We assumed the Unnamed God had abandoned us. We turned to Makba, god of the sea, to provide us with food. You have brought the old stories alive. I believe you are a prophet of the Unnamed God, I have faith you will show us the way to Him again." He removed his headdress. "No longer will I serve Makba."

"What? He shows you a tattoo and you worship him?" Kadar burst out. His eyes blazed and the veins on his neck stood out.

A guard slapped the side of Kadar's head. "Quiet, you!"

"Kill the liars!" one spectator chanted, and they all joined in.

Pellas wore a confused expression, looking from Guy's hand to the natives. His face drained of color.

Nadun raised his staff and tapped it three times on the ground. "So be it!"

Guards hefted the two to their feet and started dragging them away.

Guy's pulse drummed in his ears. Moments ago, he had faced imprisonment or death. Reprieved, he felt a surge of pity for the two now facing death. "No! Do not kill them on my account! My God is a merciful God!" Guy held out his arms, pleading. "Stop!"

When all turned their eyes toward him, he tried to think of a solution to satisfy them all. "Send them home to Canteor."

Arguments broke out among the spectators.

Nadun pounded the staff and the villagers quieted down.

Guy glanced around the room. At some point, the women and children had crowded in the back of the meeting hall. With fifty pairs of eyes on him, he searched for the words to touch their hearts.

"The Unnamed God created us all to know and love Him. If these two men agree to worship Him, will you spare their lives?"

For the first time, Nadun turned to his subjects. Some nodded "yes," a few "no."

A small boy came running over and grabbed Nadun's legs. "Papi, Pellas teach me to make bird from wood. Make their calls." His face puckered, the boy pleaded, "You save Pellas!"

Nadun's face softened. "Go back to your mother, Didi." He looked at the Canteorans, a flicker of compassion in his eyes. "If they agree to worship the Unnamed God, I will allow them to depart on the next ship that visits the island."

Guy's tension bled away. Their fate was no longer on his shoulders, but their own. He, Nadun, and those present confronted the prisoners.

Kadar spoke first. He glared at Guy as if he would kill him. "I serve Panmin, god of my forefathers. Death to the unbelievers." He spit at Guy's feet.

Guy's heart dropped. His pleading words were for nothing.

Pellas scowled at his companion. He dropped his eyes to the ground. Everyone waited to hear what he would say.

Lifting his head, Pellas looked at Nadun, then Guy. "You were right about us. We did try to attack Reina Lauressa. I stabbed you in the side. I deserved your exiling me here." He swallowed. "But I've been happy here in Bidori. These are good people, peace-loving people. If their god brings them that sense of inner peace, then I want to follow Him and have it for myself."

"Traitor!" Kadar shouted as men dragged him away.

Didi's small voice cheered as he raced to Pellas and hugged him. He swung around to his father. "Can he stay? Not go away now?"

Pellas ruffled the boy's hair but gazed at Guy. "I would like to join you and find the Unnamed God's shrine." A pleading expression replaced the earlier shame in his dark eyes. A slight flush spread across his face. "If you would have me."

Guy hesitated a moment, then nodded. He knew there was risk involved. Pellas might say he converted with his tongue but may not have in his heart. But his words rang sincere. And the small child hero-worshiped Pellas, who seemed genuinely fond of him. Guy would trust the child's instinct.

"Let us celebrate and make a feast for the Unnamed God and His prophet." Nadun clapped his hands and the villagers dispersed.

Nadun didn't seem so formal without his headdress as he walked over and joined Guy and Pellas. "I will have my son show you to a place where you may bathe and rest. Tonight, you come to our feast."

Nadun motioned to a teenage boy. "My son, Barbu, will take care of you."

Barbu, who Guy guessed to be fourteen, had skinny arms and legs. The bright, white grin on his dark face gleamed with enthusiasm. "Follow me." He gestured and led them from the meeting room toward a cluster of huts near the jungle.

"Is it true you can walk through air? What is your land like? Are all your tribe light skin?" Barbu tilted his head to one side, his eyes shining with curiosity.

Guy couldn't help chuckling. "Slow down. I don't walk through air. I open a doorway which lets me cross vast spaces in a single step."

Pellas rubbed the back of his neck. "It's my fault Barbu and the others think you're a magician. That's the way I saw it.

"We sailed from Canteor, intending to ambush your forces. Our archers disembarked first and distracted your warriors. When twilight came, a group of us fighters came off the ship and stole into the enemy camp. Our leader wore a ring with the symbol on your hand. Fog came out of nowhere. My companions disappeared into it. One minute Kadar and I were ready to step into the mist, the next minute you ran at us. I tried to stop you. Then suddenly Kadar and I were swept away by a giant hand of wild wind."

The three of them stopped outside a hut, Barbu's eyes even larger than before.

"The hurricane force lifted me off my feet. The rain battered me from all sides. I swear I was suspended high in the storm." Pellas eyes reflected the fear of that moment. "Next I knew, I was sprawled on the beach half a day's walk from here. I managed to crawl up the beach before passing out."

Barbu nodded his head and took up the tale. "My friends and I were combing the beach for storm treasure. We found you instead that morning and took you back to the village."

Guy wondered if a waypost were on this island. As soon as he got the chance, he would hunt for it.

"Please understand, Pellas. I had to send you away. Your force meant to attack the palace. I pledged my help to Reina Lauressa. Your warriors nearly killed her."

"Actually, I am grateful. Being here has brought me peace. I have come to appreciate a simple life. Even if you won't have me, I will not go back to the life I led." Pellas' eyes shone with sincerity and his mouth twisted in a wry grin. "I use my dagger now to carve birds and animals for the children."

Guy studied the man. His guilt at what he had done to the man eased a little. "It's in the past now." Guy extended his hand.

Pellas shook it. "And I'm sorry I stabbed you."

"You're friends now. Good. You can share quarters." Barbu shifted from one foot, to the other, grinning from ear to ear. "I'll have the girls bring you food and water." Barbu strode away.

Entering the hut, Guy saw a chipped mirror for shaving on the middle pole between two pallets. Guy realized Pellas had shared this space with Kadar.

Guy felt a lump in his chest. "I'm sorry for your friend Kadar."

"We weren't friends." Pellas grabbed some gear, presumably Kadar's, since he dumped it in a heap by the doorway. "I didn't know him before the mission. He hated it here and was anxious to rejoin the army." Pellas shrugged. "He made his choice."

Barbu returned, a bundle in his arms, followed by two girls carrying a pitcher of water and a plate of fruit. They shyly glanced at the visitors and giggled when Guy thanked them. Putting down their offerings, they put their hands together and bowed as they left. More whispers and giggles came from outside as they scurried away.

"Forgive them." Barbu rolled his eyes. "Traders mostly come from other islands or Canteor. They are unused to your pale skin and hair."

Guy self-consciously smoothed his blond curls.

"For you." Barbu unrolled the bundle of clothes and a pair of sandals.

"Thank you." Guy longed for a bath.

As if reading his mind, Barbu offered to take him to the swimming hole.

After washing away the salt water, Guy dried himself and donned the borrowed clothes. The tunic was tight and the trousers slightly big. He'd need to find a belt or rope to keep them up. At least the sandals fit.

Barbu leaned on ta tree trunk, his eyes bright with curiosity. "Tell me about your land." Barbu had previously asked Guy the same question.

Guy rubbed the back of his neck. "Valdeor is not an island; it's a continent which is much, much bigger. We get freezing weather—so cold the rain becomes hard and builds up on the ground as snow. I worked on a farm planting crops, chopping wood for the fire, taking care of chickens and pigs. But once I left home, I found Valdeor is vast. Mountain ranges as tall as your volcano for long, long distances. Sandy deserts, which take weeks to cross, where few things grow. Fields and plains that stretch to the horizon. Many of us are pale-skinned, but we have dusky-colored people too in Motari and Samarantha. But I have never seen skin as dark as yours."

"I would love to see Valdeor." Barbu smiled and his whole face lit up. "Maybe you can take me there some day. I can witness hard rain. Ha, ha."

They walked back to the hut.

"If there's anything else you need, I will be watching outside the door. I'll keep away any curious visitors so you can rest." Barbu brought both hands together and made a slight bow from the waist before taking up his position as guard.

Pellas loaned Guy a comb.

They sat cross-legged on the pallets and ate the fruits, which Pellas called mangoes, star fruit, and melon. Sweet tasting, they dripped with refreshing juice.

The bird calls had quieted with the afternoon heat. The mud walls muted the sound of the waves.

Exhaustion caught up with Guy as he wiped his sticky fingers. Stretching out on the pallet, he fell asleep.

10 Competition

$\mathcal{S}$ ince entering the Jugara desert, they had not seen any dwellings. But that changed today as the wagon left the canyon lands. Fields of grass stretched endlessly. The sun still beat down from a blue sky, but no longer reflected heat from the packed earth. After hours on the flat prairie, the road ran beside a stream. Soon they saw signs of habitation. Cows stood in groups. Laborers scythed the grass on the side of the road. Women followed, bundling it into shocks. The scent of sweet grass wafted in the breeze.

The wagon rolled into a village, which was just a cluster of mud houses with straw roofs. Set apart was the only wooden building.

Agomeisa parked outside it. The walls were weathered gray, as was the crude pig on the signboard above the door. Gensard translated for Donella, The Red Boar.

Handing over the reins to his wife, the slaver entered.

Donella could smell the charcoal-cooking food, making her stomach growl. She could not help but imagine roasted beef and potatoes slathered in gravy.

How she longed for the freedom to walk through that door and order what she liked.

She looked at her gaunt traveling companions and saw the

same hunger in their eyes. But just like the cattle nearby, they waited on their master.

Twelve days on the road had taught her that Agomeisa's will was paramount. She didn't voice an opinion or ask a question unless she wanted a slap across the face. She finally understood Jiana's reluctance to talk in those first days.

A wave of depression and homesickness rose in her throat. She choked back sudden tears.

Gensard must have seen it on her face because he leaned over and whispered, "What's wrong?"

"What do you think? I'm a slave, a possession. If we were in Valdeor, I would have a chance of getting us home. My skills as a waykeeper mean nothing in a place with no wayposts."

Even though she knew Guy said he sensed only one waypost in Canteor, on the coast, she had kept an eye out for them along their route. She had hoped he was wrong and that she would find one.

Gensard grunted. "That's nothing new. I have no standing, either, in this strange new land. I have never felt so powerless." He sat with his chained hands dangling between his legs. His deep brown eyes met hers openly with none of his usual superiority.

She was continually surprised he seemed so approachable these days. It all started with his kindness to Jiana. By fixing her sandal, her limp was barely detectable.

"What else?" He genuinely seemed to want to know what bothered her.

"Do I need a reason beyond hunger and sorrow at our situation?" She knew she was whining, but frustration pressed on her heart like a dammed stream waiting to burst.

"It's not like you. That is all. You're the one befriending the others. Keeping everyone's spirits up with your chatter." He glanced around, making sure the others weren't listening. "Sharing the food you find." He sat back and studied his nails. "I think Hazibal would take you to be his wife."

Donella glanced toward the big man, whom they had learned was a blacksmith by trade, and back to the grinning Gensard. Shock tingled in her middle.

Gensard tried to hide his grin, but she saw it.

A second wave of shock rolled over her when she realized Gensard was teasing her. This episode had changed him as well. He was no longer Prince High and Mighty.

She tried to put herself in his place. She was a commoner chafing at the bonds of imprisonment. How much more difficult for someone born to privilege, used to having every whim answered?

Donella dug deep to understand why she wanted to cry. "I have no purpose. And no hope."

His laughter gone, Gensard's dark eyes gazed at her intently. She was aware how handsome he was, even covered in road dust with stubble growing on his chin. Her heart fluttered at his attention.

"Your purpose is to survive." His expression hardened. His casual pose became rigid muscle. She was aware of strength emanating from him. "That's all that matters. Live each day so you can live tomorrow."

It seemed he must have thought about it a lot. His words sounded like they came from deep inside him.

Their conversation was cut short as Agomeisa and three men exited from the tavern. Agomeisa gestured at their cage. The men strolled over.

Donella's pulse sped up.

Agomeisa pulled out the key that he always kept on a cord around his neck. He opened the door. "Hazibal, step out."

The red-headed giant clambered out awkwardly with his feet chained a foot apart. The slaver proceeded to point out his good points. "He's strapping, as you can see. Look at those bulging muscles. He can wrestle an ox with his bare hands. He's never lost a fight. I'll stake him against any man of your choice."

A man with a squashed face like a toad chuckled. "I'll take your bet." He turned to one of the others. "Get Chad."

The man took off at a lope toward the field workers. He yelled something at them as they looked up and gestured at the wagon.

A man who was hunched over scything, straightened. He passed his scythe to another. He dwarfed the villager leading him to their group. As they neared, Donella studied the fighter. He was a head taller than anyone else, even several inches over Hazibal. A sheen of sweat glistened on his corded arm muscles. He had a thick, dark beard and his eyes were slits under his bushy eyebrows.

"Chad. This man wants to wrestle."

The giant merely grunted and removed his tunic. He acted as if he were often challenged.

Agomeisa unchained Hazibal and stepped back.

Several people wandered over from the tavern and gathered with the workers who crowded round, their scythes forgotten. They formed a loose circle around the competitors. Donella and the other slaves stood, gripping the bars for a view.

Hazibal stretched his arms back, loosening muscles, then cracked his knuckles. He obviously had fought many times before.

The wrestlers bent at the waist, intently watching one another. Suddenly they closed. Chad grasped Hazibal around the waist and Hazibal clasped the other around the head. They strove mightily to unbalance the other. Muscles strained. Their feet scuffed the dirt. They grunted.

Donella put her fist up to her lips.

Chad lifted Hazibal's feet off the ground and dashed him down. Hazibal lay there.

Donella gasped, covering her mouth with her hand.

Agomeisa knelt over the fallen wrestler. When Hazibal sat, grasping his side, Agomeisa yelled, "You fool! You cost me a bag of coins! You are worthless, you hear me!" He grabbed the whip from the wagon's seat and struck several times at Hazibal, who covered his face.

Gensard gritted his teeth. He longed to grab the whip and lash Agomeisa.

Throwing down the whip, Agomeisa stomped off toward the tavern. The crowd dispersed, many patting Chad on the back as they returned to the fields.

Zaniah hustled Hazibal to return to his prison. The red-headed man favored his right side as he climbed aboard. Gensard reached out a hand to help him, unconsciously. The girls cried beside him.

Hazibal had fought well, but his opponent, besides being bigger, fought better. What did Agomeisa think would happen? He hadn't even taken the time to consider the opponent before boasting of Hazibal's prowess—a tactical error.

"You didn't do us any favors. Now Agomeisa will take out his anger on all of us." Sad-alah shook his head.

Donella reached out and touched the giant's side. "Are your ribs broken?" She boldly turned to Zaniah, standing nearby. "His ribs should be bound."

When Zaniah squinted her eyes at Donella, but made no move, the girl gestured. "He will not fetch a fair price if he's damaged. So he lost once! He wouldn't have if he was better matched to his opponent."

"You have much to learn, girl," Zaniah hissed. But she must have seen the logic of Donella's argument, because she brought Donella a piece of frayed material.

Donella tore it into strips. Gensard intervened as Donella tried to reach around the big man's chest. "Let me." Gensard wrapped the material tightly and tucked it in.

As Gensard helped Hazibal into a sitting position, he winced. "Why do the two of you care what happens to me?" Hazibal shifted until he seemed comfortable.

Gensard had no ready answer. A few weeks ago, he would have walked by a slave and never even thought of how it felt to be someone's possession. He didn't personally own any slaves, but he had many servants in his father's house. He never considered their feelings or desires. What kind of person did that make him?

Donella's voice intruded on his thoughts. "You are a companion in our suffering. One of the Creator's children. We all matter to Him. And as His followers, you matter to us." Donella knelt as she looked for other bruises.

Hazibal rubbed his beard. "No stranger has ever treated me as you have." His face softened as he gazed on Donella.

She blushed and stood. "Rest will help." She retreated to Jiana's side.

Gensard had teased her about Hazibal's interest, but he might have been righter than he knew.

He moved to stand on the shady side of their prison. He longed to escape from the baking sun. His tongue cleaved to the roof of his mouth. If only Zaniah would give them water. But Gensard feared Sad-alah was correct. Agomeisa would take out his anger on all of them.

"You are so brave." Jiana's faint voice penetrated his thoughts. He glanced down to see her admiring gaze on Donella. Tendrils of loose hair curled on her brow. "You stood up for Hazibal. Where do you get the courage?"

Donella pushed back her damp ringlets. "I don't like standing by and watching evil win."

"But Zaniah almost beat you." She clasped her hands in front of her. "Hazibal wouldn't stand up for you."

"My Creator would see me. And I couldn't live with myself if

I were able to help but refused to do so." Donella brushed hair from her eyes.

"Even if you win over Hazibal, you won't change Agomeisa or Zaniah. Kindness is not their nature."

Gensard felt compelled to speak. "You're saying one man cannot make a difference. But history is full of men who have instituted change. It starts with one person, man or woman, who leads by example."

Like his brother Leander, who refused to watch his father kill starving men.

Would he be as brave in the face of exile?

Wasn't his desire to accomplish the Reina's mission really a bid for his father's praise?

Hours later, when the afternoon was far gone, Agomeisa staggered out of the tavern. He came over to the wagon. Putting his hands on the bars he stared at them with bleary eyes. The slaver licked his lips. He reeked of alcohol. He focused on Gensard. "You. The one who carried a scimitar. Can you use it?"

Gensard narrowed his eyes at his captor. Something was up. If Gensard said yes, would he get a chance to use his weapon against this monster?

Pulse thrumming, he leaned forward. "Of course. Why else would I carry it?" He gave a reckless answer, one that might enrage the other, but he didn't care.

Agomeisa either didn't hear the sarcasm or was too far gone to notice.

"Zaniah!" He stumbled away. "Feed this one and Sad-alah. They duel one another in the village ring this evening."

His muscles tightening, Gensard glanced from Agomeisa to Sad-alah. Dark eyebrows together, Sad-alah seemed to be measuring him, just as Gensard measured him back.

While his father's swordmaster had schooled Gensard in technique, Leander, his brother, taught him strategy.

Now Leander's 'Rules for a Warrior' flowed through Gensard's mind. *Know your enemy. Study him and learn his weaknesses. If you can anticipate his move, you can counter his attack with one of your own. If you can discover his pattern of thinking, you can outwit him. If you can surprise him, you can beat a more experienced opponent.*

And the thin, wiry Canteoran had the nimbleness of an experienced fighter. He constantly played with his deck of cards, dexterously slipping the cards through his fingers. Gensard could easily imagine him with a dagger blade in his hand. More than any of the other prisoners, Sad-alah also exhibited keen awareness of his surroundings. Just as Gensard kept an eye on their captors, always scanning for ways to escape, watching for deviations in Agomeisa's behavior, so Gensard often caught Sad-alah doing the same.

Whereas Hazibal seemed lost in his thoughts, or merely asleep, Gensard frequently caught Sad-alah watching him and the girls out of slitted eyes, even when his body position indicated slumber during the day.

Sad-alah reminded Gensard of a coiled snake ready to strike at a moment's notice.

As the villagers came in ones and twos to stare at the prisoners on display, Gensard wondered what they made of him. Covered head to foot in dust and dried sweat, assuming he looked like his companions, he didn't present a formidable appearance. Combine that with his thinness from lack of food, he didn't think they would bet on him. He was forced to listen as they argued over the two men's ability, placing bets.

"This one seems cunning." A fat man pointed to Sad-alah, who ignored him.

"Ah, but this one has muscle under his filthy attire," a man with a squint countered.

Gensard vowed he would never again talk around servants and courtiers as if they couldn't hear him. He had no idea how humiliating it felt.

He was beginning to think he was not a very pleasant person. It hadn't mattered before. Courtiers flattered him. The Samarantha populace bowed to him. His servants hurried to answer all his whims. But what did they really think of him? He hadn't cared, until now.

11 Island Feast

The smell of cooking fish permeated the air as Guy woke from his refreshing sleep. His mouth watered in anticipation. Rolling over he saw he was alone. He quickly combed his mussed hair.

Passing out of the hut, he heard laughter and singing. He followed the sound to the beach. All the villagers gathered in a circle. Three men beat drums, their bodies clad in bright yellow skirts. Flower garlands graced their bare torsos. They sang a lively chant in their own language. Young boys clapped to the rhythm, while girls in white frocks with flowers in their black hair swayed in a graceful dance. Women in modest robes of bright colors prepared the feast.

As he stood at the edge of the festivities, two girls broke away from the rest. They came over, taking his hands. Giggling, they led him to a place of honor next to Nadun.

The chief sat, a red robe over one shoulder, showing one bare ebony shoulder and muscled arm. A woman with a broad nose, and salt and pepper hair, sat beside him. She wore a billowing, sea green gown and an abalone necklace. As he joined them, her white teeth gleamed against her dusky skin in a welcoming smile. She stood and draped a garland of white flowers over his neck.

Their heady fragrance reminded Guy of Donella, and how she

would enjoy the festivities. He could imagine her joining the dancing girls, giggling as she did. His heart sank, heavy at the thought of her. *I failed her. I failed all of them.* The appetizing smell of food no longer appealed to him.

Barbu sat on Guy's other side. One seat down from him sat Pellas, also wearing a garland. Didi leaned against him.

At the end of the performance, Nadun clapped his hands. The drummers and dancers took their seats. When they settled, Nadun addressed the gathering in his own language, which sounded like clicks and whistles.

Barbu spoke in the common tongue for Guy's sake, "We gather today to honor the Unnamed God of All and his messenger."

The company chanted and clapped in rhythm.

Barbu translated, "They sing, 'May the sea be calm on your voyage. May the moon and sun smile on your journey. May you be blessed in your ways.'"

Nadun glanced around the assembly. He raised his eyes and his hands and spoke.

"And may the Unnamed God show his messenger the way to the sacred shrine of old," Barbu related.

A cheer went up.

Nadun's wife signaled the women, who brought dishes and laid them before the chief. Platters were heaped with several types of fish in sauces, what looked like tentacles in a broth, clams and mussels, seaweed, and some unidentifiable courses. Nadun made a gesture over them, similar to the priests of Valdeor when blessing.

Nadun's wife stood, scooped samples of the food into a wooden bowl, and passed it to Guy. "You try." She nodded at him, encouragement in her expression.

Although a mantle of guilt sat on his shoulder, Guy did not want to offend her hospitality. He tried an unfamiliar morsel and found it surprisingly tasty, if somewhat chewy. He nodded at her and she beamed back. She served Nadun, then sat for the women to serve her.

Guy forced himself to try different items, chewing slowly. The food was delicious. It was his appetite that was lacking. His friends should be here with him.

When the dinner was over, there followed more songs and dancing. As the moon rose, some couples clasped hands and moved down the beach, including Barbu and a graceful dancer.

Guy's heart was not in the entertainment, even though it was for his benefit and message of good tidings. He could have danced with one of the native girls making eyes at him. But how could he enjoy himself when Donella and Odem might be in distress or dead? His unworthiness was like a cage, locking him in a lonely place, even though joyful people surrounded him.

As soon as he could leave without giving offense, Guy thanked Nadun and his wife. He wished goodnight to Pellas. Then he walked back to the hut in the moonlight. The only thing that could make the night perfect was the company of his friends. Especially one dark-haired beauty.

The crunch of a footstep sounded behind him. Guy half-turned, thinking Pellas had followed him. A hand shoved him, and Guy landed in the sand. Before he could cry out, something hit the side of his head.

Pain exploded, then blackness engulfed him.

When Guy came to, his head throbbed. Moaning, he opened his eyes, but the world was dark. His cheek laid on a cold, hard-packed surface. He could hear the nearby crash of the surf. As he tried to touch his head, he realized his hands were bound behind his back. He moved his legs, but they were tied together. His shoulders cramped as he struggled, and he realized his hands and feet must be bound with a rope between them. He was trussed like a chicken.

The only person who would do such a thing was Pellas. But the man had seemed so genuinely sorry for his actions.

Who else?

A light shone in his eyes. He instinctively tried to raise his hand to block it, pulling on his bindings and sending waves of pain up his arm into his shoulder, causing the old injury to ache.

"Awake, are you? Your timing is perfect. This way you'll suffer as you die."

Kadar!

"I thought the natives killed you!" Guy squinted at the figure standing over him, holding a torch. He couldn't make out any details, but the voice was unmistakable.

"You don't think I became an assassin of Prince Pashmi without knowing a few tricks."

"Assassin?" Guy swallowed. How did Kadar plan to execute him?

"Oh, yes. Pellas is just a grunt who follows orders. His job was to guard the portal, while I was part of the elite team sent to rid Valdeor of Prince Pashmi's rival, the Reina. I failed my mission because of you. But the prince only wanted her out of the way so she wouldn't stop the coming of our god, Panmin. Your death will do that even better. There will be no pilgrims going to the Isle of Origin."

As his eyes adjusted, Guy saw the gleam of vindictiveness in Kadar's eyes.

"Your unnamed god will have no chance against Panmin. Why doesn't he have a name? A good name gives power," he sneered.

Guy squirmed in his bonds. "Little do you know. He has no name because he *is* so great. He is the Creator, the Uncreated One Who Fashioned All Things. The unending light who forever shines in the darkness. *He Is who is.*"

Kadar grunted. "Foolishness. Let him release you before

Makba, god of the sea, takes you to his depths." He kicked Guy in the ribs.

As he fought the sudden pain, Guy was aware of their voices echoing. The torchlight made shadows on the walls. He guessed they were in a cave. The sound of the waves had grown louder, as if the sea grew closer.

His eyes widened at the thought. He remembered the shore where he washed up and the high tide marks.

"Greet the Sea God in my name." Kadar chortled and walked away, his feet sloshing in the water as he disappeared outside the cave.

Guy made an earnest effort and managed to sit up. Not that it would help. The sea foam tumbled through the cave entrance.

Scooting over to a wall, Guy leveraged his back up against it, pushing with his feet. He couldn't stand, but half crouched.

He grunted. His ribs were bruised, but not broken.

O He Who Fashioned All, as I witnessed for you, please hear me! I need to complete the mission you asked of me. Help!

Brushing his fingers along the wall, he felt a sharp jut of rock. He put his wrists against it and sawed the rope. Scratches stung his skin, but he ignored the pain. The water swirled around his legs. He worked harder. The piece of rock broke off. He strained to stand up, but the rope between his ankles and his wrists held him.

Shuffling along the wall, he headed for the entrance, but fell as a bigger wave knocked him over. Chilly water engulfed him. His eyes stung. Sputtering, he lifted his head out of the seawater, and gulped fresh air. The next wave slammed into him, keeping him from rising. Finally, he gained his knees, but the waves splashed his face. He coughed. He bent his head back, gasping.

When Guy couldn't rise above the incoming tide, he figured all was lost.

Something grabbed him around the neck. His pulse hammered furiously, afraid a monster of the deep had him in its tentacles.

Guy surfaced as it pulled him up. He breathed in convulsively.

"I've got you! Don't struggle!" He heard a voice over the sound of the sea.

Someone swam and dragged him toward the cave opening. Then the current grabbed them and swept them out to sea. His rescuer was a strong swimmer because he fought the sea, eventually dragging Guy to safety on the beach.

As soon as Guy hit the sand, hands pushed on his back, causing him to vomit out seawater.

His rescuer loosened his bonds and turned Guy on his back. The whites of Barbu's eyes stood out in his frantic concern.

"Thanks." Guy eased his shoulders and thighs while he searched the surrounding area. "Kadar—watch out for him!" His voice came out in a rasp. He coughed to clear it.

"No worries. He is gone. I went to check on you, then I saw him hit you. I followed you here."

"I think he may have killed his guards."

Barbu made a sound at the back of his throat. "What? I saw Kadar escape on a boat, and I let him! But it was more important to that I save you. You can walk, yes?"

Although stiff, Guy stood and followed Barbu along a barely visible track along the sea cliff. He would never have been able to find it on his own.

Barbu woke the chief and the three of them hurried to the hut used as Kadar's prison. Nadun was outraged when they found the guards strangled.

"We must warn the nearby islands. Kadar will try to board a ship at one of the bigger harbors."

Guy's responsibility for sending Kadar to the isles made him speak. "I'll tell them as I travel in search of the great shrine."

Barbu stepped forward. "May I go with you?" He turned to the Chief. "Papi?"

Nadun pursed his lips, then solemnly nodded. "Very well, my son. You may be the first pilgrim from our tribe to discover the shrine of the Unnamed God."

12 Gensard Faces Sad-alah

*W*hile Agomeisa was gone, Zaniah had purchased supplies. Now she released Jiana to help her prepare a meal.

As Donella watched them with a tight expression, Gensard wondered if Zaniah was still angry at Donella for demanding her help with Hazibal.

The women pressed and baked the usual barley cakes, but Zaniah also prepared a spit of meat. The savory smell wafted in the air, making Gensard groan with hunger.

When Jiana passed two barley cakes to him, Gensard popped most of one in his mouth. He stopped at the look of desire on Donella's face. He broke part of the second and was ready to pass it to her.

"No need." Jiana held out a barley cake to Donella, then Hazibal. Her chin was set in a stubborn line, glancing back at Zaniah. Yet the older woman didn't say anything. She humphed but followed with the waterskin.

Jiana's shoulders relaxed. Gensard wondered how much that gesture of defiance cost her. She was normally so timid.

Meanwhile, Agomeisa had rinsed his head under the tavern pump. Now, he sat cross-legged on the ground and greedily ate more than his share of the cakes and meat.

But after eating half the meat, he motioned to Zaniah as she finished her cake. "They need strength. Give it to the fighters."

Astonishingly, Zaniah walked to the prison and held a portion of meat out to Sad-alah, who snatched it and chomped it down quickly.

Gensard accepted his from Zaniah, but before putting it in his mouth, he glanced at the girls.

"You need to fight and get us away from this place," Donella spoke softly so only he heard. She averted her eyes after he took a bite.

The meat was warm, crisp on the outside and soft on the inside. Gensard would swear he never tasted anything so good. He ditched his pride and licked the fat from his fingers.

Jiana shyly offered Gensard more water to wash it down. Gensard gulped until he was satisfied. His fingers brushed hers as he handed it back, sending a jolt through him. Her eyes widened and she locked eyes for a heartbeat. She lowered her head and moved to offer the waterskin to Sad-alah. Leaving Gensard to wonder if she felt the same connection as he.

One at a time, after the meal, Agomeisa led his prisoners to an area of privacy.

Gensard was last. He stretched his muscles as best as he could, chained as he was. It wasn't enough. Frustration made him grit his teeth.

"I need to stretch if I am to fight."

Agomeisa ruminated, rubbing the back of his neck. He seemed to make up his mind. "Very well. Zaniah!"

His wife appeared around the bend of the road, her birthmark standing out in the early evening light.

"Take his sister and chain her. Bring her to me."

A tightness constricted Gensard's chest. This was not what he bargained for.

A short time later, the woman led Donella to the clearing where they stood. Zaniah shackled Donella's ankles so she could barely take small steps. She glanced around, a surprised expression on her face. Huge eyes in her pale face met his gaze. Their pleading nearly undid him.

A dagger in his hand, Agomeisa pulled Donella's arm, bringing her close to him. She stared venomously at her captor. He only chuckled, tickling her throat with the dagger tip.

"Let us see you practice." Agomeisa bared his teeth in a grin. "Zaniah, unbind him."

As his shackles fell, Gensard stretched his limbs. Stiff at first, it felt glorious to move. He turned his focus inward, so as not to see Donella's fear. He went through his limbering routine, one he had worked out and practiced numerous times. He spent time on each arm and leg muscle, stretching, bending, loosening. Then he reached for a tree limb on the ground.

He ignored the panicked intake of Donella's breath, as Agomeisa laid his dagger against her throat. But it cost him his sense of peace. His breath caught in his throat. If only he could reach his scimitar strapped to Agomeisa's back. But he couldn't endanger Donella.

He fought for control. Spinning away from the three pairs of eyes, he swung the limb, thrusting and jabbing while he did an intricate dance with his feet.

After twenty minutes, Agomeisa called, "Enough!"

A fine sheen of sweat coating him, Gensard came out of his trance-like state.

"Very impressive. I think you'll make me a lot of money tonight." He pushed Donella toward his wife.

Donella tripped and landed in the dirt. Landing on her knees, she pushed herself up, stubbornly refusing to cry, though Gensard saw the tears gathered as he leaped forward and helped her up.

Agomeisa was there instantly with his dagger touching Gensard's back. "Ease away. Drop the branch."

Gensard did as he was told. He forgot he even held the branch in his desire to help Donella.

Instead of putting them back in their cage, the slaver and his wife led them to the far side of town where the villagers gathered. Sullen faces lit up when Agomeisa shoved Gensard into the ring. Sad-alah was already there, armed with a sword.

The giant, Chad, stood over the figures of Hazibal supported by Jiana. She turned a concerned expression on them. Her gaze went from Donella's chains to Gensard's face.

His scimitar offered to him, Gensard gripped the familiar hilt. Agomeisa grabbed the bound Donella and pulled her toward the other slaves, dagger still prominent. A warning not to try anything or Donella's life would be forfeit.

Sad-alah stepped in view and Gensard shut off his feelings, burying them deep. This man was his enemy now. He would do whatever it took to survive.

His opponent lunged. Gensard stepped aside, bringing his blade down. Sad-alah spun on his toes, barely missing the steel. He came at Gensard again, more controlled. Their blades met, clanging. In and out their weapons slashed, almost too fast for the eye to follow.

Sad-alah smiled grimly, his eyes alight under dark brows. "You have some training. Not such a hick after all."

Gensard's anger rose at the remark. His face suffused with heat, pride pricking him to lash out. He thrust violently. Too late he saw the trap as Sad-alah feinted and drove his sword at Gensard's legs. He skid away, but not before he felt warmth spread down his thigh.

Anger was a poor weapon. Gensard would not let Sad-alah provoke him again.

Gensard slowed his breath and focused on each move. Blow, parry. Thrust, retreat.

At the back of his mind, he studied his foe as they fought. The man seemed made of wires, nimble and quick. Overconfidence was

Sad-alah's failing.

Gensard let his sword arm droop slightly, as if he were tiring. Sad-alah pressed him harder, just as Gensard knew he would. Sad-alah bared his teeth in a grin, no doubt believing he had more stamina. Gensard waited for Sad-alah to overplay his hand. When next they engaged their blades, with a quick flick, he sent Sad-alah's weapon flying.

Eyes wide in shock, his competitor's face contorted with anger.

Gensard knew the thin, dark man would seek a way to kill him in the future.

The men fought in a ring of smooth dirt. The villagers surrounding it elbowed each other for the best view. The noise from the crowd only added to the tension.

Donella ignored the villagers around her and the prick of Agomeisa's dagger at her side. She could only concentrate on Prince Gensard. He reminded her of a slim rapier. Even grimy, the prince exuded forcefulness. His moves were smooth and measured, powerful like himself.

Sad-alah's scar stood out from his droopy left eyelid to the corner of his lip as he exerted himself. He grinned wolfishly as his sword snicked in and out, wickedly fast. He danced around his opponent as if he were a whirlwind, not sinews and muscles.

Donella's pulse hammered in her throat as she watched Prince Gensard and Sad-alah battle each other. She clenched her hands into fists. Of all those gathered, only she knew how excellent a swordsman Gensard was. But still, she tensed at every blow.

The two opponents were serious. She had been peripherally aware that they didn't like each other but pitting them against one another had seemingly heightened their rivalry.

His thin nostrils flared, Prince Gensard thrust at close quarters and miraculously managed to knock Sad-alah's sword from his hand.

A cheer went up from half the crowd, while the other half hissed with disappointment. Many in the audience exchanged coins.

"It seems your brother is my new champion." Agomeisa's sour breath tickled her cheek.

Donella drew away as far as her chains allowed.

After that moment of triumph, Gensard's eyes met hers. She thought she saw a flicker of struggle on his face as he moved toward them, scimitar in hand.

The dagger point jabbed her, making Donella wince in pain.

Gensard stopped and the feral light in his eyes dimmed as he glared at Agomeisa.

She read his thoughts as if he had spoken them aloud. He meant to kill Agomeisa. But she stood in his way.

The three of them stood frozen, then men crowded around, offering payment to Agomeisa. The moment passed.

As Donella lay awake that night, she wondered if Gensard would have sacrificed her life.

"Are you awake?" Jiana's soft voice whispered next to her ear.

"Yes."

"I saw the look on your brother's face." She grew silent. The pause was so long, Donella wondered if she would continue.

"I wish my brother loved me the way yours loves you."

Startled, Donella jerked. "What do you mean?"

"My brother didn't care about me. The vineyard owner offered him work but refused to hire me. He said my limp would hinder me." Jiana's voice held great sadness. "My brother could have tried to find work elsewhere, but I didn't matter to him." Her voice broke. "My brother sold me to the highest bidder so that he could continue to live well."

"Maybe he was scared." Donella realized that might sounded callous. "What happened to you?"

"I was deemed unfit for farm work. So a lady bought me to work in the kitchen. I swept the ashes from the fire, carried jugs of water, fetched for the cook and housekeeper. Sometimes I was too slow and got beaten."

"How old were you?"

"Eight."

Her heartstrings wrung, Donella exclaimed, "How awful! You were just a child." She swallowed the lump of sympathy which formed in her throat.

Donella reached out and took Jiana's hand, squeezing it. "How came you to be in Agomeisa's possession?"

"Recently my mistress sold me. I—I was no longer needed."

When Jiana didn't elaborate further, Donella wondered what was unsaid. Something had happened. After training a slave for eight or nine years, it seemed odd to suddenly sell her.

"My background is so different from yours." Jiana withdrew her hand.

"Nonsense. I'm no fine lady. I grew up at an inn, doing the same chores as you. I washed customer's dishes, swept their rooms, made up their fires. When my mother died, my Uncle Warun and Aunt Sinlindra treated me like an unpaid servant. They said I must earn my bread and the roof over my head."

"And your brother, Gensard? What did he do?"

Donella bit the inside of her cheek. Whatever she said, she would have to fill in Gensard later so he wouldn't trip up. Not that it mattered. In a few more weeks, they'd be separated from Jiana. From each other. She pushed that dreadful thought away.

"He worked in the stables. You've heard him speak of his love of horses. That is where he got it." She didn't really know much about his youth, growing up in a palace.

13 Queen Nerea

*A*n enormous volcano rose above an island, like the hump of a brooding black beast. A wisp of cloud snagged upon its mouth, adding to the image of a breathing animal. Below, lush green foliage swept down its hills to the shore. A white castle perched on a hill overlooking the town clustered around a large natural bay. A big ship floated in the harbor. Smaller fishing boats gathered around it, the islanders offering their wares.

From his vantage point on a small boat bobbing in the current, Guy didn't recognize the ship's flag as Valdeoran or Canteoran. The green strips on white background must be those of another nation.

Barbu sailed their little native boat past the larger one. As they approached the shore, he asked Guy to lower the sail. Pellas grabbed the oars and rowed them until they hit sand.

The three disembarked in the shallow water. Barbu dragged the boat further up the shore, then deftly flipped it to dry. "Welcome to Cressava, largest of the island nations."

Feet crunching on the crushed shell beach, Guy gazed around as they trod across it. With two-story wooden houses, this town was larger and more civilized than Bidori, but cruder than Tulken Harbor.

They entered the busy landing. Several men unloaded sacks

of goods from the sailing ship's dinghy onto the shore. A lean fisherman touted his catch of fish to stout women. Sailors jostled past, whistling at a group of young women strolling the quay. A cooper loaded the last of his barrels on a wagon.

An unkempt man with twisted hands begged for coins. Guy dropped a bronze yiza in his dirty palm. "Blessings on you, young man," he cried, clutching the coin.

Barbu seemed to know the way as they walked down wide streets. The gray-weathered buildings seemed to lean together, huddling from the elements.

Tantalizing aromas of cooking meat seeped from a tavern.

"Let us eat before we wait for hours to see the queen." Guy knew palace routine, having spent months at Mintala. After two days at sea, with only bread to eat, Guy's mouth watered at the thought of real food.

"What'll it be, gents?" A server half-heartedly swiped the crumbs from their table.

"Three ales and three daily specials." Pellas put down a handful of coins and grinned at the other two.

"Coming up." The server left.

Guy glanced around. Dark-skinned islanders in their bright knee-length wraps conversed in their dialect at tables. The sailors that passed them a few minutes ago sat at the wooden bar, drinking and rowdy. Cooking smoke mingled with tobacco smoke in a comforting smell.

As the server delivered a fresh fish dinner and crisp potatoes, Guy's stomach grumbled. He savored each bite.

Suddenly a hand clamped on Guy's shoulder.

"You're sitting at my table."

Guy swung around and faced someone he never thought to see again. A one-eyed man loomed over him, a menacing expression on his face.

"You!" Drake, the deck master of the *Indomitable* pirate ship, recognized Guy at the same time. "Deserter!"

As Drake yanked Guy to his feet, Guy's stomach threatened to heave his meal.

Out of the corner of his eye, he saw Pellas surge into action. "Let my friend go," Pellas demanded. The muscular man grabbed Drake from behind. The deck master's hand released its death grip on Guy.

The two men wrestled like a wolf hamstringing a bear. Patrons leapt out of the way as crockery and tables went over.

"Stop! Stop!" The server tried to break up the fight.

A burly man wearing a greasy apron, whom Guy assumed was the tavern keeper, stomped over. "Stop, you scum!" He effortlessly yanked the men apart and twisted Drake's arm behind his back. "I told you before, no brawling in my tavern!"

"He deserted my ship!" Drake twisted, trying to free himself, but he had met his match.

The taverner eyed Guy. "Then your judgment is poor. He's not up to weight. He couldn't man a rowboat!"

The taverner marched Drake to the door and shoved him outside. "Look for crewmen somewhere else. Or next time I'll call for the queen's guards."

As the owner passed by their table, Guy thanked him.

He humphed. "Choose your mates more careful-like. That one's a pirate."

As they sat down to finish their meal, Pellas asked Guy who the attacker was. Guy explained how pirates aboard the Canteor ship, the *Indomitable*, had made him the mast boy. And how with the help of another boy he had eventually escaped.

Guy cautiously followed the others from the barroom, keeping watch for Drake in case he lurked nearby. "I came to Cressava to see the Queen of the Isles, but I'm glad it won't be as a prisoner.

Thanks for your help back there."

"I owe you a debt of gratitude." Pellas rubbed the bridge of his nose. "Instead of using my skills for the wrong purpose, I can use them as your bodyguard."

"The queen should be listening to petitions today. I have met her before with my father." Barbu motioned them to hurry up.

Barbu led them up the hillside toward a castle perched on a ledge overlooking the town. As they neared it, Guy marveled at the construction. Seashells of every size, shape, and color entirely covered the outer walls. It looked as if it had risen from the seabed. The entrance was scalloped like a shell.

Guards stood at the entry way, their bored gazes taking in the travelers. Their deep blue cloaks fluttered in the sea breeze.

The three joined the other petitioners streaming into a courtyard.

After a twenty-minute wait, a man in black ceremonial robes with seashells embroidered around the hem requested the petitioners' attention. "The most bountiful Queen of the Isles will judge your cases. Step into the entry hall and let your request be known."

As the crowd surged forward, he demanded, "Keep order!"

A scribe at his side noted the citizens' names and nature of their petition.

When it was their turn to enter, Barbu stepped forward. "It will be faster to explain in Bidori speak." And Barbu relapsed into his native whistling dialect.

Guy assumed Barbu told him enough to enlist the queen's help.

Fortunately, Barbu switched back to the common tongue. "My friends, Pellas and Guy."

"I am Mauga, Queen Nerea's Master of Ceremonies. You must wait for me to call your names before Her Benignity will hear you."

Guy studied the hall inside of the shell castle. He was expecting white marble halls like those of Lauressa's palace. Instead, these were only whitewashed plaster. But, he reasoned, marble quarries were far from the islands.

After an hour, all the petitions were recorded.

Barbu, leaning on one foot, then the other, making little huffing noises all the while, left their side and went to speak with the scribe. Grimacing, he returned. "The scribe says it may take days for the queen to see us. We are at the bottom of list."

"I'll wait here and explain our need for guidance to the Isle of Origin while the two of you find us a place to stay," Pellas offered.

Guy led Barbu back to the tavern where they ate and paid for rooms with the money Chief Nadun had given them on their departure.

The days dragged on.

Guy and Pellas took turns waiting for an audience with the queen. Barbu was too impatient. He spent his days roaming the city, picking up fragments of news.

On the third day, Barbu offered to show Guy the sights.

"What I could really use are clothes that fit. And boots."

"I know a place." Barbu grinned.

"Of course you do." Guy was learning how resourceful the native boy was.

First, Barbu led Guy to the top tower of the shell castle. The town lay at their feet and the glimmering blue sea stretched endlessly before them. "I visited several days in Cressava with my papi last year. He worked on trade agreements. He wants our island to grow in importance. I snuck away and climbed Old Varu." Barbu gestured at the volcano brooding over the landscape.

Guy was impressed.

He thought of a way to repay his friend. "Valdeor experienced years of civil war, but Reina Lauressa ended it. I spent months at the Reina's court. I am sure she would open trade agreements with your father."

"I will tell my papi. He will be glad. Bidori is small, but closest to your continent."

Guy leaned on the tower's wall overlooking the island. "As I told you when we first met, I grew up on a farm. But when my father was still alive, it was an inn. Travelers used to sit around the fire and talk of faraway places. Places like this island were the most exotic sounding to me. I can hardly believe I traveled so far from my home."

Next, Barbu took him into the trade district. Cooper smith and blacksmith yards gave way to the shops of butchers and bakers. Instead of an open market, shops lined the streets. Guy was amazed by the number of different goods: tiny shops selling spices which enticed his nose, fabrics displayed in a waterfall of every color and texture, rolled carpets, shiny brassware, and bright beads of shells and mother of pearl.

"Where does all this come from?" Guy had never seen so many varieties of wares.

"Cressava is the biggest island in the chain. Ships from all over the world stop here. You can purchase things from everywhere."

That explained the use of the common tongue that Guy heard spoken everywhere.

Soon Guy was outfitted more as he was accustomed to be.

Not watching where he was going, Guy bumped into three girls carrying baskets of shopping. "Uh, sorry. My fault." Heat rose in his cheeks as the girls stared and giggled, passing on.

Barbu struck a pose, wagged his finger, and spoke in a mock whisper, loud enough for them to hear. "You have a girlfriend back home? If not, I find you a nice island girl." He winked at the girls, who were glancing back at them over their shoulders. More giggles.

Guy's ears were burning. *Was he that immature when he was*

fourteen?

An image of Donella rose in his mind. How he wished she shared his adventure. He automatically reached out with his mind trying to sense a waypost.

"Ah, you do like a pretty girl back home! You never make eyes at island girls. Is she pretty? Does she feel the same way?" Barbu was nearly dancing in excitement as he circled Guy.

Guy's concentration broke. "She's pretty with dark ringlets and super talented. But it is not like that. I mean, she can have anyone she wants."

"But you wish she was yours."

"I didn't say that!" Guy went around Barbu.

"But you meant that. What's her name?" Barbu stopped and blocked Guy's way.

"Donella. We're friends. She's a waykeeper like me . . ."

Guy glanced around, looking for something to distract Barbu. They neared the end of the street where a wall kept out the jungle.

A familiar-looking post stood there. But Guy felt no tingle in his hand. *Could that be a waypost?* Pulse beating, Guy headed for the marker, teasing forgotten.

The trinity symbol of interlocking ovals, same as his birthmark, was faintly etched on the weathered marker. "Look, Barbu! A waypost here on the islands!"

Guy automatically touched it. Nothing. No mist, no tingle. Guy pulled his hand back. His birthmark was faint but distinctly there. Guy tried again. Still nothing. A weight settled in his gut.

For the first time, he truly believed that he was being punished for using the wayposts for the Reina's spy mission. The Guardian had given Guy a quest to find the great shrine. Guy hadn't listened to his inner voice telling him not to obey Reina Lauressa's command to infiltrate Canteor through the portals.

"What is it?" Barbu's insistent question drew Guy from his thoughts. He had a feeling that Barbu had asked the question more than once, by the concerned expression on his ebony face.

"Guy, you scared me. You went away, inside." Barbu grabbed his arm and shook it. "What happened?"

"The waypost doesn't work for me. I never wanted the gift of travel through the portals, and now that I accepted it, the Guardian has taken it away from me." Emptiness, like a gaping hole sucking joy away, pressed on Guy's heart.

"I had grown used to my power. Now it's a part of who I am. But I misused it. I knew it was wrong to do so." Guy put his head in his hands. He'd never find his friends now. Especially a dark-haired girl who haunted his dreams.

Barbu tugged on his arm. "Come. We'll visit Queen Nerea's court. Maybe we will finally see her and she can help."

"No one can help," Guy swallowed past the sorrow closing his throat, the panic building in his gut.

Please, please, just let me know she is alive and well. Guy pleaded in his heart.

He put both hands on the waypost and rested his head on them. He opened his mind and sent his thoughts toward Donella. A slight vibration under his palm made him open his eyes. A puff of mist pooled at his feet.

A commotion broke his concentration. Focus slid out of his grasp.

Four men carrying a closed litter had stopped. Four guards in the queen's blue tunics stood at attention. Fancy blue curtains parted, and a dark woman's face peered out. The onlookers bent their knees.

Barbu yanked on Guy's sleeve as he knelt. "Queen Nerea!" he hissed.

Guy bowed.

The queen spoke to one of the attendants who then approached Guy. "Our munificent queen wishes your presence in her throne room this afternoon."

The entourage moved on, but a hand flickered at the curtains and a baleful eye stared at Guy.

At the start of the afternoon petition session, Guy, Pellas, and Barbu gave their names to the scribe. He must have seen their names at the top of his list because he immediately motioned the guards to open the doors and let them through.

They passed from the entry hall into the great chamber. Here the splendor of the decor made up for the lack of marble. The floor design was a shell mosaic. Pillars studded with coral reef life held up the two-story ceiling painted in shades of swirling blue. Sea mammal statuary frolicked in realistic poses complete with carved splashing waves. Torches flickered in teal-colored glass surrounds. The effect of the room made Guy feel as if he were undersea.

Dark-skinned natives dressed in bright colors mingled with Nyrmidion warriors in horned helms and dusky sailors with pearl earrings.

At the center of the scene, an ebony woman sat upon a giant carved shell seat. The scalloped shell engulfed her as if she were a pearl of worth sitting on a pink cushion. Her elaborately braided dark hair was piled on her head and topped with a pearl encrusted crown. She wore a kimono style robe of gold fabric that shimmered in the light. As they approached the throne, Guy saw tiny seashells picked out in silver thread. Around her neck hung a giant mother of pearl pendant, catching all the colors of the rainbow. A light blue topaz graced one finger and an opal another finger, twinkling as she moved.

Noticing the trio's arrival, Mauga approached her and whispered in her ear. She replied softly to him. Mauga turned to those gathered and clapped his hands for attention.

"The Queen's audience is suspended. Her Benignity will listen to your petitions next week. Anything needing urgent attention, please follow me."

The courtiers and petitioners followed the departing Master of Ceremonies, curious glances aimed at the three who stayed.

As Barbu knelt before her and Pellas and Guy bowed, Queen Nerea raised her brows over almond-shaped eyes. Up close, crow's feet at her eyes and strands of gray in her hair showed her age to be older than Guy first thought.

"You may rise." She tapped one ringed finger on her armrest.

When she asked what brought them to her island, Guy told her of their quest for the Isle of Origin. "The winged one of light gave me the mission to find the great shrine of the Unnamed God."

At the name, her eyes widened for a heartbeat. Her glance flickered over Guy, then her expression shuttered once more.

"Show Her Benignity your birthmark," Barbu urged.

Guy stepped closer and put forth his left hand.

The sudden tightening of her hands made Guy wonder if she knew something.

Her ebony hand reached for his and she held it, turning his hand this way and that. Queen Nerea's hand was papery thin and cool to the touch. She smelled of cinnamon.

She let Guy's hand go and sat back, her face unreadable.

"What were you doing earlier? You acted strangely."

Guy had an odd feeling. Odem would call it a gut instinct and told him to listen to it when it happened. "I, uh, felt dizzy. I leaned on the post to catch my breath."

Guy wondered if her sharp eyes could tell he was lying. He resisted the urge to brush his sweaty palms down his trousers.

"And why have you come to me?"

"We were hoping you knew the way to the Isle of Origin, Your, um, Benignity. I was told you were wise." Guy decided politeness would serve him best.

"Well, I don't. But I will inquire about it. I may consider helping you on your journey. Now let these old bones rest." She waved a dismissal with her ringed hand

"Thank you, O most noble Queen." Guy bowed and added, "May you reign long, and the seas be calm on your shores."

"What if she will not help us?" Barbu kicked a stone as they hung around the wharf, watching the ships unload their goods.

"Then I will purchase our passage aboard a ship," Pellas announced. He pointed at a ship in the harbor. "That one looks fast. I heard the captain was looking for cargo or passengers."

Guy and Barbu turned to stare at him.

"Where will you get the money?" Guy wished he had not lost the coins the Reina had given him. All his possessions had washed overboard during the storm on the raft.

Pellas dipped his finger under his collar and pulled out a gold chain. Attached to it was a golden goat amulet.

"I invested a lot of my pay in this good luck charm. I figured it was an easy way to carry money on my person." He made a sour face. "I actually believed in Panmin's power once."

He glanced at Guy. "But now I am searching for your Unnamed God, it seems like a good idea to rid myself of superstition." He smiled. "Let's get ourselves a ship."

Over the next few days, the captain and crew outfitted the one-masted schooner, the *Diadem*, for sailing.

Pellas made friends with the crew, while Guy and Barbu shopped for supplies.

14 In The Ring

The prisoners' lives had settled into a new routine. One fraught with danger. As they traveled across the Canteor plains and encountered more villages and towns, Agomeisa would visit the tavern upon arrival. He would wager his fighters against the locals.

He would allow Gensard, Hazibal, and Sad-alah freedom to stretch and prepare for fighting. He let them know that the girls were hostages for good behavior.

The men no longer fought one another. Agomeisa forced them to battle the strongest, most worthy opponents in the town. Sometimes Gensard fought with his scimitar. Other times Hazibal was up against a wrestler. Sad-alah was best at knife fights.

Donella tended to their open wounds, strains, and broken bones afterwards as best as she could. Donella used every skill she had. Jiana wasn't squeamish and became a good helper. As Donella worked, she taught Jiana what she knew.

Donella could sense Gensard's restlessness for freedom. She feared one of these times he would give in to it and leave her behind. Not that she could blame him. This wasn't the life of a prince.

She thought of this as she searched for food—roots, berries and seeds—which she would hide in her secret, deep pockets to supplement their diets. Only when Agomeisa and Zaniah dozed during their daily siesta did she distribute it.

Jiana was also becoming an apt student at identifying food under Donella's tutelage. She limped behind Donella as they foraged for food. The strap holding Gensard's wedge to her shoe had broken after a week's use.

"See those brown stalks by the big stump?" Donella whispered as they gathered twigs and branches for the cook fire. Nearby, Zaniah arranged rocks in a circle.

Jiana nodded, her glance slipping toward Zaniah to see if she watched.

"Fennel gives flavor to fish dishes and prevents sickness." Donella strolled over and casually picked a few stalks to stuff them in her pocket.

"What are you doing, girl?" Zaniah was suddenly beside her.

"I thought we could catch fish in the stream. It would be a tasty addition to the barley cakes." Donella stared back at the woman, not letting her eyes slide to the splotched birthmark on her face. Zaniah was very sensitive about it, and liable to slap her if Donella stared at it.

"Impudence. I decide what we eat. What are you doing with that weed? Are you going to catch a fish with it?" Zaniah slapped it out of her hand. "Get the fire going."

Donella lugged her branches to the ring of rocks and dropped them. She mourned her rough hands. Would she be able to play the zythrin after this? She tried to start the fire by spinning a branch. She cursed as it refused to start, then bit her lip at her coarseness. She was picking up bad habits from her captors.

Tending the fire in the heat of the day caused fresh sweat to break out on her forehead. The grass and trees were tinder dry, so she worked without shade.

Zaniah and Jiana were doing something by the cool stream. She pounded barley flour for cakes by herself.

The women were gone so long, she wondered if they washed clothes. Or maybe bathed their feet? She wished she could trade places with Jiana right now.

Her gut clenched. What was she thinking? Did she wish Jiana to suffer the heat in her place?

The slave girl still held back part of her story. Donella was sure of it. Any mention of her brother or her previous mistress and Jiana would clam up. Donella gathered that something awful had happened to make Jiana's mistress sell her after so many years. What was it?

"Hurry up, woman. Where is my dinner?" Agomeisa roared, shaking his skin of ale and throwing it down.

"A treat for you, husband. See, I have a fish." Zaniah smiled, ingratiatingly pointing at the gutted fish as she placed it in the pan.

"One? You think I have your womanly appetite?" He stumbled over. With unsteady hands he fumbled for his key. "Hazibal, can you fish?"

"Yes, master." The big man rumbled from inside the cart.

So Agomeisa released him and Hazibal caught many fish using a branch sharpened by Sad-alah's knives as a spear. Zaniah let Donella add fennel and watercress from the stream to the dish, which she wrapped in leaves and steamed in the coals. Donella's mouth watered at the aroma.

When she bit into her meal, the licorice smell of the fennel and peppery watercress disguised the fishy taste of the crisp morsels.

"Plenty to go around, for a change." Gensard met her eyes as he ate his portion.

"I may have to keep you on as cook," Agomeisa praised Donella, licking his fingers. "Why can't you serve me this well?" he chided his wife.

Donella squirmed. For his praise, she knew when the slaver wasn't looking Zaniah would beat her where it wouldn't show.

Jiana glanced over at her as they settled on the ground for the night. As usual, Zaniah had tied their hands through the bars at either end of the rope.

"I have learned more of the art of cooking from you than at my last station. Maybe Agomeisa will advertise me as a cook, if I can learn it as well as you. Nobody wants a cripple girl, but every great house needs a good cook."

"You are an apt student, Jiana. I only wish I could do something to better your life." The thought of the beautiful girl as a mistreated slave made anger bubble up in her gut, as sadness weighed her down. "What can I do, a slave myself?"

If only she still had her ring. Then if they ran across a waypost she could escape and take Jiana with her. *Why, oh why, did something have to go wrong when we crossed the sea? Was it too far?* She recalled lightning before they separated from Guy. *What caused it? Did the Guardian punish us for misusing the portal?*

"You have helped me, Donella. Your strength gives me courage. You have banded us together. We traveled as strangers before. Now Hazibal is protective of my safety in the towns. He tells the villagers to back off if they approach me. And he seems less despondent. Even Sad-alah leaves you alone since you tend his wounds. His barbs can be as sharp as his knives."

Donella pondered Jiana's words silently as she drifted to sleep. She didn't think her rebellious attitude was an asset. It usually got her slaps and beatings.

After the fish incident, Zaniah hardly let Donella out of her sight. She seemed to be lying in wait to catch Donella in an infraction.

The only good outcome was Agomeisa required Donella to cook, so they ate better. He spent an inordinate amount of his winnings on drink, but Zaniah managed to beg a few coins before his binges to buy supplies.

They pulled into a town in the interior of Canteor which was larger than the ones on the outskirts. An eight-foot-high stone wall, three feet thick, surrounded the town. Donella saw this when the wagon passed through the gates. The cobblestone streets were wide. Buildings stood two-stories made of wood and plaster.

Agomeisa directed the oxen to the town center where an amphitheater dominated the landscape. Seating three stories high curved halfway around a dirt ring.

"What is this place?" Donella stood, grasping the bars, and staring. Nausea rose as she feared it was a slave market. She took quick breaths trying to ease her roiling stomach. She didn't want to be separated from her new friends.

The men moved to her side of the wagon, knuckles white on the bars and staring at their future.

"This must be the amphitheater of Kiwan where slave combatants show their skills." Sad-alah absently ran a finger over his scar. "The rich enjoy the sport of fighting, keeping slaves for just that purpose. There's seating for the well-to-do and standing room for the general populace. It's a three-day event every quarter of the year, drawing huge crowds." He seemed amused at her discomfort. His sly eyes taunted her. "Don't you have this form of entertainment in Valdeor?"

"No. It's barbaric." She leaned away from his close presence.

"It's part of our culture. In the bigger towns, no longer do the local villagers pit themselves against slaves. Slaves are trained to combat one another." His smile was mocking. "Agomeisa has been testing us for this event."

"And then he'll sell us to the highest bidder." Hazibal's deep voice sounded resigned.

At these words, Jiana's face paled as much as Donella imagined her own did.

After that, Donella noticed a change come over the prisoners. Gensard withdrew from his companions. Jiana's shy smiles at him dried up. Sad-alah was more boastful and irritating. The only one who acted the same was Hazibal. He had not lost a fight since his rib-breaking episode.

Storm clouds moved in late afternoon the next day, when the games began. The spectators made bets and cheered on their champions.

Hazibal was up first, pitted against a man equal in size, but lacking technique and style. The opponent tried a headlock, but Hazibal broke it by flipping the other slave over his knee.

Several owners challenged Agomeisa to let their champions try and best Hazibal, who was victorious against them all.

Donella's pride in her friend's skill soon evaporated when a rich man approached. His flowing robe was made of silk with vertical stripes of cream and red. He wore rings on every finger. Several slaves accompanied him, one holding a parasol over his head in the strong sunlight.

"What price for the wrestler? I'll offer you 50 silver yiza."

"He is unbeaten. I'll accept 100 silver yiza."

"Outrageous!" The rich man began turning away.

"Fine, fine. Seventy-five silver yiza and he's yours." Agomeisa rubbed his hands together.

The buyer angled back. Touching his short, pointed beard, the man considered. "Sixty-five. My final offer."

"Sold!" Agomeisa grinned and motioned Hazibal over.

The rich man counted out coins into Agomeisa's hands.

Donella was aghast. Her hands trembled. They couldn't sell her friend. "No! He's not cattle. You can't bargain over a person!"

Ignoring Jiana's tug on her arm, she stepped forward. "He's a man, the same as you. This is wrong!"

The sharp eyes of the seller inspected her from head to toe. "He is nothing like me. He's a slave." Red-faced he told Agomeisa, "You had better teach your slaves manners if you want to sell them."

As big drops of rain began to fall, he withdrew haughtily, Hazibal added to his retinue.

The giant wrestler directed a sad look at Donella, then lowered his eyes and followed his new master. The big man's shoulders slumped.

Agomeisa slapped Donella hard across the face. "Be quiet! You nearly cost me a sale, girl."

Her head snapped back at the force of the blow. Tears gathered in the corner of her eyes. She fought them back. She wouldn't show weakness before this bully.

She paid the price for her insolence. Zaniah denied her food that night. Donella's stomach grumbled as she watched the rest eat. No one met her eyes. Jiana and Gensard looked embarrassed as they ate their meal. Sad-alah was indifferent. There was a hole in the corner where Hazibal usually sat.

The rain came down in torrents, gusts of wind bringing drenching spray as they huddled under Agomeisa's hastily rigged wagon's tarp.

So many people were lost to Donella—Guy, Odem, Usher, and now Hazibal. How could she keep going? Soon she would be sold and ripped away from Gensard and Jiana, too.

Her reality had become scarier with the passing of time. No one was going to rescue her. She was never going home. Panic gripped her gut as the truth hit her.

Starting the next morning, Zaniah tied Donella's left wrist with a rope which she looped around her own waist.

"You will learn to keep your mouth shut. You think to win favor from my husband. You're nothing but a slave girl. Whatever freedoms you had are gone forever. Get that through your thick head." She shook Donella and glared at her.

From then on, she always kept Donella on a short rope near her.

That afternoon's competition was hand-to-hand combat with

weapons. Sad-alah held his own against the knife-wielders, only getting a few scrapes.

Donella held her breath during Gensard's fight. His black-bearded opponent wielded a mace, a ball with spikes on the length of a chain, with great skill. Gensard dodged in and out of the mace's way, his shield blocking. He thrust when an opportunity presented itself to cause damage. Between his opponent's swings, Gensard slashed the bearded man repeatedly until, with a roar, the man charged.

At the last second, Gensard spun out of the way. Donella flinched as the mace grazed Gensard's upper left arm. His face a grimace of pain, he finished his spin and managed to use his momentum to slice between his enemy's ribs.

The judges deemed the contest a draw at that point.

Sweat glistened on Gensard's face and soaked his clothes as he staggered toward them.

When Donella surged forward, Zaniah tugged the rope tying them together. "I forbid you to tend to your brother. You will learn your place. You can do nothing, say nothing, without my permission." Her red birthmark stood out on her face in her anger. Her eyes gloated at Donella's helplessness.

That left Jiana to minister to Gensard using the skills Donella had taught her.

Making Donella carry a water jug, Zaniah dragged her away to the town well.

The joy had gone from the sun. The birds soaring in the blue sky only mocked her with their freedom. Donella was in a dark place. Despair dogged her steps.

Guy was gone. Dead. She didn't know.

She couldn't return home. Without her ring she was just another slave girl. Zaniah never allowed her away from the camp, so she gathered no information about the war preparations of Canteor. Their whole mission was bust.

And to top it off, today she turned seventeen. In captivity. Tears stung her eyes, although she refused to let them fall. She wouldn't show weakness in front of Zaniah.

Setting her jug on the stone's edge, she lowered the pail into the well. A lone teardrop ran down her face and splashed into the water. She sniffed and wiped her eye with the back of her hand, pushing her hair out of her face.

As she poured the water into her jug, advice from Reina Lauressa came floating back to her. "Seek the Almighty Father's glory, not yours. Search your heart to discover your true talents. Not what you think them to be."

How could Donella do that in her situation?

"Do what you do best," the Reina had added.

What did Donella do best? Get into trouble? Voice her opinion?

She recalled Jiana's words of the day before, "You have helped me, Donella. Your strength gives me courage. You have banded us together. We traveled as strangers before."

As Zaniah led her back to the group, Donella wondered if helping others was her strength.

Not that she could help them escape.

Observing Gensard fight challenged everything Jiana believed in her nineteen years.

Apparently in their land of Valdeor, gladiators were unheard of. In Canteor it was a popular entertainment. Jiana had never questioned the good or bad of it before.

Yet all she heard from Donella about the One Who Fashioned All made her question her own beliefs, such as fighting to the death as a sport, slavery, and acceptance of tyranny in order to maintain peace.

Obedience was the guiding rule of her life. But her new friends believed courage to challenge wrongness was more important.

And yet, for her boldness, Zaniah punished Donella and curtailed what little freedom she had. Jiana glanced to where Zaniah made Donella stand and watch as her brother faced his opponent. Donella tried to inch forward for a better view, but with a smirk Zaniah yanked the rope holding Donella, moving them further back in the crowd.

But it was watching Gensard face his opponents in the ring that shook Jiana to the core. With clenched hands and taut nerves, she felt every clash of the swords. Her heart galloped with fear for him. He was so brave and strong.

After the contest, Zaniah dragged Donella away, leaving Jiana to cope alone. She summoned her courage, gripped her satchel of herbs, and entered the building where the gladiators gathered.

As she patched up the slash on Gensard's arm, she finally admitted how attracted she was to him.

So close to him, she could admire his hazel eyes with yellow flecks, surrounded by long eyelashes. She longed to sweep back his curly hair from his face.

She could feel the rock-hard muscles in his arm as she passed the bandage around it. Strong as he was, he was like a lamb in her care.

Jiana didn't know when her blossoming feelings first appeared. Maybe it was the day he said he'd like to take her on his horse, Fiery, and ride with her on the wind. Or was it the daily interactions, catching his dark eyes on her as she went about her chores? Or his protective stance when they moved among strangers, and he put himself between the rough men and her?

He was about six years older than she was, but she was of marriageable age in her culture. Other girls settled down at seventeen through arranged marriages.

If she gave her heart to Gensard, there was no guarantee they would stay together. Married slaves were sometimes sold separately. Jiana wasn't sure she could risk being hurt.

She daren't give her heart. Although she feared Gensard already held it in his hands.

15 Slave Block

As he sat on a bench in the contenders' barracks, the pain in Gensard's arm was intense. He gritted his teeth as Jiana tended it as gently as she could. Her pale face and shaking fingers let him know she felt for him. He concentrated on her long eyelashes that hid her light blue eyes. Wisps of ash blond hair that worked their way out of her braid fell over her soft cheek. She bit her pink lip as she concentrated.

She was so close he could feel her breath on his cheek. He fought his desire to kiss her.

She glanced up at him, and her beautiful eyes widened, as if she could read his mind. Suddenly she moved away from him.

"That's the best I can do," she mumbled, blushing.

"Thank you." His voice came out husky. The words tripped off his lips without conscious thought. Words he rarely spoke. Heat rose in his cheeks as he wondered what kind of person he was, taking all his good fortune for granted until this last month or so.

He flexed his left arm, the pain sending a shockwave through him. Although the bone wasn't broken, the power of the mace's hit had caused damage. He felt a sweat break out over his body. Jiana's bandage held it immobile.

"At least it's only my non-dominant hand," he flashed a reassuring grin at her, although it felt more like a grimace.

She blinked at him, then reached out a tentative hand and touched his wrist. He could tell she didn't buy his brave act. "I have some willow bark." She dug in her healer's satchel and pulled out a nasty bunch of stuff.

He gagged at the thought of chewing it.

"I'll make some tea." She hurried away.

He watched her slender figure as she left the central room and went to the healers' area.

"Lovely, isn't she?" A voice intruded on Gensard's thoughts.

He turned to see Sad-alah's narrowed eyes appraising him. The knife-wielder strolled over and sat on a nearby bench, casually putting one leg over the other. "Too bad you are both slaves. The chances of being bought by the same master in Dabbori is too slim to contemplate." He played with his little dagger, flipping it in the air and catching it, barely missing the point. His grin was pure malice.

Gensard knew Sad-alah only waited for a chance to get back at him for his defeat by Gensard in the ring. Gensard judged Sad-alah the type to egg him on with little pricks, and stab Gensard in the back if he ever let his guard down. Which he had no plan on doing.

Gensard longed to punch the slimy creature in the nose. His hands involuntarily curled into fists. If only he could declare himself a prince in this cursed land. But he would never share anything with this scum.

"I wouldn't, if I were you, lover-boy. Agomeisa might just sell you out of hand. Or take it out on the lass." The dagger spun impossibly fast as Sad-alah worked out his constantly pent-up energy.

Pretending a lack of interest in Jiana might turn Sad-alah's attention away from her.

"Keep your thoughts to yourself. She doesn't mean a thing to me. Pretty maids are plentiful. It doesn't do to get caught by one."

Gensard put his best sneering face on and stared at his tormentor. "Don't push me, or you will regret it. Your parlor tricks don't scare me." Gensard narrowed his eyes at his foe.

Sad-alah's lips pulled into a snarl. He hurled the dagger at Gensard, who flung himself off the bench.

The dagger pierced where Gensard had been.

Ready to spring at Sad-alah, Gensard was stopped by the sound of breaking crockery and Jiana's cry. Gensard swung around to see Jiana's empty eyes and a stain spreading where she had dropped his mug.

Agomeisa stormed in behind her.

"You weasel! I saw that! I have a mind to sell you today. In fact, the lot of you have been more trouble than you are worth." He flung out his hand to include the three of them.

Gensard had a sinking feeling as he smelled the alcoholic fumes as Agomeisa approached him. There was no reasoning with him in this mood.

Bleary-eyed, Agomeisa raged at them. "Insolent males and opinionated females! I've had enough!"

Gensard glanced at Jiana's face. She was even paler than before. She looked as if she were ready to pass out. He took a step toward her, reaching out a hand. She caught his eye and glanced away. Her rigid posture made it clear she didn't want his support. He dropped his hand back to his side.

Whatever connection he thought was between them was obviously not as strong as he imagined.

Jiana stood alone, arms wrapped about her middle. Agomeisa was stomping about, threatening to sell them this very evening. Her gut twisted at the thought. Yet a greater pain squeezed her heart.

She doesn't mean a thing to me. Pretty maids are plentiful.

Gensard's cruel words played themselves over and over in her head.

She had returned from the healers' room with the pain-relieving tea to hear his sneering voice. She flinched as the dagger flew and missed Gensard, embedding itself in the wooden bench. Fear for his safety caused her to cry out. The mug slipped out of her numb fingers.

She had seen the look in Gensard's eyes earlier, the same look that Pim had on his face before he grabbed her and kissed her. And then Pim's mother, her mistress, had walked in on them. Jiana felt the same shame spread up from her chest onto her face.

"She doesn't mean a thing to me, mother." The words of the two men eerily similar.

The blood drained from her head.

Pim's face overlaid Gensard's handsome one as he stepped toward her, his hand out.

Could a heart really shatter?

Unwanted. Unworthy.

She turned her face away.

At that moment she felt a pang of desire that Agomeisa go through with his threat. Let him sell her. Then she would never have to face Gensard's scorn again.

The women's slave quarters had thick stone walls. A pile of straw laid in the corner to distribute when it came time for sleeping. Zaniah had left Donella here after the match and fetching water at the well. She stood at a tiny, barred window, waiting for any sign of her friends.

Jiana was an apt pupil. Donella trusted she could patch up Gensard. But waiting was still hard. Donella absently rubbed her chafed wrist where the rope had cut into the skin.

A movement caught her eyes. Agomeisa was dragging Jiana with one hand. They strode toward the women's quarters. She couldn't make out what he shouted. There was no sign of Gensard.

"—be free of the lot of you!" Agomeisa yelled as he approached. With a shove, he opened the door and unceremoniously pushed Jiana inside. Slamming the door, he slid the locking bar into place and stormed off.

Jiana brushed tears from her streaked face. "Oh, Donella! We're to be sold to the highest bidder!" Jiana wept as she collapsed to the ground.

Donella's curiosity was replaced by dread like a stone in her stomach. Her mouth dry, she knelt beside her friend. "What happened? I thought Agomeisa was going to sell us in Dabbori. I thought . . . I thought we had more time!"

Jiana lifted her wet face. "Sad-alah p-provoked your b-brother. They nearly f-fought but Agomeisa st-stopped them. He said we weren't w-worth the tr-trouble anymore."

Donella sat back on her heels. This couldn't be happening! She wasn't ready!

Jiana was inconsolable. Donella didn't have the energy to try and cheer her. Her own stomach clenched with fear at the thought of what tomorrow would bring. No words of comfort came, as sorrow penetrated her own soul. The two girls clung together wordlessly.

She hardly slept that night. She heard Jiana tossing and sobbing sporadically.

Early the next morning, Zaniah brought some flat bread for their breakfast. Donella could barely choke down a mouthful. When Zaniah realized they were not going to eat anymore, she escorted them to the washing area and left them.

The bath house smelled of soap and perfume. Warm steam came from the copper tub. A hairbrush lay on a bench beside a clean, coarse gown. A simple sash was folded on top.

Donella had longed for these things for weeks. Now the sight of them twisted her stomach.

She was supposed to bathe and groom herself so she could go on the slave block in a few hours.

Lies and deceit had brought her to this point. Why had she thought that becoming a spy was a good idea?

She longed for Mother's arms to wrap themselves around her and tell her it was only a bad dream. She wished Usher or Odem would walk through the door and say they were here to take her home. But no one was coming to rescue her.

Help me, One Who Fashioned All. I cannot do this. To be sold. I am your child. Please hear me!

Anguish making her limbs weak, she buried her face in her hands. Tears poured down her cheeks.

After a burst of crying, calm settled over her.

Trust. All will be well.

She lifted her head. No one was in the room with her. She took a deep breath. *I can do this. Just get through each moment as it comes.*

She shivered as she prepared herself.

As she stepped into the next room, she found Jiana combing her wet locks. The girl was so pale she looked like a ghost. Jiana's hands shook and her hair was tangled.

Donella reached for the comb and took it out of her friend's unresponsive hands. She divided the silky blond strands into sections and tackled them.

Jiana's huge eyes watched her in the mirror. "How can you be so brave?"

"Brave?" Donella snorted. "If you only knew how much I want to throw up or fling myself on the floor and scream. My heart is literally trying to come out of my chest with fear."

"I know how you feel."

"But I won't let them see my fear. I won't give them the

satisfaction." Donella stiffened her spine.

Jiana turned in her seat and faced Donella. She cried out, "I don't want to be separated! You are the first friend I've had. I'm so scared! What if my new master is a monster?'

Donella put her hands on Jiana's shoulders. "More of a monster than Agomeisa?"

Jiana's smile flickered, though worry filled her eyes.

"We are the daughters of the One Who Fashioned All. He has us in his hands. I was as scared as you, but I prayed. The answer I heard was 'trust.' We are not forgotten."

"How can you trust your god, when you are headed to the slave block? If he cares like you say he does, why doesn't he rescue us?" Tears pooled in her eyes and traced a line down her cheek.

Donella rubbed her forefinger along her bottom lip. She searched for an answer to bring her friend hope. "He brought us together, didn't he? Our friendship has gotten me through the worst weeks of my life." She gave a weak smile. "The wisest woman I know told me to seek the Almighty's glory. If this brings him glory, then I will trust him to bring it right."

Jiana bowed her head as she squeezed her eyes shut. After a moment, she lifted her head and locked eyes with Donella. "I don't have your faith. But I trust you." She brushed away her tears. "I will try to be brave."

Donella hugged her friend. They clung together. Tears stung her eyes.

Only the appearance of Zaniah pulled them apart.

A flash of compassion seemed to flit across her face for a second. She opened her lips as if she were going to speak. Then her expression hardened. "It is time. Follow me."

16 Entranced

$\mathcal{G}$uy stared at the back of his hand as he stood in front of the waypost. He could not resist visiting it again and trying to open the portal. His birthmark of intertwined ovals was barely visible. He turned his hand back and forth, hoping it was just a trick of the light. But it had simply faded.

Then tendrils of mist floated by. For a moment, Guy thought the portal was reacting to him. Looking up, he realized it was only fog drifting in from the harbor.

"Come on!" Barbu grabbed his arm and dragged Guy along with him. "You are pale, like you have seen a spirit. Queen Nerea may know someone able to help you. All's not lost, my friend."

But that's exactly how Guy felt. First, he lost his sense of knowing what was right. Then he lost his friends. Now he seemed to be losing his abilities—his gift from the Unnamed God that he had taken for granted.

No! This can't be happening. I shouldn't have jumped through the portal when my intentions were not what they should have been. I am separated from my friends because of my decisions. But I know I was wrong. I want this gift. I really do! Guy silently prayed as they climbed the street to the castle.

Panic clawed at the edges of his conscience. What if his powers never returned?

Guy pushed the thought away as they entered through the main gate and into the castle courtyard. The white shells making up the walls blinded him. The fog swirled below in the town while the castle remained in the sunlight. The awe he had felt earlier at seeing the edifice failed to manifest, wrapped up in his numbness as he was.

The guards let Barbu pass, Guy in his wake.

He barely registered the sea statuary and spraying fountains as they made their way down the main hall to the throne room.

Stopping before the elegantly decorated white doors, Barbu spoke with the guards stationed on either side. "The queen said yesterday we were to come back and see her."

The guards let them pass.

The throne room was empty, but a side door Guy hadn't noticed on his last visit stood slightly ajar. Barbu headed for it.

Even in the anteroom, the sea motif was ever present. On the far wall was a mosaic mural of nymphs playing in the sea with large, bottle-nosed fish leaping from the foam. The floor tiles were alternating shades of blue. Two oval windows faced each other from opposite sides of the room. One had a magnificent view of the town, and the other overlooked the brooding volcano in the distance. As Guy watched, the sun dimmed and fog rolled in from the sea, blotting out the views.

Queen Nerea sat in the center of the room on a carved wooden chair. She wore a royal blue gown today and an elaborate headdress of tiny shells and pearls stitched on a matching turban.

Three men were gathered around her. They looked up as Guy and his friend entered.

The first man wore a gold and red-striped robe fastened with a gold cord around his waist. His dark hair was slicked back, and he sported a pointed goatee.

The second man was stout, his belly protruding over his trousers. He wore a white tunic open at the neck. His pasty white skin contrasted with the dark chest hairs exposed.

The third man was deep ebony. He wore a necklace of sea monster teeth and his earlobes had multiple piercings with what looked like bone pieces sticking out. His robe was dark maroon, almost black, with strange runes embroidered over it. He carried a black staff with a blood red gem twinkling at the top. His thin-lipped stare seemed hostile, though they hadn't said or done anything yet.

"O, Mighty Queen of the Isles," Barbu made a deep bow. "Forgive our intrusion. My friend has a problem and comes seeking your wisdom."

The queen raised a hand to the others, "Please excuse us." As the three bowed, she added, "Lemmo, you may stay. Your guidance may be necessary."

Guy's spirits plummeted when the hostile man remained.

When the other two men departed, the queen motioned for Guy to speak.

He swallowed past his dry throat. "Your Majesty, Barbu and I were strolling through your town the other day, when I happened to notice a waypost. I can usually, um, feel the presence of a waypost before I find it. They are markers to help find the Isle of Origin. But I've lost the ability to sense them." Guy did not want to reveal he could transport from one to another.

Guy looked away from them, concentrating on the tip of his foot. "The being of light who gave me my quest told me not to use the wayposts for anything but finding the great shrine I spoke of. I traveled with friends . . ." He let the sentence hang, not wanting to divulge the mission. "But we were separated through my fault. I've hunted for them, but they vanished. I don't know what befell them."

"And you feel guilty." The queen nodded at him when he glanced up. "That's to be expected. Maybe your feelings interfere with your abilities. It sounds like you lack concentration."

"I can't help my fears." Guy ran his palm down his trousers.

Her rings twinkled as she tapped her chair arm. "You must practice clearing your mind. Let go of your guilt."

Guy reluctantly held out his hand. "But the mark on my hand faded."

She motioned him forward and took his hand in her papery thin one. She turned it this way and that.

"I think it looks the same as when you showed it to me before. Again, in your emotion, you are imagining things." She dropped his hand and turned to Lemmo. "Will you work with him? Meditation may help the boy concentrate."

"Of course, My Queen." He bowed. A swift glance passed between him and her. It was a mere suggestion of a raised brow and a twist of the lips, gone in a flash.

He swung to face Guy, towering over him at six and a half feet. Lemmo's intense eyes pinned him. The expression might look bland, but the eyes were menacing. "Come with me and we will start the exercises." He smiled, but it reminded Guy of a wolf spotting prey rather than a friendly gesture.

"I'll see you later." Barbu glanced from one to another. Guy thought he glimpsed a look of concern on his friend's face, but he couldn't be certain.

Guy followed Lemmo from the queen's presence, through a door leading from the antechamber. He was surprised when the man led him out of the castle. They walked through the courtyard.

The fog soon swallowed them, causing the castle and outbuildings to disappear. The path was made of broken shells, which crunched under their feet. The lack of other sounds and feeling of isolation was eerie.

A shiver ran up Guy's spine.

It wasn't just the cutting off of everything familiar, but

Lemmo himself projected an aura. Guy didn't trust the adviser to Queen Nerea.

A domed building appeared out of the fog. An iron studded door reminded Guy of a prison.

Lemmo removed a key from a pocket in his maroon robe and put it in the lock. The door swung open with a creak. Through the opening, torches flickered.

"This way." He gestured for Guy to enter first.

Reluctance made Guy drag his feet. But the thought of focusing exercises made him move. Stiffening his spine, he entered.

Lemmo followed, shutting the door firmly.

The walls seemed to move closer, suffocating Guy.

With another wolfish grin he said, "Not much farther to my sanctuary."

They walked down a short hall and entered a large room. Circular in shape, it spiraled up to a vaulted ceiling. It made Guy think of the inside of a conch shell. Torches flickered along the walls. Benches circled the room facing a dais. On it was a stone slab holding a copper basin.

A strange smell hung in the air. An unpleasant mix of metal and burnt wood.

As Lemmo marched up to the dais, Guy realized the slab was an altar and this was a place of worship. And not a pleasant one like the churches he attended. He hung back. Sweat broke on his forehead and his skin crawled. He got a bad feeling about this place.

Lemmo mounted the dais and beckoned the frozen Guy.

Guy forced one foot in front of the other. When he was close enough to examine the copper basin, he saw it was stained a dark color inside. Hot coals burned in the bottom.

"Breathe in the aroma of life." Lemmo intoned, waving his staff, the red gem picking up the firelight.

The strange smell was stronger and made Guy gag.

The low light caused Lemmo's shape to melt into the darkness. The black man's eyes were the only distinct feature and they bored into Guy's with deep intensity. He stretched out his hands over the copper brazier and gestured for Guy to look down at the coals. "Empty your mind. Focus on the embers. See how they pulse with life."

Lemmo's words enthralled him. Involuntarily, Guy glanced down. The burning coals did seem to be alive with little flickers of blue flame dancing around.

With a quick flick of his wrist, Lemmo added a pinch of something stringy that caused the flames to leap. The little strips twisted and curled. A sickly, sweet smell wafted from the basin.

Everything around Guy seemed to melt away. The embers filled his mind with their pulsing glow. He seemed detached from himself. Time seemed to stretch.

He was barely aware of a swishing noise behind him.

The dancing flames held his attention.

"Tell me about your power," Lemmo's voice whispered from the dark beyond the basin. "What does it do? Where does it come from?"

"I-I can travel from place to place with a thought."

Why did Guy say that? He struggled with the desire to hide his abilities from this wizard.

"And?" The voice was sharp. "Go on."

The urge to unburden himself was strong.

Guy found himself continuing, "It c-comes from m-my b-birthmark."

"Why does it no longer work?"

He longed to confess his failings and his weakness. He longed to unburden himself of the guilt he carried.

He longed for absolution.

But this felt wrong on so many levels. Lemmo entrapped him

with his wizardry. Guy fought to regain control of his thoughts and tongue. He brought Usher's training to mind. He must focus and push away all distractions.

He closed his eyes against the spellbinding flames. He clenched his hands until his fingernails dug into his palms. He searched his memory for a happy moment. He imagined standing at his front gate, after he and Donella had repositioned the waypost. He relived the tingling in his hand as it went up his arm when he first touched a post.

"Get him to tell his secrets," a new voice hissed.

"I was getting to that," the deep voice whispered. Louder, Lemmo's voice intruded into Guy's focus. "How can I gain your power? Tell me, how do I open the portals between places?"

Guy snapped his eyes open.

A familiar face peered at him beside Lemmo's dark one. Headdress discarded, a dark cloak wrapped around her form, Queen Nerea gazed at him with parted lips. Her claw-like hand gripped Lemmo's arm. A waykeeper's ring glinted on one finger. Her yellow teeth were as those of a fox.

Perspiration gathered above Guy's lip.

"Answer me."

How did Queen Nerea obtain a ring? Then Guy remembered how he sent three men through the portal to Bidori: Pellas, Kadar, and the ring wearer who drowned.

Now he understood their interest.

Lifting a vial above the basin, Lemmo poured a thick red substance on the hot coals. The flames hissed and a metallic smell burned Guy's nose. The same awful smell that greeted him when they entered the temple.

Blood!

Evil forces swirled around him.

Guy's pulse elevated with the desire to run as fast as he could from this place. But he forced his eyes back down, as if he were still under Lemmo's control.

"Tell me how to open the portals."

Guy bit the inside of his cheek, letting the pain push away the urge to answer truthfully.

He let a few heartbeats pass, giving himself a moment to come up with a sufficiently complicated answer.

In a measured tone, Guy said, "A creature lives in the ocean's depth. A blob of jelly with tentacles. It squirts black ink when afraid. Gather its ink. By the full moon's light, draw the design of three ovals on the back of your hand. Then you can access the portal and go wherever you wish." He hoped they believed him.

His armpits wet, Guy felt the walls closing in again.

"And how do you choose your destination?" the queen's voice whispered.

Guy answered with the first thing that came to his mind, "You say where you want to be three times in a row."

Lemmo and Queen Nerea broke the silence with their whispers to each other.

Guy tuned them out. He had to get away from here. He swayed and groaned. Then he let himself drop to the floor. The cold stone was unyielding.

"What should I do with him, My Queen?"

"Leave him for the moment."

At those words, Guy inched toward the dais' edge. The two conspirators were in deep conversation. He slid closer to the edge. Watching them from narrowed eyes, he slipped over the edge while they seemed to argue.

Guy heard the words, "over the side of the ship", "Barbu" and "Kadar" but he couldn't stay and listen.

Crawling between the benches, he kept himself below the seats as he scooted for the doorway. He was nearly there when he heard the queen screech from behind.

Giving up on stealth, Guy stood and rushed for the exit.

17 New Mistress

*M*erchants and well-dressed nobility filled the first six rows of benches of Kiwan's amphitheater. In the center of the sand ring stood a wooden platform built for the occasion. On the back side of the platform was a roped-in area where masters showed their slaves to those gathered to buy them. Dust and sweat and fear permeated the area.

Donella's hands tingled and her pulse was elevated as she clung to Jiana. She hadn't seen Gensard since his fight with the mace wielder the night before. The girls had been housed in the women's slave quarters where they slept—or tried to—before bathing and readying themselves to go on the slave block.

Zaniah stood outside the ropes and presented them to interested buyers.

Up and down the line, slave traders hawked their human wares. Zaniah made Jiana and Donella turn around, showing their lithe shape, or open their mouths and show their teeth, all the while playing up their good points.

"See, they are young and strong. Many years of labor will you get from them."

She pulled Donella closer to a fat, balding merchant whose heavy cologne made Donella wonder if he bathed in it. "She is a fine cook, something I am sure you can appreciate."

The man reached out a hand and pinched her hip. "She's as thin as a stick. I doubt she knows fine cooking."

Donella lifted her eyes and glared at him. The merchant took a step back. "Humph. Too spirited for me."

"Nothing a cane won't fix." Zaniah gave her a quick slap on the ear where it wouldn't detract from her beauty.

Donella's eyes stung, but she bit her lower lip.

The merchant's eyes lit on Jiana's pale face. "She's a pretty little thing. Aren't you, pet?" He couldn't tear his eyes away from Jiana, missing Zaniah's flash of jealousy. "What skills does she have?"

"Besides being pleasing to the eye?" The woman couldn't disguise her bitterness.

"Yes, besides that, which I can see for myself." The merchant licked his lips as his hungry eyes caressed Jiana.

Donella fought the urge to gag.

"She is a tolerable cook. She has some skill with herbal medicine. And she is very docile." Zaniah made Jiana turn around again.

"Walk about," the merchant ordered, ogling the girl. As Jiana limped along the roped in area, the man's face changed. "A cripple! What are you trying to pull? You should have said that from the start." He glared at Zaniah.

Donella shook with anger. An urge to talk back to these inhuman monsters replaced Donella's earlier dread. How dare they treat them like cattle? She wondered if she made a scene would Zaniah take her off the slave block? More likely Zaniah would sell her cheaply to an abusive master.

The merchant stomped away. Although she was glad the man wasn't likely to purchase Jiana now, she was mad at his dismissal of her friend's worth.

Clenching her hands behind her back, Donella took deep breaths.

Trust.

The word echoed in the air. Donella lifted her head and gazed around. No one was looking her way. Most of the slaves wore a resigned expression. Many had gone through this before. When they first met, Jiana had said, "I could tell you weren't a slave. You're too confident. You speak too much and ask too many questions. Most slaves learn to hide their feelings and thoughts. It's better not to have them. You cannot get hurt if you don't feel."

Maybe that is what Donella should do. Not feel. Not care. Resign herself.

But it felt wrong. A betrayal of all she was and had to offer.

Trust in the One Who Fashioned All. This time she heard the words in Lauressa's voice.

A horn sounded, breaking into Donella's musings.

"Ladies and gentlemen, take your seats. The auction is about to begin." A tall, fat man paced on the platform waiting for the audience to comply. He was nondescript, with a long, plain face, but his voice was resonant and compelling.

The buyers settled into their seats.

By ones and twos, the slave masters and mistresses led their human wares onto the platform. Again, they showed off their finest features. Then the bidding began. Once an agreed upon price was reached, the slaves descended, and their old masters led them to their new masters. Money changed hands while the next slave took their place.

Please, please, help us! Don't let us go to an evil master! Please let us stay together! Donella repeated the same desperate prayer over and over while clinging to Jiana's cold hand.

All too soon it was Jiana's turn. But Donella gripped her hand so hard she was halfway up the stairs before Zaniah turned and saw her.

"Not both of you. Donella, return to the ring," she hissed.

Reluctantly, Donella let go of Jiana. The blond girl gazed at her sadly, bit her lip as tears welled in her eyes, turned away and finished ascending the steps. Donella stood where she was until an overseer motioned her back down with his whip.

The auction for Jiana began.

Donella scanned the crowd bidding on her friend. She couldn't see a friendly face as several men shouted out their bids. They had the same look as the merchant earlier.

Fear for Jiana and herself brought on nausea. She broke out in a sweat.

Jiana looked ready to faint.

"I'll pay twice as much!" A woman's voice suddenly rang from the benches.

Donella snapped her gaze around to find a heavyset woman who pushed through the crowd. They moved back to let her and her attendants pass, like waves pushed aside by a warship. She was dressed in a dark green gown edged with gold trim which hugged her full form. Her shawl was intricately woven in shades of green and purple. One attendant held a pink, flower-shaped parasol above her head to shade her from the bright sunlight.

Zaniah's face gleamed with greed.

"But I have one condition." She sailed up to the forefront of the crowd.

Zaniah stared at the woman warily. "And what is that?"

"I want the dark-haired girl as well." Her double chin wobbled as she spoke. "They make a pretty contrast."

Donella glanced around to see who the woman meant. Zaniah and Jiana looked her way. It took another second to realize it was herself the buyer wanted.

After a nod from Zaniah, the auctioneer announced, "Sold!"

Legs wobbly, Donella climbed the steps to the platform and followed Zaniah and Jiana down the other side, across the sand, to the seating area.

At least Donella had skipped the humiliation of standing

before the crowd as people bid on her.

Jiana grabbed Donella's hand as they came to a halt before their new mistress.

Up close, she had crow's feet at the corner of her eyes, as if she squinted a lot or smiled often. Her face was lighter in tone than most people Donella had seen in Canteor. She had jowls and dark, bright eyes. Her ample bosom and taller than average frame made her stand out in a crowd.

"They'll make me the envy of my mistress," she said as one of retinue passed a small bag of coins to Zaniah.

She surveyed the girls from their heads to toes and gave a nod of satisfaction. "Come along." And she whisked away, Donella, Jiana, and her three attendants following, like support ships in the wake of a battleship.

A beautiful villa sat on the outskirts of Kiwan, near the river, surrounded by lawns and shade trees. From the front windows, Jiana could just see the tops of the town's houses.

She and Donella posed in sleeveless white robes holding palm leaf fans as their mistress painted them. Standing for hours was tiresome, but nothing compared to the fate they could have faced if a brutal master had bought them.

"Normally I'd spend the springtime painting scenes of my orchard. But I can't resist painting the two of you for my mistress," Lady Beccah had commented when she positioned them for painting.

At the far end of the property were many acres of apple orchards that the girls wandered around in their free time.

The apples were not sweet for eating but used for making sweets. After the laborers picked the apples, they pressed the fruits for their nectar. Confectioners mixed the nectar with chopped nuts, pectin and sugars. They heated the mixture. They poured it into molds in the shapes of flowers and leaves and left the mix to cool. When they were done, the confectioners sprinkled them with fine sugar powder and packed them in painted wooden boxes. The delicacy was highly prized among the nobility.

All this Jiana had learned since Lady Beccah brought them here.

After standing for several hours each day for the last week, Lady Beccah dismissed Donella to work in the kitchen. She retained Jiana to organize her things.

"Now, if you can just find me this shade of red, I will be able to finish it up."

Jiana placed the palm against the wall and searched through the paint pots until she matched the color her new mistress wanted.

"Ah, you found it." Lady Beccah dipped a tiny brush in the red paint and proceeded to add touches to her miniature painting of a sultry young woman on a throne. "I am going to turn this into a fan and give it to my mistress."

Jiana hadn't figured out yet how a lady could have a mistress, but she knew better than to ask.

Lady Beccah was not as formidable as she looked. Jiana spent her days as a slave mostly fetching items such as her mistress's shawl, her jewelry, and her afternoon drink. She sorted paints as she did today while her ladyship painted fans. Side by side with Donella, she attended her ladyship on walks and visits. Most of Lady Beccah's friends exclaimed how her new slaves made a pretty pair, and how envious someone named Sefira would be.

Jiana sent up a little prayer of thanks to Donella's god for her good fortune.

She had been expecting the worst, especially after those men leered at her as she stood on the auction block. She had wished herself dead rather than in the power of one of those men. And yet

Donella said suicide was evil and her god frowned upon it. Panmin, the pagan god of Canteor, allowed the killing of oneself in some rituals. But Jiana was thankful to leave aside the teachings of Panmin and follow the One Who Fashioned All. He sounded like a more merciful god.

She had prayed to him as she waited for someone to purchase her. "And see how praying to him had turned out?" she told herself with a smile. She didn't know all his laws, but she was willing to learn.

"There. I'll let this dry." Lady Beccah put down her foot-long scroll.

Jiana admired the details in the painting of the girl. She had black hair and pouting lips. She draped herself on a golden throne. Two female attendants held frond-shaped fans on either side of her. Jiana recognized herself and Donella by their attire and hair colors. At the throned figure's feet lay a large tawny animal. Jiana couldn't make out whether it was a dog or a giant cat.

"You are so talented, my lady. Whoever receives this will admire it."

"Yes, I hope so." Lady Beccah removed the giant apron she wore over her dress.

A tap at the door, and the porter stuck his head in. "A message for you, my lady. Came by special courier." He handed it to his mistress, bowed, and left.

"Huh. What could this be?" Lady Beccah spoke to herself as she used an ornamental knife to cut through the red wax seal. She walked over to the window that looked upon the street and read it.

Jiana busied herself putting the lids on the paint pots since the session was over.

"Still a month away," Lady Beccah mumbled to herself when she was done reading. Then she flipped back to the start and reread it again.

"Jiana, fetch my parasol and Donella. We have some visits to make."

The aroma of baking bread filled Lady Beccah's kitchen. The cook was dressing the beef hind. The scullery maid fetched water and poured it in a pot.

Donella still couldn't believe her luck in working as an assistant to the cook's assistant. Even if her eyes did water from the pungent task of chopping onions to flavor the meat. She added them to the pot.

"A pinch of rosemary and oregano," the assistant cook ordered Donella.

Taking a stool from the corner, Donella stepped upon it to reach the correct bunches of herbs hanging from the low ceiling. Her herbal training came in handy.

She sorted the amounts, adding them to the palm-sized mortar and using the pestle to grind them into tiny pieces. She held the mortar in her left hand and gripped the rounded pestle in her right, twisting the ingredients. She was careful not to break the ceramic bowl by pressing too hard.

She offered the ground spices to the cook. Donella watched as it was the exact amount needed to coat the meat.

"Lucky guess," was the rotund little woman's only comment. She was a surly type, with never a good word or praise for her helpers. But her cooking was superb. By the time they were done, the pastries she made would be flaky, the creams fluffy and light, the pies not too sweet and not too tart, the roast succulent, the potatoes crisp.

Lady Beccah's servants always ate the leftovers as there was plenty for all. Which was good, seeing how Donella's mouth watered at the thought.

"Psst," a sound came from the open door.

Donella turned around to see Jiana beckoning her.

Wiping down her hands on her apron, Donella strolled over. "What is it?"

"Lady Beccah received a letter. She's all excited about it. She wants us to accompany her to her friend's house."

Shortly after, the girls were trailing behind their mistress as four male slaves carried Lady Beccah's chair through the streets.

As they passed the amphitheater, Donella wondered what happened to Prince Gensard. The men had been auctioned off after the women and children. Was he still in town? Was he on his way to a distant part of Canteor? Would she ever see him again?

As Jiana reached over and clasped her hand, Donella figured she was thinking the same thing.

Thank you, One Who Fashioned All, for keeping Jiana and me together. Watch over us. Please take care of Gensard. And Guy and Odem, Hazibal too.

The chair stopped at the gates of an imposing mansion, the residence of the governor of the province. Guards stood on either side of the iron embossed door of the two-story building of gray stone. Bushes lining the path to the entrance were trimmed neatly. Not a piece of gravel was out of place. The window curtains were all matching in a bright shade of yellow.

Lady Beccah's bosom friend was the governor's wife, whom she visited frequently to gossip about all the news of the kingdom.

Donella and Jiana followed her down the formal hall. The stone floor was patterned in checkers. The walls were of dark wood, interspersed with paintings of men and women sitting stiffly, frowning as if they disapproved of the lowly visitors.

The sitting room was formal. The chairs were stiff, covered in thick gray fabric. The floor was covered by a black and white rug. A low table would soon hold beverages and delicacies. The only hint of color and life was the yellow curtains. Donella idly wondered if they were from a previous owner because they didn't seem to fit the style of the governor's wife.

When the ladies were seated, Donella stood in the background in case her mistress needed her. Lady Beccah had sent Jiana to the chair conveyance to fetch her forgotten shawl.

Donella studied the governor's wife. Unlike Donella's plump mistress, she was thin as a reed with a long, narrow face and a very slight mustache. Her dress was black with a froth of lace at the neck and hands. Her hair was pulled back in a tight knot, giving her face a severe expression, or maybe that was due to her disposition. The two women were a contrast, and yet they put their heads together and enjoyed a good gossip.

"And the grand event is a month away," Lady Beccah was saying.

Donella remembered Jiana mentioning a letter. This must be it. She kicked herself mentally for not paying attention to the earlier part.

"And so you must leave soon if you are going to partake."

"Yes, the princess will turn twenty-one. It will be a celebration I cannot miss. Though Dabbori at that time of year is not as cool as it is here in the country."

The conversation turned toward the latest fashions in Dabbori.

Donella tuned out.

So Lady Beccah was going to the capitol city Dabbori, where Agomeisa had meant to sell them before Gensard and Sad-alah angered him.

Jiana entered and brought the shawl to Lady Beccah just as the servants brought the afternoon refreshments.

"You must come and visit after your journey," the governor's wife said. "I'll look forward to your accounts of all the court scandals when you return."

When the girls were getting ready for bed in the attic room they shared, Jiana brought up the subject.

"What did she mean when she said that about our mistress visiting the court? What court?" She sat on the bed and brushed her hair.

"Lady Beccah spoke about Prince Pashmi's oldest daughter turning twenty-one and how she will be traveling to the celebration." Donella tucked her shoes under her side of the bed. "Do you think she'll take us? I wanted to see the capital city when I first arrived in your land." She didn't add, "a lifetime ago, when I came on a mission."

Donella wasn't sure if she'd ever see home again. A great sadness filled her heart at the thought.

"I've never seen the great city. It's supposed to be splendid." Jiana's hands stilled, suddenly. "But what if our mistress decided to sell us at the slave market . . ." Her voice trailed off.

"Don't be silly." Donella reached out and touched her friend's hand lying limp in her lap. "You are Lady Beccah's right hand. She depends on you every day."

"Yes, I suppose so." Jiana's face lost some of its tension. "And she doesn't have a son."

At the odd remark, Donella wondered if Jiana were finally going to talk about what happened to her. She remained quiet.

"My last mistress had a son, Pim. He spent most of his time away at an esteemed school in Dabbori, studying the law. He didn't show any interest in me until I turned eighteen. He returned home and suddenly he began watching me. He cornered me in the pantry once, the linen closet another time. I tried to avoid him. I was careful to always be around others." Jiana stared at her intertwined hands.

"But one day he found me laying out refreshments when no other slave was around. He grabbed me and scolded me for avoiding him. I tried to break free, but he was too strong." She put her hand to her mouth. "He kissed me. I tried to push him away, really, I did. Eventually I went limp."

A tear formed in the corner of Jiana's eye. "That's when his mother walked in. She accused me—*me*—of chasing her son and trying to win his affection. She called me horrible names.

"I was so agitated I didn't know what to do. I didn't even defend myself, hoping she'd calm down. But in a matter of days, I was on the slave block. Agomeisa bought me. You know the rest." Jiana hung her head.

"Look at me." Donella put both her hands on Jiana's shoulders and made her look up. "It was not your fault. You did nothing wrong."

A tear slid down Jiana's cheek. "But I felt so dirty."

"Listen to me. Pim sinned, not you. I mean if Hazibal had grabbed me, do you think I could have broken free?"

Jiana's dimple showed as she smiled slightly. "Not likely."

Donella sat back, trying to think of something to say to cheer her up. "If your previous mistress hadn't sold you, we wouldn't be friends."

Jiana wiped her eyes, then she nodded. "And I wouldn't know about your merciful god. Our merciful god," she corrected herself.

18 The Diadem

*A*s Guy raced down the main aisle for the exit, his heart thumping wildly, the door flew open. Kadar blocked the exit. His sword drawn; he wore a ferocious expression.

Guy's heart stuttered at the sight of him.

Trapped! Guy zigged to the side and ran down a row of benches, his breath ragged. Escape, but how?

Kadar advanced into the room. He glared at Guy.

Guy glanced toward the dais.

The shaman held a ceremonial dagger in one hand and his dark staff in the other. The symbols on his robe shimmered in the light, as if they had life of their own. Eyes narrowed and nostrils flared, he looked like what Guy pictured the sea god Makba to be.

"Kill him!" Queen Nerea pointed a bony finger at Guy as she commanded her henchmen.

Suddenly the glass window across the room shattered. Pellas climbed through, a sword in his hand.

Guy was truly hemmed in on all sides. He had thought Pellas his friend. Had he and Barbu conspired to bring Guy here? After all, Pellas knew the power of the wayposts.

"Is this how you treat visitors? Or only ones that threaten your absolute sway over the island chains?" Pellas' words had a bite. Without turning his head, he addressed Guy. "Get behind me."

Guy's adrenaline rush calmed as he realized Pellas was on his side. He climbed over the benches between them and joined his sword-wielding friend.

In the blackness beyond the window, Guy caught sight of Barbu's huge eyes peeking around the frame. As soon as he caught Guy's gaze, he motioned him to climb through.

Guy debated. Did he trust the island boy? Why had Barbu brought him to Cressava? And into the queen's web of deceit? Only his desire to escape the situation made him move his feet.

Pellas was trading insults with Guy's captors, so Guy took advantage of it to retreat. He shoved a bench over to the broken window. Barbu was already clearing glass off with a stick.

"Hurry!" Barbu only waited until he cleared the window, then he led the way, Guy following, reluctantly, his senses alert for any trick.

The fog remained thick, muffling their footfalls as they ran. After a burst of running, just when Guy felt a stitch in his side, Barbu slowed down. Guy leaned against a tree on the edge of the path, his hands on his knees, catching his breath.

"What happened to you?" Barbu huffed.

Guy straightened. "Lemmo led me to the temple. He did something to the burning coals on the altar and it was as if he mesmerized me." Guy watched Barbu's expression closely. "He asked me about my mark, and I felt compelled to answer. I was under some sort of spell."

Guy bit his lip as he stared at his friend. Was he involved? Barbu seemed genuine. He searched Barbu's open face. He saw no guile, only concern.

He hated to be the one who told Barbu that he had led them into a trap, but he had to learn sometime.

"Then when I fought against it, I found Queen Nerea was guiding Lemmo's questions," Guy reluctantly told the young teen.

Guy straightened up but remained silent, letting his words sink in.

Barbu's eyes widened. "She was behind the attack?"

"Yes. She wanted to know the source of my power so she could travel anywhere. I think Kadar gave her a ring which has the symbol on my hand." Guy watched Barbu's face fall as he took in the news. Guy rubbed the back of his neck. "I'm sorry."

"Why? I'm the one who should apologize." Barbu spread out his hands, palms up. "I brought you here to her. I thought the queen would know of the whereabouts of the Isle of Origin. She receives news from all over. Her spy network is famous."

"I'm sorry I doubted you, Barbu." Guy shuffled his feet. "For a minute, I thought you and Pellas were there to keep me from leaving."

Running footsteps made both boys turn around, ready to bolt.

Pellas dashed out of the fog. "To the ship! Hurry! Kadar's dead but the others aren't far behind me."

"I know a shortcut! Follow me!" Barbu hissed. He left the path that led to the courtyard, sprinting through the trees.

A ringing bell cut through the silent fog. The 'To Arms' signal!

Guy forced himself to move faster.

The three wound through a barely perceptible footpath. Trees, ornamental bushes, and statues of nymphs appeared and disappeared in the fog, which was thicker as they went downhill. Guy realized this must be a garden. Barbu must have found it on his ramblings.

The footpath eventually ended in a gate. They passed through to a set of steep stairs cut in a cliff that led to a private cove. They jogged along the smooth beach until they came to the larger harbor.

As Barbu sought for someone to row them to their ship, the beggar, seeing Guy, pleaded with Guy to take him with them. "I was outside the throne room and heard your destination. I have desired to see the great shrine since I was a boy at my baba's knee." He must have noticed Guy's reluctant expression. "I'll be no trouble. Please!"

Guy stared at the man's red eyes, the gnarled hands clasped in supplication, and could not turn him away.

In another forty-five minutes, they climbed aboard the *Diadem* from the dinghy Pellas had paid to row them out. The boat was nowhere near the size of the *Indomitable*, the pirate ship Guy had served aboard. Nor was it as large and majestic as the Valdeoran fleet ships of King Stepan.

The *Diadem* was an island hopper. Long and sleek, holding up to twenty crew, it boasted one mainsail and a jib. It had room for cargo in the aft through a hatch on the deck. The crew consisted of Captain Anaru and five others.

"We are all here and ready to sail." Pellas saluted the captain.

"The tide is an hour away." Captain Anaru replied.

"We'd like to get underway as soon as possible."

"Well, the breeze is freshening. We can unfurl the sail. Should be able to pick up the current a few knots out."

The captain ordered the crew to get the ship underway.

The beggar found a coil of rope and settled in. The sailors glanced at him and then ignored him.

Pellas led Guy and Barbu below deck. The main cabin held bunks and a tiny galley in the prow. Everything was tidy, stored neatly or lashed down.

Although they had escaped Queen Nerea and her shaman, Guy's shoulders were still tense.

When they were alone, Guy asked Pellas, "Can we trust the crew?"

"I think so. I have spent time with them. None of them are originally from this island and they don't have ties with the castle. They're simply a merchant ship for hire."

"But won't they be suspicious at our sudden hurry?"

"I drilled it into the captain's head that you are impetuous, Guy," Pellas grinned, "and you were likely to want to get on with your business at a moment's notice. So, no, I don't think they're suspicious."

Pellas pointed out their bunks. "I took time to stash our belongings on the ship, beforehand."

His grin faded. He crossed his arms and glanced at Barbu. "I don't know if you want to hear this, but I've had my suspicions since we arrived here. No offense to your father, Barbu, but I heard rumors swirling around the taverns. Queen Nerea is not the benevolent ruler like your father thinks. Sometimes important visitors disappear. They might eventually be found floating in the harbor. An unfortunate accident is the usual story. The queen would confiscate their ships under a new law of the islands. A law she enacted.

"So when I arrived at the castle today and Mauga told me you were closeted alone with Queen Nerea and her advisor," Pellas scowled at Guy, "I feared the worst."

Barbu looked from one to the other. He rubbed his forehead. His skin was too dark to show a blush, but he spoke reluctantly. "I overheard soldiers when I waited for Guy in the courtyard. Talk of traders drinking too much and drowning. The soldiers treated it like a joke." Barbu's eyes fell. "I live on a tiny isle, not important. People think me stupid. But I listen."

Guy flopped down on a bunk and put his head in his hands. "I had no idea that anything unusual was going on." He rubbed the back of his neck as he looked up at the other two. "Why didn't either of you tell me?"

"I feared you would not believe me." Barbu hung his head.

"You're not stupid, Barbu. You are very bright. You could have trusted us. We will always listen to you," Guy reassured him.

"And I had nothing but a gut feeling to go on." Pellas

scratched his cheek. "Something felt off."

Guy thought of Odem's lessons in situational awareness. He had failed to heed them. He determined to be more vigilant. Trust should be earned, not given.

The *Diadem* caught the current leading away from Cressava, when an hour and a half later a deep rumbling noise interrupted Guy's meal. The ship vibrated in sympathy. Barbu stopped in mid-bite of a tube-shaped fruit. He dropped his fruit from his limp hand. Leaving his bowl of stew, Guy followed Pellas up the ladder toward the deck, Barbu just behind. Just before they exited, the ship slammed to the right. Guy's hands automatically gripped the rungs as they hit the wall, his legs swinging free.

Barbu cried out as he fell the short distance back into the cabin.

"What in Panmin's name was that?" Pellas exclaimed.

They regained their feet, climbed the ladder, and burst on deck.

Off the port bow, black smoke belched from Cressava's volcano. Plumes of rock and ash shot up for a league, then billowed out in all directions. The spreading eruption soon blocked the sun. Darkness swept over them like the wings of a beast.

The white of Barbu's eyes were pronounced in his dark face. "Varu has awakened." His voice held awe and fear. He glanced askance at Guy. "Queen Nerea must have promised you for a sacrifice to Varu, and now he's upset that you escaped him."

Guy opened his mouth to say that volcanoes weren't alive, when another earthshaking rumble sounded. The ground didn't move, since they were in the sea, but a huge swell of water did. Traveling from the shore, another wave hit the side of the sloop, tipping her at a dangerous angle.

Unprepared, they went tumbling. Fortunately, it was smaller

than the first wave and they crashed into the ship's side. Guy grasped the oarlock, and held out a hand to Barbu, who grasped it. Pellas clasped a freshwater barrel lashed down several feet away.

The ship righted itself. Captain Anaru had the crew and passengers attach themselves to the ship with ropes around their waists until they were free of Varu's influence. But as they sailed farther away, a new menace threatened them. The ash cloud dimmed the sun, settling over the sea. An unnatural stillness hung in the air.

Captain Anaru approached the passengers. "We can't sail into the cloud. The fumes will choke the life out of a man. It's better if we put out to the deep sea and circumvent the volcano's destruction."

Pellas nodded his agreement.

Guy didn't know where to head, anyway. He had a general idea where the shrine's waypost lay. He walked to the prow of the ship, careful not to tangle his line with anyone else. He gazed over the choppy, gray water. Stretching out his senses, Guy pushed away the distractions—the stench of sulfur overlaying the seawater smell, the cool sea spray stinging his face, the movement of the deck under his feet, and the voices of the others.

A tiny thread of a pull to the east teased him and was lost. *He had felt something! Not much, but a familiar tingle. All was not lost. Maybe he could still redeem himself.*

Gripping the rough wood of the prow, he took several breaths. Closing his eyes, he formed an image of Donella with her black ringlets and how she twirled them with her fingers when she was anxious. He tried to sense her. Nothing.

He blew out a breath, exasperated. *Don't give up so easily,* he heard his mentor Usher's voice in his head. *Clear your mind and focus.*

Closing his eyes again, he imagined her smiling and biting into an apple. Guy concentrated on her mischievous eyes. He dove deep into his very core. He remembered how the between-place inside the portal felt. He reached out. A waypost very far south twinkled and went out.

Guy opened his eyes, smiling. Even though she was very far away, just knowing she was alive made him step lightly as he sought out the captain.

A hand clutched him, and Guy swung to face the intruder. The beggar asked his forgiveness. "I didn't mean to startle you, young lord. My baba, that would be my mama's mother, told me the Isle of Origin lay past the eastern isles, at the end of creation." He pointed in the direction that Guy had discerned.

"I am not a lord. Just a simple farm boy. Guy, at your service."

"You can call me Eliu. Thank you for rescuing me." His eyes watered, his hands were arthritic, but he was not as ancient as Guy had thought. His crippled state only made him seem old. He was likely only just past middle age.

"You'd never guess I was one of the watchmen on the docks. I kept drunken sailors from falling into the sea. I kept the peace. Until I became sick with the ague. Months I hung on by a thread. But when I recovered, my hands were stiff. They only grew worse over time. I sought out two healers. Eventually my money ran out. Nothing for me but to beg." He hung his head in shame. Lifting it he grasped Guy's arm. "My baba said many miracles happened at the great shrine. Maybe I will regain the use of my hands."

He rubbed his watering eyes. "I will forever be grateful for your kindness. May the One Who Fashioned All bless you, Guy." He slipped away to take up his position near the cargo hatch.

Guy headed for the wheelhouse, his step lighter. He was glad he had taken a chance on Eliu and Pellas. Maybe sensing the waypost was a reward for doing the right thing.

"Excuse me, captain. But do you have a map I can study?"

Soon, Guy was leaning over a chart in the wheelhouse, Pellas and Captain Anaru speaking nearby. A lit lamp hung over the table, swinging gently, allowing him to see in the obscured sunlight. Guy traced his finger from Bidori to Cressava and beyond to the east. Too many islands to count strung out to the east. He sighed. The Isle of Origin could be any one of them.

To the south was a stretch of sea and the land of Canteor, his original destination, where he sensed Donella was.

Both destinations were equally far away. Guy longed to tell Captain Anaru that he changed his mind and wanted to sail to Canteor. He could catch up with his friends.

Donella was alive, but was she alright? She could be a prisoner or injured. The possibilities were endless. Anxiety came back, as strong as ever.

He glanced at his birthmark. He couldn't tell in the dim light whether it was still faded or not.

Not doing what he was supposed to is what got him into this mess.

He stiffened his spine as he stood. As much as he longed to go to Canteor and find Donella, he would complete the mission the Guardian gave him. They would sail east and find the Isle of Origin.

"If only I knew where to go," Guy complained for the umpteenth time in the days since they sailed from Cressava. He kicked the leg of the bunk he sat on.

Every day he had stretched out his senses, searching for the shrine's waypost. Tiny glimmers sparked and faded.

Did that mean the Guardian was still angry with him? *I'm so sorry. Really, I am. Let me prove myself. Just one more chance.*

Guy wasn't sure if the being of light could hear him. Guilt for his friends' fate swirled in his gut.

Forgive yourself.

Guy took his head out of his hands and glanced around.

Barbu was stringing sea monster teeth on a necklace. He had told Guy it was a talisman of the sea god Makba against unforeseen disasters like storms and Varu awakening. Since leaving Cressava, Barbu had reverted to his pagan superstitions. The volcanic eruption had turned away his questions about Guy's beliefs.

Guy had to find his way again, not just for himself, but for Barbu and the pilgrims the Guardian told him would follow in his footsteps.

Pellas sat nearby, carving a bird from a piece of flotsam.

Neither one was looking at Guy.

Pellas put down his work and scooted around in his chair. "You know, we haven't asked Captain Anaru for his opinion. He has many years of experience. Maybe he could point you in the right direction."

"And the crew may have heard tales," Barbu chipped in, his eyes alight.

Guy seriously doubted the crew would know anything. The island had been lost for centuries. But he was willing to give it a try.

They made their way onto the deck. Black volcanic clouds still hung over them, blotting out the sun. Days had passed and the gloom had only deepened. They seemed to sail continually into the twilight.

Guy's spirits plummeted. He hoped they had sailed past the reach of the volcano.

"Varu still angry." Barbu shook his head.

"If we find the Isle of Origin, will you consider agreeing the Unnamed God is more powerful?" Guy liked the boy and wanted him to embrace the true God.

Barbu screwed up his face. "Your god has not been on your side so far." And then his white teeth gleamed in the dark. "If your god shows himself more powerful than Varu, then yes, I'll convert."

By this time, they had crossed the deck to the wheelhouse. Captain Anaru glanced up from his charts.

He updated them. "We're still trying to go around the ash cloud, but it's spreading as fast as we can sail."

Guy usually let Pellas, as the eldest of the group, speak to the captain. But this was his quest, so he asked the question. "Captain, sir, you said you sailed these islands extensively," he began.

"That's so. Since I was about your age, a lad of sixteen."

"I'm actually seventeen," Guy corrected him. "Anyway, I'm trying to find an isle with a great shrine on it."

"Ah, you spoke of the Isle of Origin. That is a myth I have heard but have no knowledge of. But a shrine . . ."

Guy's breath hitched. Maybe the choice of words was important.

"I have heard of a spectacular temple, but I don't know where it is."

Guy's heart plummeted into his shoes. It had been too much to hope for.

The captain scratched his head. "There is someone who might be able to guide you."

Hope surged back up like a fountain.

"Enri, do you remember that old hermit? Wasn't he from your village?"

A sailor standing at the wheel and steering the ship glanced at them. He was mostly bald on top. His most outstanding feature was his long, white, drooping mustaches.

Taking one hand from the wheel, he rubbed his nose. "Aye. He were a strange one. Muttering to himself, claiming to speak to an unseen person. Predicting storms and disasters as punishment for our sins. Finally, he went to live on a uninhabited rock, claiming to wait for a sign from above." Enri tapped his forehead. "Touched in the head, he were." He touched the giant tooth on a cord around his neck, in a sign of warding off evil.

Guy didn't like the sound of this man, but he didn't have much choice but to search for the hermit. "Do you know where he lives now?"

The sailor spit in his hands and grabbed the wheel. "Sikarta is the island where I'm from. He lives near it."

Guy glanced at his friends, who nodded at his questioning look. Guy turned back to the crewmen. "Then, Captain Anaru, please take us there."

19 Gladiator

Standing in front of a pack of boorish merchants and foreign nobles, sold like cattle, was the most humiliating thing in Gensard's twenty-four years of life.

Agomeisa had ordered him to bathe and coat his chest and arms with oil. Half-naked, he inwardly seethed as would-be buyers checked out his strong points.

If he had a blade, he would've cut them down where they stood.

The latest gawker was a wizened man leaning on a cane. His hair, what little was left, was a wispy halo about his round head. He barely came up to Gensard's shoulder. But his purple robe of fine silk was intricately patterned with lozenges and Gensard recognized the dye as one only nobility could afford. The man wore several gold rings, one with a large emerald. He smelled of expensive cologne.

Speaking to Agomeisa, he said, "I saw your man fight last night. What is his record of wins?"

Agomeisa bared his teeth in a grin. "Unbeaten."

"Hmm." The nobleman faced Gensard. Spinning his thin, bent finger, he commanded, "Turn around!"

Gensard ground his teeth and glared at the nobleman staring at him.

Agomeisa whipped Gensard across the shoulders. "Obey!" he roared.

Jaws clenched, Gensard turned around in place.

His gaze landed on two giants who attended the nobleman. They looked familiar somehow. Their features didn't match the rest of the Canteorans. These men had wide noses and deep black bodies which absorbed light. As he looked closer, Gensard noticed strange diagonal slashes stood out on either cheek. He had a flashback to defeating a giant with similar markings in the Laketown battle.

Soon after, the auction began. The auctioneer presented Gensard first.

"Ladies and gentleman, here is the finest specimen you will see today."

Staring from the slave block, Gensard sneered at the sea of faces calling out pittances for him. The nobleman easily outbid the others in a fierce battle to own Gensard. At least his skill was recognized.

Immediately after the auction, his new master's ebony attendants claimed him. One of the hulks shepherded him, Sadalah, and another slave to the blacksmith. Gensard suffered his second most humiliating moment, as the blacksmith fitted a slave collar around his neck.

Bile rose in his throat. How dare they! He opened his mouth to tell them he was a prince. His father would ransom him. The only thing that stopped him was the thought that his father might disown him, as he had his older brother, Leander. No, better to suffer in silence than to hear that his father refused to ransom him.

Never let your enemy know what you are thinking. Always take him by surprise. Taking breaths through his nostrils, Gensard expelled it through his lips. His heart rate slowed.

Gensard longed to hit out as one of the giants attached a chain to the ring on his slave collar, its metal links rattling as he was chained to the two other men his new master had purchased.

He should have escaped before now! But he hadn't had the heart to leave the girls behind. A chance to free them had never presented itself. He was stuck now.

Never to see Jiana's lovely face nor Donella's determined one. Never to set foot on Samarantha, his kingdom. Nor ride his steed, Fiery. Never to be a free man again. Never to claim his princely birthright. He had taken it all for granted. Despair sucked the heart from him.

Gensard shuttered his thoughts. They were too painful.

They were led like a string of horses to an inn. The two-story building was made of clay bricks, seeming grand next to the smaller wooden buildings around it. Window boxes decorated the bottom floor windows. As the nobleman entered, Gensard glimpsed slate floors and a rich wooden bar with pewter tankards on the shelves.

One of the giants attended his master, the other led the slaves around the back to a simple wooden building beside the stable. One high window let in a little light, which shone on a pile of straw. Gensard and the other two were made to sit down. He assumed the pile of straw was meant for their beds. Other than that, the room was bare of furnishings.

"I'm Elozma, Lord Paitar's bodyguard and your new boss until we arrive at his estate." The giant stood in front of them. Legs apart, thick as tree trunks. Oiled arms held at the ready. Face carved of granite with cold eyes. From their position, they had to look up at him.

"Don't give me no trouble," Elozma rumbled, catching each man's eyes. "I don't know what Lord Paitar sees in you scraggly bunch. But he owns the finest gladiators in the land. If you do well in training and the ring, he might let you into his elite corps. But you cross me, and I'll see your sword arm broken so you can't fight again." He smacked his fist into his palm. "Then my master will send you to his mines where life is as brutal as it is short. Understand?" He must have been satisfied with what he saw in their faces because he ceased threatening them. He strode out and Gensard heard a padlock clicking in place.

He studied his current companions. Sad-alah smirked and laid himself down in the straw as if he didn't have a care in the world. The other was older with corded muscles and graying hair. His bare back was crisscrossed with old whiplash scars. He was probably a veteran military fighter. But that many lashes denoted a defiant attitude.

The scarred man spit at the giant's retreat, but he waited until it was only the three of them. "Thinks hisself better'n us. Naught but a slave hisself."

"He's not the one chained up like a dog." Sad-alah played with a bronze yiza, spinning it through his fingers.

"I'd rather die in the sunlight with a sword in my belly than a dark pit underground." Gensard made his sentiments clear as he tested the strength of the slave collar. In the short time he wore it, the collar already chafed his skin. Too bad Hazibal wasn't here. He might be able to rip it off with his bare hands.

Several days of traveling followed Lord Paitar's purchase of the new gladiators. Their mode of travel was identical to that of Agomeisa, a barred wagon for the three slaves. Paitar rode in an elegant carriage while his two attendants with wickedly big scimitars rode on enormous horses on either side.

They eventually pulled up to an enormous estate on the outskirts of Dabbori. A three-story mansion set on a hill dominated the scene. Made of yellow clay, surrounded by shade trees, it overlooked a large training ground. What at first look seemed to be a town behind the house, turned out to be barracks for the gladiators, a blacksmith's shop, a weapon master's shop, a leather worker's shop, a mess hall, and a stable.

The first morning in the training yard, Gensard joined the others circling the yard. Twenty-five hardened fighters stared back at him. Like him, they were naked to the waist, some had even oiled their chests. They had bare feet for traction and wore brown homespun trousers held in place with belts.

At the other end of the yard were straw dummies attached to posts.

A burly man with a square jaw, penetrating eyes, and gray in his temples walked the ranks of the slaves. The barrel chest, muscled legs, and many scars on his bare, corded arms showed him to be a fighter. But he wore no slave collar. The men showed him respect by standing at attention as he inspected them.

He stopped in front of the three new men. "I am Master Doza. Lord Paitar might own you, but I rule here. This is my training ground. You follow my rules. Anyone who doesn't gets sent to the Lord's mines."

Doza's eyes lighted on the man with the scarred back. "What is your name?"

"Gerd," he answered sullenly.

"Call me sir or master, dog."

Gerd curled his lip, then lowered his eyes. "Gerd. Sir."

"You look like trouble, Gerd. I'll be watching you."

Doza moved in front of the line of men, placing his hands behind his back. "Prince Pashmi has planned a tournament for his daughter's birthday in a month's time. He declared he would honor Princess Sefira's wish for the winner to be set free."

Freedom!

A murmur went around as the men took in his words.

After a moment, Doza held up his hands for silence. "I will choose only Paitar's best gladiators to represent him."

Gensard was determined to be among their rank.

Each man was assigned a straw dummy to attack.

Gensard did some stretches first. Right leg extended, knee bent. His arm parallel to his leg. He lifted the sword until it was straight up in the air. He changed feet and did the same with the left side. He pushed through the pain of the mace's injury in his left arm.

He saw the nearest man smirking and pointing him out to the fighter on his other side. He heard their snickers. Ignoring them, he finished his stretches and inhaled. He imagined Agomeisa standing there and threw himself at the straw man.

Slash the left shoulder. Spin. Slash the right shoulder. Thrust low and hit the right thigh. Step away, swing backhand through the neck. Straw stuffing burst from each blow.

He repeated the movements over, more stuffing flying. Now it represented Elozma and Paitar, and whoever bought Jiana. Everyone who stood in the way of Gensard's happiness.

He fought until his muscles ached and his breathing was ragged.

Stepping away, sweat dripping down his back, he glanced to the right. The man wore a grim look, hacking at his dummy but with less precision. It was Gensard's turn to smirk.

Doza called a halt, inspecting each straw figure. When he came to Gensard, he paused and raised his eyebrow at Gensard's spent dummy.

Two boys brought pails of water and ladles for the men to refresh themselves.

That afternoon, Doza separated the men into pairs to spar. Gensard was paired with a man of medium height. His most noticeable features were his wide shoulders and black brow, which was one unit, the dark hair extending from eye to eye across his nose.

Gensard gripped his wooden sword's hilt. It was heavier than his scimitar, and not as well-balanced. But he had fought with his father's sword master many a time with wooden blades. This was not a battle to the death, but a training exercise.

At the signal to start, they took each other's measure. Unibrow thrust first and Gensard countered. Another thrust and parry. They circled around each other. Gensard went on the offensive as Doza strolled over to observe. He made a flurry of moves. Thrust overhead, blocked. Continue his arc to the right, thrust up. The swords clicked as they connected over and over. Leading suddenly with his left foot, he changed to backhand hits, taking his opponent by surprise. Gensard smacked Unibrow's wrist, causing the other to drop his blade.

Stepping back, Gensard used his left hand to wipe his brow. It throbbed with the exertion.

With his hands behind his back, Doza regarded Gensard. "Let's see how you do against a more seasoned fighter." Doza indicated another combatant who had bested his challenger.

Gensard walked over and faced a new adversary. This man was taller and broader. He had a gap between his front teeth as he grinned. "Bring it on, brother."

They both moved toward each other, blades striking. They disengaged, then struck. On the third time, gap tooth went for an overhead strike. Gensard ducked under his reach and smacked his adversary in the stomach. The man made a loud oof and clutched his middle.

Doza's lips twitched when Gensard stepped away to catch his breath.

Doza signaled Elozma to ring a bell to get everyone's attention. "Enough one on one. Report to the mess hall for dinner."

Gensard was sure he had made a good impression on the overseer.

The rough wooden mess hall wasn't very large, especially when filled with hot, sweaty men. Unwashed bodies' odors mingling with savory stew smells made Gensard grimace. Men jostled him in the line to receive their portion.

He missed the lightly perfumed courtiers of the palace and the deference shown him by servants and nobles alike. He had always been served after his father, Prince Xander. No waiting for his turn.

He sniffed at the stew slapped in his bowl before putting in his wooden spoon.

"It's not poison, though some might call it that." A man with a shaven head, loop in one ear, and full beard sat across from him.

Gensard took a mouthful and chewed the tough beef and overcooked potatoes. The onion added flavoring, reminding him suddenly of Donella's savory additions to the plain fare on the road.

The thought of the girls made his appetite wane. Where were they? Safe? Abused?

He hated feeling powerless. He longed to do something. But what?

The conversation swirled around him, but he stared into his bowl and forced himself to eat. Using a chunk of bread, he scraped the bowl clean, not because it tasted good, but because he knew he needed the nourishment to keep fighting.

"You're handy with a wooden sword. But how do you do with a real blade in your hand?"

Gensard met the eyes of the man across the slab table whose voice boomed out the question.

"I can wield a sword better than most. You?"

"Ha. The answer of a true warrior." He threw back his head, his mouth showing several missing teeth as he laughed. "My name's Jod, and I can wield a sword better than most myself."

His eyes narrowed as he looked over Gensard. "But how do you do in front of an audience of thousands? Hmm? A street scuffle or a fight over a pretty lass is much different than a gladiator match. If Master Doza picks you, you'll be up against the greatest swordsmen in the land. Hardened fighters with many more years than you." Jod used his knife to pick his teeth.

"And how many battles have you been in?" Gensard put down his bowl. "Have you fought for your life against hundreds of enemies? It only takes one man to pierce your heart. But do you have courage to stand your ground on the battlefield for days on end? Smelling the stench of death and knowing if you don't prevail, you'll eventually be overrun?"

Jod looked at him, somberly. "You are talking about your experience, aren't you? You are saying you have faced hundreds on the battlefield? Not just one on one in the ring?"

Gensard realized the men's conversation around them had ceased while he and Jod spoke. Faces were turned their way, eyes evaluating the truth of his words.

"Yes, I have been in several battles against enemy forces."

"He is not from Canteor. He is an enemy of Prince Pashmi," a voice accused from somewhere down the table.

Gensard twisted to see who spoke and met Sad-alah's challenging gaze.

Murmuring erupted around the table.

"Every man here is either a slave or a criminal," a commanding voice cut across the room. "Your master bought you as fighters, not patriots." Doza's presence quelled the ugly tension in the room. "Which of you is a perfect model of propriety?"

The men sheepishly looked away from Doza's piercing eyes. "Here I shall judge you on your skills, not your birth. Now, fall in and get some sleep."

The men rose and filed out.

Gensard glanced at the overseer as he left, but Doza's stony expression gave no indication of his thoughts.

Doza had watched him closely today. Gensard thought he saw a spark of admiration once or twice. He needed to be one of the chosen. If he could fight and win his freedom, he could find Jiana. He longed to know if she were safe and well.

As he lay in his bunk in the stone barrack, Gensard's thoughts turned to the girls.

Donella always had a positive attitude, trusting her god. The One who Fashioned All was Gensard's God, too. But he hadn't prayed much. It wasn't that he didn't believe, just that he hadn't had a need to lean on the divine before now.

Even Jiana seemed to beseech intercession from the Creator, who she hadn't previously known. She soaked up all of Donella's lessons like a parched land soaked up the rain. She flowered and grew more confident, smiling more often, seeming less afraid.

That was until he opened his mouth and told Sad-alah a lie. He was convinced she overheard his words dismissing his feelings for her. Her expression of shock and great sorrow after she dropped the willow bark tea haunted him.

He longed to tell her he said those things to protect her. And yet, did the lie help? No, Agomeisa sold them out of hand because of what he did. He finally admitted that his own actions had separated them. Whatever evil befell her was his fault.

Self-loathing rose and choked him.

Maybe it was time Gensard prayed in earnest.

Please, please, let her . . . let both girls be alright. Keep them from evil masters. Free me and let me find them! Not for myself, but for their sakes. I would do anything, Almighty Father. Just keep Jiana safe.

20 Dabbori, Capital of Canteor

$\mathcal{P}$reparations for the trip occupied Lady Beccah's household for a week.

Early afternoon, Jiana knocked on her mistress's door after lunch, which was her custom. The lady's maid, in charge of dressing and styling her hair, said Lady Beccah was resting. Behind her, Lady Beccah's belongings were strewn about the room.

"The mistress was choosing what to wear and what to take." The lady's maid seemed frazzled, unlike her usual self.

"Let me help you put the things away." Jiana smiled shyly.

The maid usually looked down on the slave girls from her superior position in the household, but today she was grateful.

Jiana carefully smoothed each gown, more beautiful than the next, as she hung them in the wardrobe. The fabrics felt so soft to her hands. If only she could wear such lovely clothes. She picked up a dress of pale pink. The bosom was white with lacing to tie it in place. The sleeves were tight to the elbow and flared out in a bell-shape to the wrists. She held it against herself. She glanced in the mirror and sighed. She would look like a princess in it.

She imagined Gensard's face if he could see her wearing it.

She sighed and hung it up. She should be thankful that she was a servant of a noble lady who treated her decently. Dreams of finding love and being a free woman were silly thoughts.

She should concentrate on the task at hand, which was pleasing her mistress. Donella said doing one's duties in life was most pleasing to the One Who Fashioned All. Her heart swelled with gratitude when she recalled that day on the slave block.

Soon Lady Beccah joined them. "The baggage can wait. Come here, Jiana. Stand in the light."

Jiana moved near the window embrasure. Lady Beccah scrutinized her critically, making her spin slowly in place. "Your gown will not do for the court. I will not show you and Donella to Princess Sefira until I have a gown that will set off your features.

"No time to visit the shops for suitable gowns. We will just have to alter two of mine." Lady Beccah rummaged through the wardrobe. She pulled out a dress the color of a blue sky. "This will suit Donella's coloring."

Happiness washed over Jiana's when her mistress held the pale pink up to her. "Yes, this color looks better on one so young than it does on me at my age."

A servant was dispatched to bring a seamstress from town. The woman spent the rest of the afternoon fitting the gowns for the two girls. She pinned and sewed and had the girls try them on until they were just right.

Lady Beccah seemed pleased, her eyes crinkling critically as Jiana and Donella showed her the final product. She had the girls walk about, arm in arm.

"Such a shame about your limp." Lady Beccah frowned. "It spoils the effect."

"A cobbler can fix it easily," her friend quickly came to Jiana's defense. "Gensard, my b-brother made a platform and attached it to her shoe." Donella blushed for some reason. "It worked very well. Jiana's limp was barely noticeable. But he only had a leather strap to attach it with." Donella earnestly told the story. "But a cobbler could nail a piece to the bottom of Jiana's sandal. It only needs to be a little higher."

And so Jiana found herself as beautiful as a princess, with a new silk gown and new shoes that allowed her to walk easily without a limp.

Donella was right. Being sold to Agomeisa had been a blessing in disguise, for Jiana was better off than ever in her life.

Four carriages rolled out from Kiwan, each bearing the crest of a fruit tree, which betokened Lady Beccah's late husband's apple growing business. The first carriage carried Lady Beccah and her lady's maid. Donella and Jiana traveled in the second, and the third and fourth were filled with everything their mistress would need in the capital, from her sheets embroidered with her crest, to trunks filled with gowns, shawls, shoes and hats. She had also included boxes of presents for all her friends at court: delicately painted fans and the exotic delicacies made from fruit on her villa's grounds.

The road to Dabbori, the capitol city, followed the Rashir River, fed from the Zarde Heights and rushing to the sea.

The hill country was very different from the desert and plains of the northwest. The coarse grass was suitable for grazing sheep and the way was dotted with sheep ranches. Well-cared-for cottages made of dried clay bricks, topped with grass roofs, were set back from the road.

The time for shearing sheep's wool had not come, so the sheep looked like fat clouds of fluff on spindly, little black legs. They placidly roamed from grass tuft to tuft. But at a loud noise, like the cracking of a whip, the nearest ones would fall over in a faint. This caused Donella and Jiana to giggle each time it happened, once they learned the effects were temporary. The sheep soon jumped up and went back to chewing as if nothing happened.

But wolves came with the territory, living in the surrounding hills, hunting for an easy meal.

Lady Beccah's six outriders rode alongside the travelers to provide them with some safety.

Donella was pleased to notice that Jiana had bloomed in her time as Lady Beccah's servant. Her hollow eyes were now bright with delight at the sheep's antics. Her face had filled out with regular meals. Gone was the shadow of fear in the back of her eyes. And she shared her thoughts more freely than she had in all the weeks they had traveled with Agomeisa.

With just Donella as an audience, she was adept at telling stories that were handed down over generations. Donella thought she was a natural storyteller.

To while away the long hours, Donella encouraged her friend to tell her about Dabbori and its history.

"Grandpap told me Dabbori is an ancient trading city. The wealth of the Zarde Heights mines literally flow down the Rashir River to Dabbori. Much of the precious metal is minted into gold and silver yiza of different values. The great city boasts goldsmiths and silversmiths who are the finest in the world. They create lovely jewelry, trinkets, and plates and goblets for the rich.

"And the deep harbor allows ships from the islands to the north, as well as those of Valdeor and Hamleor to dock." Jiana sat relaxed.

"Do they bring spices and linens, jewels and hard woods from my homeland? These are items we are known for." Donella remembered the marketplaces she loved to wander.

"Yes, and fine wine from the Tilmuk vineyards where I worked is also traded in large caskets. Trade made the inhabitants of Dabbori very wealthy. You will see, the city supposedly has every luxury." Her eyes shone with excitement. "Grandpap said they have water in every house. Can you imagine?"

Jiana clasped her hands and giggled at the thought.

Donella didn't spoil her delight and tell her how she had experienced such luxuries in Mintala. Besides, she would have a lot of things to explain about why she was a guest in the palace there in the first place. It wasn't that she didn't trust her friend— she thought of Jiana as a sister—but she could not expose Gensard.

Her pulse quickened as they came closer to the capital. A part of her secretly hoped she would find Gensard, or even more importantly, Guy, in Dabbori.

If either one was there already, she wouldn't jeopardize their original mission. In all of her troubles, she mustn't forget war looming between her country and this one.

That night they stayed in a comfortable inn which served their mistress fine food in a private parlor. Not able to finish the extensive courses, she let her servants finish the tasty meal. The innkeeper treated Lady Beccah deferentially. It transpired that she always broke her journeys to the capital at his inn. The hospitality even extended to the room the girls shared in the attic servant's quarters with the innkeeper providing them a fire.

A week on the road brought Lady Beccah's entourage to the crest of a hill. Below was a green valley, filled with fruit orchards. Leafy trees were showing early fruit.

A magnificent walled city spread out at the far end of the valley. Small, single-story row houses were behind the city gate. Beyond them were three-story buildings of pink clay ascending three hills. A palace of quarried pink sandstone crowned the summit of the central hill.

The road before them continued alongside the Rashir River which eventually emptied into the Dabbori Harbor. Palm trees dotted the shore. Distant ships rode in the blue waters, their colorful hulls bobbing in the waves.

But Donella's eyes widened at the tent city set between the

orchards and the city's edge.

Lady Beccah must have wondered about it too, because her hand appeared at her carriage window, fluttering a lace handkerchief. One of the outriders approached her. After a moment of listening, he signaled the other riders to stay and urged his steed toward the tent city.

Lady Beccah's maid stepped out of the first carriage and helped their mistress down.

Pushing open the door, Jiana lightly jumped down and ran to her. Donella followed more slowly in her wake.

"Put my rug on a log over there, Jiana. I will enjoy the fresh air while we wait," Lady Beccah announced.

Donella retrieved the basket of food she had ordered at the inn before leaving this morning. It contained rolls, a slab of hard cheese, a tiny, corked jar holding freshly packed olives, and a bunch of grapes. She presented these to her mistress, along with a waterskin of wine and another of water.

Jiana threw down a second blanket for the servants to sit at the feet of their mistress.

Lady Beccah nibbled at the impromptu snack. The smell of the goat cheese and the olives caused Donella's mouth to water.

Lady Beccah brushed away the crumbs from her ample lap. "We will be at my house in Dabbori by dark." She motioned to the remains. "Eat your fill."

The salty taste of the olives blended well with the crusty roll and tangy cheese. Donella knew she had gained back the weight she lost as a slave because her dresses fitted snugly again. She silently thanked the One Who Fashioned All for his care and the good food.

The outrider returned shortly thereafter. "Milady, below is Prince Pashmi's training ground for war games. Fortunately, they do not start in earnest until tomorrow, so it is safe to you to pass."

"Then we shall be on our way. I wish to be home before

nightfall." The girls helped pick up their mistress's belongings, stowing them back in the first carriage. Once they climbed back in the second carriage, the entourage moved forward.

Donella and her friend each gazed out their carriage's open windows, as they traversed through the silent bare trees and into the war camp. They both instinctively pulled back from the windows as the carriage rolled through the camp.

The tent city was a beehive of activity. Men sharpened their weapons or fletched arrows. Others practiced their sword skills, while men shot arrows at targets in a field. A cook fire smelled of wood and onions. A line of horses smelled of the stable. A giant blacksmith shod a horse. Forges burned bright while smiths fashioned weapons, the sounds of their hammers ringing through the air.

"They look like they prepare for battle," Jiana whispered beside Donella. Her face had lost some of its color as rough men turned to watch the fancy carriages pass by. "I wonder who Prince Pashmi wars with."

"Valdeor."

Jiana's eyes widened as she stared at Donella's face. "Your kingdom? How do you know?"

"Because I was there when the scout ships attacked." Donella bit her lip, deciding how much to say. "I was staying in Laketown with Gensard when Canteor ships sailed into the harbor. I watched the battle from the balcony. The few Valdeor ships prevailed against the invaders, but there were only three scout ships. Our force was not prepared for war. I hate to see what a Canteor fleet could do."

The girls sat silent and still until they passed through the massive arched gate into the city. With one accord, they moved back to their respective windows to see the sights.

Poorer homes sat just inside the gates, with their small windows and gaping, dark doorways looking uninviting in a single-story row of gray. Dark alleys twisted away from the main boulevard. But as they journeyed farther into the city, the houses became larger and detached with walled-in gardens. Some were two-story made of pink clay bricks, while others towered at three stories. A few gates were open, giving glimpses of spacious courtyards filled with palm trees, ferns, and decorative urns. Windows were larger, with cheerful white shutters and attached balconies having fancy ironwork balustrades. The nearer to the palace, the fancier the houses.

"Have you ever seen such beautiful homes?" breathed Jiana from her side of the seat.

"Laketown is very beautiful. The houses are all painted different colors, and they plant their gardens on their rooftops. Vines and flowers fill the air with their scents." Seeing Jiana's expression, she added, "But this city is lovely, too. I like the pink houses."

A breeze off the sea tickled Donella's nose with the smell of salt and seaweed and ruffled her hair. She realized the carriages approached the harbor.

A sudden wave of homesickness overcame her. Talking about Laketown and remembering the last time she had stood overlooking the sea, reminded her of all she had lost. Her eyes teared up.

Thoughts of her mother, the inn where she had grown up, her mentor Usher, Seeker the horse, and Guy all rushed into her mind. She wiped the sudden tears with the knuckle of her right hand.

Jiana turned at the sound of Donella's sniffles.

"What is wrong, Donella?" Jiana's hand pressed into hers.

"The smell of the sea made me long for home. It's the last thing I remember before setting out for Canteor. I miss my friends and my cozy little house." The tears threatened to become a waterfall. Donella covered her face and let them come.

Jiana rubbed her back and made soothing noises.

Not wanting to distress her friend, Donella pulled herself together. She had to be strong for Jiana. But it was nice to be on the receiving end of compassion for a change. She wiped her eyes and blew her nose with a handkerchief she retrieved from her pocket.

"I wish I could see Valdeor," Jiana said, her hands clasped in her lap. "A land where I could be a free woman."

Donella's heart constricted at the longing in her friend's voice. Determination grew in her. If she could find her way back home, she would not go unless she could take Jiana with her.

Deep in their conversation, Jiana had not noticed they were at the palace until the sound of the wheels changed. Glancing out the window as Donella wiped her eyes, magnificent pink sandstone walls appeared beside her. Drawn by their beauty, Jiana scooted nearer the window. Windows arched gracefully, outlined in white paint. The courtyard was laid with crushed white shell. Palm trees, perfectly spaced, lined the area. The carriage rolled up to a massive entryway and stopped. The doorman opened the right-hand door in the arch as the carriages stopped.

He helped Lady Beccah descend, her lady's maid following behind her with their mistress's personal belongings. Jiana and Donella exited their vehicle and joined them.

Jiana stretched unobtrusively. It felt good to stand after hours of sitting.

The building had elements of a palace and a fortress about it. Four stories above her head, crenelations marked the battlements. Soldiers on guard peered down at them.

Then the doorman whisked them through the two-foot-thick walls into the cool shade of the entryway. Tapestries lined the walls, depicting scenes of war. A whiff of sweet incense drifted in the air.

The housekeeper met them.

"Welcome back, Your Ladyship. I ordered your rooms prepared as soon as I got the message you were returning." She was short and squat, her dark, smooth hair twisted in a long loop on her back. Her orange gown was shapeless, hanging down to her ankles. A red sash hung from her left shoulder to her right hip.

She inspected Jiana and Donella from head to foot. "I will have the maids prepare another room for your servants. This way."

"How is Her Highness?"

"Full of high jinks as her twenty-first birthday approaches."

The rest of the conversation was lost to Jiana as they moved down the hall. She had never seen such beauty.

The floor was intricately inlaid mosaic in a geometric pattern. Jiana's shoes made a tapping noise as she followed at the tail end of their procession. She swung her head this way and that as she tried to absorb every detail.

Torches were yet unlit in their golden brackets. Pedestals held vases of colorful flowers and small statuary. Open doors gave glimpses of opulent chambers.

They traversed many corridors and stairs, all grand in scale. Jiana could hardly believe anywhere so majestic existed.

Her delight knew no bounds when the housekeeper showed them the bathing chamber with running water.

"Oh, look, Donella! I cannot believe it's true."

Arriving at her bedchamber, Lady Beccah commanded them, "Clean off the traveling dirt and report back here. I will dine with the princess this evening. I expect you to help my maid unpack my belongings."

After leaving Lady Beccah directing the orderlies in placing her pieces of baggage in her suite, another maid ushered Jiana and Donella to their room on the floor above.

Unfortunately, the fancy bathing chamber was not for

servants, so the girls used a hip bath that servants brought and filled with pitchers of lukewarm water. But that was not enough to dampen Jiana's excitement at staying in a palace.

"I will have the servants send a tray of food here." Lady Beccah informed them afterward. "You may finish unpacking and then sup."

Jiana shoved down her disappointment. She wanted to meet a royal in real life.

The next morning the girls entered their mistress's chamber before she awoke. In the daylight, the sitting room looked even more sumptuous. Sheer drapes fluttered in the tall windows. Several chairs and couches were set in a circle with tiny tables beside them. A large wardrobe of dark wood stood on one wall. A looking glass stood on a small vanity, pots and jars of ointments and perfumes scattered on it.

"The mistress returned in the late hours. She won't stir until midmorn. Come back then," her maid told them.

Jiana and Donella returned to their room to set it in order, having been too tired the night before. It didn't take much time to unpack their few gowns and personal items.

"Do let's explore the grounds," Donella exclaimed, turning from their small window. "I want to stretch my limbs and see the gardens. They look delightful from here."

After getting lost a couple of times, a manservant pointed them in the direction of the servant's entrance.

They spent a delightful hour wandering the elaborate gardens. Palm trees stood sentinel, but they also saw fruit trees and flowering trees. Pathways lined with crushed shells led to statuary, benches, and fountains. They saw no one at this early hour except one elderly gardener.

Standing under an arbor weighted with heavily blooming vines, Jiana clapped her hands and took a deep breath of jasmine and fresh air. "It is heavenly."

"This is going to be my favorite place." Donella smiled.

Arriving back at their mistress's room, she told them, "Make yourselves presentable. I expect you to accompany me to the princess's chambers in an hour."

They quickly dressed in the blue and pink gowns the seamstress in Kiwan had altered for them. After fixing each other's hair in curled waves, they descended to their mistress's suite.

Early afternoon found them approaching the princess's suite. Jiana's fingers tingled with nerves, and butterfly wings fluttered in excitement in her stomach. The soft gown made her feel as if she were Lady Beccah's daughter rather than her maid. The glow on Donella's cheeks as they exchanged delighted glances told Jiana she felt the same. Donella fiddled with her tresses while Jiana smoothed the pink dress one last time.

The guard to the princess's rooms acknowledged Lady Beccah. He was over six feet tall, with a wide forehead, square, short-bearded jaw, and intelligent eyes. He wore a sleeveless top, showing off his powerful arm muscles. His eyes met hers for a brief second as he straightened. He looked familiar somehow.

All thoughts of him fled Jiana's mind when he swung the door open.

21 Sikarta Fortress

$\mathcal{S}$ ikarta Island rose out of the sea surrounded by odd rock stacks and arches created by the wind and wave action. In the harbor, an old fort built into the cliff brooded over the palm trees lining the steep hillside. Shoals stood between the shore and the ship. Fortunately, Captain Anaru knew the way between the sand bars that reached out to snag the *Diadem* if she went off course.

Guy and his friends disembarked into the dinghy, which Enri rowed to shore.

At first Guy thought it odd to see pinecones along the pristine white sands. Yellow scales overlapped with bird-like claws in the hole in the center. Then one pinecone uncurled and chased another.

Guy jumped as they raced passed his shoes. "What are those things?"

Barbu smirked and picked one up. It chirped. "Chameleons are considered good luck. They are rare and prized as pets. This must be their native island. I've never seen so many in one place." He petted the strange creature which emitted an eep sound. "They like to soak up the sun."

The beach was littered with chameleons. Guy carefully walked around them. He wasn't fond of reptiles.

"The fortress is the best place to start our search for the hermit." Enri motioned to a structure overlooking the harbor.

As Guy, Pellas and Barbu followed, Enri led the group, climbing the path up the cliff face.

Guy grabbed for a rock to pull himself past a steep spot. He spotted a giant blue spider mere inches away. Yanking his hand back, he pointed out the hairy spider to the others.

"Don't disturb the tarantula. Its bite is deadly," Enri warned him.

"No worries. I'm as fond of spiders as I am of weird lizards." Guy shuddered.

Barbu snorted. He still carried the little lizard-like creature, which had draped itself around his neck. "Scooter is harmless. We could collect some chameleons to sell and make lots of money."

"You named it?" Guy rolled his eyes.

"Yes, I'm going to keep him." As if reading Barbu's mind, the lizard gave a happy chirp.

"Tell me, why are we going to the fortress and not searching the surrounding islands?" Guy's leg muscles burned.

Enri's long mustaches blew in the breeze. "The island chieftain is a very distant cousin of my baba's."

Guy recalled that 'baba' was island speak for grandmother.

"He should be able to tell us how to find the hermit. As you saw, Sikarta is surrounded by small rock formations and islands. It would take too long to check them all."

After half an hour's exertion, the three reached the top of the incline. Before them stood a black arch in the wall surrounding the fort and town that had grown around it. All the buildings were straight rock walls, their windows outlined in painted white arches, many shuttered. But it gave Guy the feeling of eyes watching them.

The jungle pressed around the fort walls, thick and mysterious.

The sparkling blue sea was behind them. The *Diadem* bobbed in the harbor waves.

As they walked under the gloomy arch, Guy likened it to walking into the mouth of a beast. Enri led them through the winding, narrow streets. The buildings blocked the sunlight. Guy shivered.

The native population's olive skin was not ebony like Barbu or light like Guy, but somewhere in between. The men dressed in long, striped robes. They had dark, curly hair. The women wore somber colors and hid their hair under white veils. Dark chocolate eyes followed their progress. Some stopped and stared, then carried on with their business.

"Strangers are not common, though not unheard of. The harbor makes it difficult for larger ships to enter. Most of the trade here is done with nearby islands. Very few have ever seen a Valdeoran." Enri wove through the inhabitants curiously watching them.

As Guy thought about it, he hadn't seen anyone else with light skin and hair since landing in the isles. No wonder he attracted attention. First his birthmark made him stand out. Until meeting the other waykeepers, he had always been conscious of it, trying to hide it. Now it was his skin color, which he couldn't hide. But he wasn't meant to. The One who Fashioned All made him as he was.

He was pulled out of his thought as they approached the fort, crossing the courtyard. It had looked small from the harbor, but up close it was built with massive blocks of stone fitted tightly together. The base had been carved from the cliff rock itself.

Pellas must have been thinking the same thing. "Your people are amazing builders. Constructing this would take great skill."

Enri fingered his white mustache with his hand. "My people didn't build this. An angry volcano destroyed our original island home. Only six boats of survivors fled. Eventually my ancestors' ships hit the shoals. Some of them managed to swim through the harbor and washed up on these shores. They rejoiced that the gods had abandoned this city for one in the heavens, leaving it for my people, their followers."

Staring at the giant fort, Guy could understand how the islanders imagined that supernatural beings created such a structure.

The warm sun on his back disappeared as he entered the fort's shadow. A shiver ran up his spine. Two-story wooden doors, studded with iron nails, marked the entryway. Guy hadn't seen the man-size door hidden to the side until Enri knocked on it. A tiny window slid open. Enri spoke in his native tongue to the sentry. The enormous doors creaked open. Guy almost expected to see a giant step out.

He sighed with relief when a normal-sized man stood in the doorway.

Something about this place made him jumpy.

Guy watched, fascinated, as the sentry closed the door behind them by spinning an iron wheel attached to a chain.

With the sun shut out, an oppressive feeling permeated the cold stone hall. The ceiling soared thirty feet in the air above them. Torches flickered, throwing strange shadows. With no windows, it felt as if it were the middle of the night.

Glancing around in the gloom, Guy gulped when he saw six giants, their hands folded over their hilts, holding their swords, point down. Guy puffed out his breath when he realized they were statues standing in niches set along both walls. They wore the raiment of knights, and their features were white. Curious. Why build this place and then abandon it?

Another sentry joined them. After speaking to Enri, he led them down the shadowy length of the hall. The place smelled musty.

Guy felt the stern giants' blank eyes following him. This place gave him the willies. He shook off the strange sensation and concentrated on the far end of the hall where another set of doors stood closed. The second sentry opened them into a massive room.

Whoever built this place meant it to impress visitors.

A young man sat on an oversize throne of black granite surrounded by gesturing villagers. From the distance, it looked as if he were settling a dispute. Two guards stood on either side, both holding spears, their red robes garish in the dimness. Guy fervently hoped this would not be a repeat of the events of Cressava.

When they reached the group surrounding the granite throne, the villagers halted their impassioned speech and stared at the strangers. They moved aside, leaving an opening. As they did, Guy's glance strayed to a tall, white-haired man with ebony skin standing apart from the rest, leaning on a staff in the deepest shadows. Something twinkled on his hand. Even in the gloom, he looked familiar.

The sentry and Enri spoke, pulling Guy's gaze away. They joined the end of the queue waiting to gain an audience.

When Guy glanced back to the corner, the tall man was no longer there.

It was an hour before they stood before the chieftain.

Enri stepped forward and bowed. Guy and his friends followed suit. As he straightened, Guy took stock of the ruler. Guy was struck by his youth, looking only a few years older than Guy. Other than that, he was heavyset, of medium height, with an olive complexion, dark hair and eyes. He dressed in a white robe with gold geometric patterns along the neckline and hem. On his head he wore a gold circlet with a large pearl in the center. A black onyx ring adorned his pudgy left hand.

"Your Beneficence, these are travelers who are seeking your mighty wisdom."

Beneficence? Wisdom? Guy thought the sentry was overindulging the teen ruler.

The sentry motioned Enri forward.

"I am your loyal subject, Enri, returned to the isle where I was born. I have sailed the seas for many years. May I ask with whom I speak? The last time I was home, Faro the Wise was chieftain."

"I am Faro III. My grandfather passed away a dozen years ago, and my father but months ago."

"I am sorry for your loss." Enri's expression held shock for a moment. Then bowed his head again briefly, clasping his hands together. "My last visit was in the spring twelve years past." He hesitated.

"Faro I departed life in the autumn."

"And your older sister? She is well?" Although the question was asked blandly, his narrowed gaze focused on Faro III. Enri spread apart his hands. "I only ask because I am a distant cousin."

"Ah, then I regret to inform you that she went missing days after my father's passing. A servant saw her near the cliff at Desolation Point. We mourn her, knowing her great grief must have led to her taking her life."

Although his words were laced with sorrow, his pudgy fingers betrayed him, tapping on the throne arm in a nervous gesture.

Enri's expression mirrored Guy's own suspicion for a moment. Then Enri's face went blank, and he gestured to the companions. "These are clients aboard the sailing vessel *Diadem*. Barbu of Bidori. Pellas of Canteor. Gyfar of Valdeor." Each stepped forward at their name and made another slight bow.

The teen chieftain's eyebrows rose at their lands of origin. His close-set eyes studied them.

The back of Guy's neck pricked. He felt as if someone was watching from the shadows.

He lost the thread of conversation.

Looking from the corner of his eye, he caught the tall, dark man's eyes watching him. Suddenly Guy knew where he had seen him. He could swear he was Lemmo without all the trappings of mystical symbols and bone piercings. His staff was plain wood, not the black staff with a maroon gem at the top.

Guy's heart rate sped up at the remembrance of Lemmo's brazier and blood sacrifice. Guy felt trapped in the man's mesmerizing gaze. He forced his eyes away to find his friends waiting for him to answer Faro III.

"Uh, could you repeat that, Your, um, Beneficence?" A blush crept up Guy's neck.

"I said, what brings natives of Valdeor and Canteor to my shores?"

Guy wet his lips before speaking. He wasn't good at flowery speeches, but he didn't want to show offense to someone with the power to help. But he couldn't choke out such a silly title again. "My lord, I am seeking a wise man. A hermit that once lived on your lovely island."

"As potentate and ruler of Sikarta and the surrounding isles, I am the wisest man." Faro III smirked and looked to those gathered. They nodded, but their grins were stiff and their eyes wary.

"What is it you wish to ask?"

Just great. This was turning out to be a reenactment of Cressava.

All eyes upon him in the silence, Guy wasn't willing to state his purpose in front of these strangers.

"It is a personal matter. As you surmised, I have traveled a great distance, and I was hoping the hermit has an answer for me." Let Faro III think Guy had traveled all this way to receive personal enlightenment.

The teen's face became petulant. "And these others with you?"

Surprisingly, Barbu boldly answered. "When they were

shipwrecked on my island. I promised to help them."

"Maybe I can be of service?" A deep voice spoke from the shadows. Guy glanced as Lemmo's lookalike stepped forward and stood beside Faro III. Glancing down at the ruler, he told him, "I believe he is searching for Ikonis."

"Didn't my father banish him?" Faro asked, frowning.

"No. Your grandfather and he disputed about religious worship of Makba, god of the sea. Faro the first sent him away."

Guy glanced from one to the other. "Do you know where I can find Ikonis now?"

Faro III seemed to lose interest. "Tell him if you know, Londo. I want to be done with these villagers. I've already sat at judgment longer than usual. My stomach rumbles with all these heavy duties." He slouched on his throne.

Londo snapped his fingers and a servant appeared. "Get me the map of the kingdoms." With a deep bow, the servant left. The old man leaned heavily on the staff as he led the companions into a side room. In it was a circle of six chairs around a table. Torches in iron holders along the walls lit the meeting room.

After waiting for twenty minutes, Guy's nerves were stretched thin. His pulse pounded in his ears, forced as he was, to be in the same room as the wizard. At least Enri entertained Londo with stories of his sailing exploits since leaving Sikarta. Guy watched him surreptitiously, but Londo seemed engrossed in Enri's tale.

Barbu absently stroked his chameleon as he listened.

Only Pellas seemed as wound up as Guy, pacing the room as they waited.

Finally, the servant returned and passed a rolled scroll to the tall, black man. Londo unrolled it on the table. They all gathered round. As Guy stood next to Londo, he got a whiff of pungent incense, making his mind snap back to Cressava's sanctuary. He broke out in a sweat.

Londo's long, wrinkled finger pointed at the fort on the map.

He traced an imaginary line toward several tiny islands surrounding Sikarta. "There. Ikonis resides on this tiny island, Hipopo Tree Isle." Dark eyes swiveled sideways and met Guy's. "He might not welcome you. He is mad. He talks out loud to someone and yet I've seen no one there. He waits for the end of the world. You will not get any answers to your life's questions from him." He hesitated as if he would say more.

A whiff of incense struck Guy's nose as Londo shifted. "Inform me when you are ready to leave."

The old man re-rolled the scroll, and taking the servant with him, strolled toward the door.

Surely, he's Lemmo's brother.

Londo swung around.

Did I say that out loud? Guy groaned inwardly.

"Yes, I have a brother Lemmo." Londo narrowed his eyes at Guy. "He is my twin. He practices black magic. I don't follow his path. We haven't spoken in many years."

Londo pursed his lips and fastened his gaze on Guy. "I see you have met him." He rubbed a shaky hand over his face, and suddenly he didn't look so scary to Guy.

"Lemmo and I parted ways when I began to follow Ikonis' god. I saw your mark of the Unnamed God." His eyes went to Guy's hand, and Guy fought the old urge to hide it in the folds of his tunic. "I hope Ikonis can help you, but I fear he's not what he used to be."

He shook his head sadly, but an odd gleam flashed in his eyes as he glanced at Guy's birthmark again before he turned and left.

Heat bloomed in Guy's chest, realizing he had judged Lemmo's twin by his looks, assuming him evil because he looked like someone who was. But Londo hadn't earned Guy's trust yet.

Guy was missing something. He was sure of it. He just needed to figure out what.

They stayed anchored in the harbor for another two days. Captain Anaru oversaw taking aboard supplies.

Enri visited his many relations, while Pellas spent his time in the taverns, gleaning gossip and news.

A new passenger joined their crew, Enri's nephew. He met them on the beach as they made ready to return to the ship with the last of the supplies.

"Uncle Enri! It's me, Yarto, your sister's son." The youth was a little older than Guy. He was lank, all elbows and edges. His face was narrow, with a long nose. He smelled of fish.

Enri hesitated a minute, as if he didn't recognize Yarto. Then Enri threw an arm around the boy. "My, how you've grown." He stepped back, a wide smile on his face. He sobered as he gazed on the lad. "I was sorry to hear your mother died."

Yarto lowered his eyes. "She died nearly two years ago now. It happened the day after her mistress, Faro III's sister." He shuddered. "Strange things have happened since the last chieftain died."

"Like what?" Enri was all business.

Even though no one stood near them on the beach, Yarto lowered his voice. "The rumor in the servant's hall is Faro III poisoned his father to gain power. And when his sister accused him, he had her thrown from the cliffs. Mother acted odd that day and wouldn't tell me what bothered her." He wrung his hands. "I found her dead at Desolation Heights the next evening."

Guy thought it odd that Yarto's face showed no expression at the mention of finding his mother dead.

Out of the corner of his eye, Guy thought he saw movement at the edge of the wooded path. His gaze darted around. A bush rustled and he thought he saw a hand withdrawn. Leaves fluttered in a gust of wind, and he couldn't be certain if he imagined it.

Goosebumps rose on Guy's arms at the possible menace.

Yarto rubbed his nose, the white of his eyes showing as he glanced behind him. "Oh, uncle, take me with you from this place!"

"I'm not surprised at what you say. Faro has the demeanor of a despot. I felt the presence of evil while we were there."

Enri threw his arm back around Yarto and led him to the dinghy. "Come, I will speak to Captain Anaru on your behalf. There is room for another sailor."

And so they gained another crew member.

A light drizzle fell as *Diadem* crested the waves. The fresh, salt air did wonders for Guy's mood. His spirits buoyed up after leaving the oppressive fort and the isle of Sikarta behind.

The ship sailed beyond the rocky pinnacles surrounding Sikarta and into the deeper water. Islands appeared like mountain tops rising above the sea.

On the third day, Barbu pointed at an odd sight as they were sailing past an island. In a steep canyon, a tree hung by one large root from the cliff, suspended free in the air.

Yarto must have noticed Barbu pointing, because he strolled over.

"The Floating Trees are only found on this cluster of islands in the Husa Channel." Yarto leaned beside Barbu and Guy as they gawked at the side rail. "They are a type of air plant, according to my mother."

"I am glad to leave Sikarta. Those statues creeped me out." Scooter rolled up into a ball at Barbu's outburst.

"Is that your pet chameleon?" Yarto reached over curiously but pulled his hand back when the lizard hissed at him.

"Yes. I name him Scooter." Barbu coaxed it with soothing words until it relaxed and draped itself around his neck.

"I thought Londo was even creepier. I know he said he began

following the One Who Fashioned All, but something is off about him. Something he said or did. I just can't recall it." Guy tapped his fingers against the railing.

"Faro spooked me. My mother was a servant of Faro's sister." Yarto hunched his shoulders. "Strange that she disappeared the same day as her mistress. I fear she saw or knew something."

Enri walked past the knot of boys, so Guy snagged him.

"What do you know about Londo, Enri?"

"Me? I've never seen him before."

Guy frowned. "He's old enough to have served under Faro the Wise. And he spoke as if he were there when the chieftain banished Ikonis. He seemed like the prince's adviser. The servant treated him like a master."

"Well, he wasn't there a dozen years ago. Maybe he captured Faro II's ear." Enri shepherded his nephew toward the chow line.

Two days later, a small island appeared off the port bow. It was a rocky crag like all the rest they had passed, but this one had weird trees growing along the shore. They only grew fifteen feet tall, and their grayish bases appeared as if four or five trees had grown together. Two little spindly branches sprouted from the top. Instead of leaves, it had what looked like bloated pine needles.

Guy stood with Pellas at the prow.

"Those trees looks as if someone pasted a cactus on each branch end." Guy had never seen anything like them.

"Hipopo trees must be named for the hipopo, a huge, gray-skinned animal that lives along riverbanks in Canteor," Pellas mused.

As they rounded the island, a natural harbor appeared around the next bend. The *Diadem* anchored and the sailors prepared to lower the dinghy.

Guy gathered some flour, sugar, and caffeine beans and stuffed them in a sack as a gift offering for the hermit.

After discussing it with his friends, they agreed that one

stranger was less threatening. Barbu and Pellas would stay on the *Diadem*. Enri would row Guy ashore, and he would wait with the dinghy. If Guy didn't return in two hours, Enri would seek him out.

The land was rocky, with succulents growing between orange-colored stones. Other than the slap of waves, it was silent. A hawk circling lazily overhead was the only movement.

Guy set off on a path which wound from the shore through the well-spaced, bizarre trees.

Upon reaching the top of the rise, he beheld a clearing. The ridge across the way encircled the area like a bulwark. At the base, the green of a garden and a few fruit trees stood starkly in contrast to the wall of stony hills. In the center of the oasis stood a dwelling carved from a dead hipopo tree.

As Guy strode toward the abode, a man emerged from the tree's opening. He was of medium height, wearing a tunic made of hide, a wide-brimmed hat blocking his features. He must have seen movement, because he whirled to face Guy. He wore a patch over his left eye. He stood and watched Guy advance.

"Are you lost, sailor?" he asked Guy warily. "I have nothing of value."

"I am not looking to rob you," Guy reassured him. "My name is Gyfar, but my friends call me Guy. I seek information only." Guy stopped at a respectful distance. "I brought you a gift of some things you could use." Guy held out the sack he had filled.

The hermit met him and reached for the sack. Opening it, he exclaimed, "My, my!" He took a deep whiff of the bag. "Years since I smelled caffeine beans." He looked Guy over and seemed satisfied. "Come, come. Why stand here? I'll brew a little pot now."

Almost as an afterthought, he said, "You may call me Ikonis."

"Doesn't that mean 'knowledge' in Canteor?"

"Yes, yes. And I am knowledgeable." He chuckled.

Instead of feeling uncomfortable with the strange hermit, Guy found him approachable.

Guy followed Ikonis to his little dwelling and peeked in the doorway. The only furniture consisted of a table made of a ship's hatch propped on logs and a chair obviously carved by hand. A straw mat for sleeping was visible tucked in the corner. Rough planks of salvaged wood were stacked to make shelving against one wall.

A cookpot on an iron tripod sat over cold embers outside the door. They pulled up nearby logs and sat around the fire that Ikonis started. Seeing his one battered tin mug, Guy politely refused his offer of boiled caffeine beans.

After savoring his first sip, a blissful smile appeared on Ikonis' face.

His good eye speared Guy like a gimlet. "Now, what information do you require of me?"

22 Selection for the Games

$\mathcal{G}$ ensard had grown accustomed to his routine. Up just before dawn. Onto the sandy ring. Exercise and stretches. Into the mess hall, where the sweaty men lined up for a bowl of porridge and a chunk of bread. Morning practice with Doza's handpicked opponent for him followed. The overseer closely observed the men's skill and technique.

Perspiration dripped in Gensard's eyes as the day wore on and the heat beat from above and below, sand reflecting the sunlight. Then an afternoon meal break, this time a form of stew and hard bread. A short siesta at the hottest part of the day. Then practice and competition until dinner. The men were allowed to wash up and soak in a large bathhouse, the pool as large as Gensard's room in the palace back home.

Tonight was no different.

After weeks of practicing and competing, the number of top gladiators stood at ten. Gensard was in the running, as well as Gerd and Jod. Lord Paitar would only take his five best competitors. One more round and Gensard would go to the Dabbori Games.

As he finished off his opponent with a stroke of the wooden sword, he brushed his hand over his grimy face. Sweat rolled down his back. He tasted grit on his teeth.

A few groups still strove in competition as he headed for the bathhouse.

He eased his body into the warm water. He ducked his head under to wash off the grime and sweat. Flipping his head back, water droplets flung in all directions as he surfaced. His muscles eventually relaxed.

New scars and bruises dotted his body.

Gensard had not made any friends. Each man was a possible threat to his freedom. Better not to get familiar with another. No sentimentality would stand in his way.

The next afternoon, the final trials began. The ten top men would fight until only five remained.

Gensard was paired with Gerd, who stood half a head shorter, but broader in shoulder. But he made up for his smaller stature with his intensity.

When the bell sounded, Gerd charged at Gensard like a bull at a red cloak. Gensard stepped slightly to the side to avoid the full brunt of the blow. Gerd's wooden sword slammed down repeatedly in a vicious arc on Gensard's shield, denting the metal.

The blows rained on Gensard's shield, bruising the forearm it was strapped to with the fury of the strokes. He slashed back with his sword around the shield. At a slight pause of Gerd's, Gensard pushed the metal circle at his opponent's face and slipped under his guard.

He launched himself forward, sword swinging down from an overhand stroke. Now it was Gensard's turn to hammer the other's shield. Gerd cowered beneath his.

With Gerd's shorter arm span, his thrusts from behind the buckler didn't hit the mark. Eventually, Gerd's shield broke under the blows.

Yelping, he flung the pieces at Gensard and backed away.

Bringing up his shield, Gensard flipped the broken pieces to the side, then attacked.

Sides heaving, Gerd parried Gensard's blows as best he could, but it was soon over. Gensard held his wooden sword to his opponent's throat.

"I give!" Gerd spat out the words of surrender. But his eyes blazed in hatred.

"Winner," declared Elozma, and chalked an x by Gensard's name. He moved on to the next combatants.

"You deliberately took the unbroken shield!" Gerd followed on Gensard's heels as he headed to the bathhouse, grabbed his shoulder and spun him around.

"What? Get your hands off me!" Gensard's nostrils flared, and he glared at the man. A pulse drummed in his neck as men nearby turned their attention toward them. Several of the competitors Gensard had beaten smirked. "Are you calling me a cheater?"

"If the shoe fits, wear it!" Gerd pushed him in the chest, eyes burning.

The pent-up energy of weeks burst like a dam in Gensard's chest. He let go with his right fist in an uppercut to the chin. Gerd stumbled back.

"Stop!" a commanding voice shouted.

Anger clouded Gensard's judgment. He wanted this fight.

With a roar, Gerd lashed out at Gensard with his left fist, then his right, in quick succession. Gensard deflected the blows as best he could, though he felt blood dripping from his eyebrow.

Gensard's next blow fell squarely in the middle of Gerd's face, breaking his nose.

Suddenly, Elozma and Ishmi were between them. The giant black men twisted the combatants' arms behind their backs.

Doza strode over, a stern expression on his face.

"I knew you were trouble the moment I laid eyes on you," he spat at Gerd. Nodding at Elozma, he commanded, "Take him to the guardhouse."

Turning his dark gaze on Gensard, he frowned. Disappointment glinted in his eyes. "You were my pick for the

Dabbori Games. Gerd was never going to make the cut. You should have stopped when I ordered you to. Lord Paitar won't stand for disobedient slaves." He gestured at Ishmi. He strode away, his chin tucked down.

As Ishmi led Gensard to the prison barrack, his anger drained away. *What have I done? I am the best warrior here. My place was sealed. But I let my temper get the better of me.*

They entered the low ceiling, stone building. Ishmi led him to chains attached to the wall and shackled him. Gloating, the giant stepped back. "Now you go to the master's mines. Life is short for those he sends there."

Gensard glared at his tormentor.

"Even your blazing spirit will break in hard labor." He bared his teeth and left.

When he was alone, except for Gerd chained in another corner, Gensard bowed his head. Of all the low moments since he stepped into the portal, this stung the most.

To be so close to his one chance at freedom!

He groaned. It was his own fault he was here. Not Gerd's. Gensard had taken his measure the first day they met. As Doza said, the man was trouble. Gensard knew he shouldn't have let the man get under his skin. But no, his pride had caused him to defend himself because others gathered to watch.

Pride was always his downfall.

The sun beat upon Gensard's bare head. His hands were shackled in front of him, jangling as he kept up at a trot behind Elozma's horse. The bay horse kicked up dust from the road, choking him with every step, coating his throat. His tongue felt too big for his mouth.

Gerd was beside him, jerking on his chains, barely keeping up.

Gensard could strangle the idiot for getting them in this situation. Anger was the only thing that kept him going. Despair was hunkered just underneath the surface, like a chained dog ready to lunge.

They had traveled the road from Lord Paitar's estate through scrub bush, to grasslands, and now woods. Trees sporting new buds surrounded them as they ascended the Heights.

Was it only a day ago that they had set out for Lord Paitar's mines in the Zarde Heights? It felt like a week.

Eventually, Elozma stopped to let the horse drink at a mountain river.

"About time," Gerd whined, dropping to all fours and lapping the water like an animal.

Gensard stumbled forward, fell to his knees, and scooped water in his hands. The refreshing taste washed out the lingering dust. He gulped another scoop, then another.

A twig snapped. He scanned the area. A fallen tree lay in the woods across the river from them. He thought he glimpsed stealthy movement behind it.

So he was more prepared than the other two when an arrow came flying toward them. He flung himself behind a stump.

Unaware of his surroundings, Gerd was in the process of pushing himself up when he took an arrow in the chest. He gave a strangled cry. He collapsed and his head sank back into the water.

Startled, Elozma stopped digging in the saddlebag and reached for his sword.

Gensard scanned the forest for the archer's location. Whang! The enemy launched another arrow.

Hearing a grunt, he turned to see Elozma with a hand tugging at the arrow lodged in his throat. Blood gushed as he yanked on it. He toppled to the ground.

Gensard was a sitting target, chained as he was to Elozma's horse. The tall grass provided scarce coverage as he belly-crawled to the dark giant's side. The diagonal slashes on his cheeks stood out in sharp relief. The sightless eyes would never gloat at him again.

Any moment another arrow could pierce Gensard. He patted the man down frantically. His hands found a cord around Elozma's neck. Pulling it from the dead man's chest, Gensard fumbled with the key. Breathing hard, he fit it in the lock and released his hands from their shackles.

A movement out of the corner of his eyes alerted him to imminent danger.

He used his elbows and knees to crab crawl to the nearest stand of trees. His heart pounded like a horse at full gallop. Seeking cover from the brush, he crouched behind it. He watched a bearded, unkempt man row a skiff across the river currents.

Gensard weighed the chances of showing his position and running for it. Winded from trotting after the horse for two days, he didn't think he could outrun the archer. He studied the trees around him.

The archer's sharp eyes were distracted when he ran his skiff aground. Gensard took the opportunity and sprinted for a large tree bole. He stood with his back against it. His drab-colored clothing would help him blend in.

He peered around the tree at the riverbank. The archer tapped Elozma with the tip of his foot, and seemingly satisfied that Elozma was dead, he went through Elozma's belongings. Hopefully he would see the chains and shackles and decide it was not worth his time to chase down a slave.

Gensard zigged and zagged from tree to tree, making as little noise as possible, just in case the man did pursue him. He stopped every so often to listen for pursuit.

After nearly an hour, he decided he was safe enough to make his way to the river. He slaked his ongoing thirst and picked some berries growing in the bushes. Thanks to Donella, he knew which ones were safe to eat. He made a bed under a half-rotted tree as the stars twinkled above.

The next day he openly walked on the road, heading back to Dabbori. Except for his slave collar, he could be free. If only he had some money, he could hire a blacksmith to remove it. But Canteorans seemed accustomed to slavery, and none might choose to help an escaped slave.

The sound of hooves had Gensard diving into the bushes. His knee ached as it hit a rock. He bit his lip and it bled.

He was startled to see Ishmi riding a horse at a gallop toward the Zarde Heights and the mines Elozma had been headed for.

What would bring him chasing his brother out here?

Back on the road, Gensard walked until the afternoon. The trees had thinned out, then disappeared. Grasses waving in the wind made a swishing sound. He was still a day and a half's walk from Lord Paitar's residence outside the royal city.

Gensard didn't have a plan on what he would do on reaching the city outskirts.

Horse hooves behind him sent him scrambling for cover, but there wasn't any. He laid low in the ditch.

The horse stopped beside him. Looking up, he saw the whites of Ishmi's eyes glaring at him from atop the horse. His expression gleamed with satisfaction.

"Get up, dog!" he barked.

With as much dignity as he could muster, Gensard stood. He pulled his wrinkled tunic down.

Behind Ishmi's horse was the bay. Elozma was slung over the animal like a sack of potatoes and tied into place.

Ishmi's voice was harsh. "What happened back there, slave?"

A tic started in Gensard's jaw. "We were attacked by an archer. Elozma was busy with the saddlebag. While his back was turned, an arrow pierced Gerd. Before your brother could pull his sword, another arrow struck him. I hid and ran away while the archer was rowing his skiff across the river."

Ishmi's eyes roved over his face, as if seeking the truth. Seemingly satisfied, he pointed toward Dabbori. "March!"

As if he didn't have a care in the world, Gensard walked ahead of Ishmi. Surprisingly, the giant didn't shackle him. But then again, where would he go? Grassy hills spread all around them, not a tree, nor a bush, nor a stone to hide behind.

After half an hour, lightheadedness assailed Gensard. The scenery blurred before his vision. He had no idea how long it had been since his last meal. His feet stumbled. He tried to ignore the feeling. Suddenly the ground came up to meet him.

After a moment, a waterskin pressed on his lips and he gulped the freshness down.

He stared at close quarters at the diagonal slashes on Ishmi's cheeks.

"What are those marks?"

Ishmi drew back and curled his lips. "My people mark their warriors, so all know to fear us. You are the first man to ask me that question. Most are too afraid."

"I killed a man with those marks, once." Maybe the dizziness loosened his tongue. Or was it that Gensard had nothing left to lose? "A year ago, Canteor scout ships attacked the city where I was staying. Aboard was a ferocious fighter with those slashes. Nearly killed me with his spiked bat." Gensard made a move to get up.

Ishmi put out a hand to pull him up. "Not many men can best us." Respect glinted in his eyes for a second. "You are lucky Doza sent me to retrieve you."

"Retrieve me?" Gensard wasn't sure he heard right. He put his hand to his head.

"Yes. One of the contestants poisoned the food. Lord Paitar's top fighters have all taken to their beds ill. You and the four alternates are going to fight at the Dabbori Games."

Gensard felt lightheaded again, this time with unbelief at his good fortune. The One Who Fashioned All seemed to have answered his prayers after all.

23 *Princess Sefira*

*P*rincess Sefira's room was opulent. Woven carpets led from the door to the sitting area, so thick that Donella's feet sunk in. Several divans had been pulled into a semicircle. Each was piled high with red cushions, having intricate gold patterns embroidered on them. Low tables were interspersed around the semicircle, holding trays of dates, cheeses, grapes, sweets, and a squat teapot with tiny cups. Sweet incense floated on the air.

Peeking through the door to the princess's bedchamber, she saw a magnificent, curtained bed was hung with red silk with a matching coverlet and pillows.

This was a backdrop to a dark-haired beauty sitting by the window. The princess's honey-toned face was flawless. Her eyes were dark under her slightly arched eyebrows. The only thing that marred her beauty was a petulant pout and a bored expression.

Her dark green silk robe had sleeves cuffed at her elbow. Her lower brown arms were bare. She wore a golden sash from her right shoulder to her waist. On her feet were beaded sandals.

Two servants were fussing with her hair. One wrapped an elaborate braid around her head, intertwined with strands of tiny pearls. The other brushed out the rest of the tresses that dangled to her waist. She wore a single teardrop-shaped pearl hanging against her forehead.

"Ow! Stop pulling my hair, Abelita." Turning to berate her servant, Princess Sefira's eyes lit up at the sight of them.

"Aunt Beccah, I am so glad you are here!

"Enough. I wish to speak with my visitor." She impatiently snapped at the servants.

The women placed their hands together, bowed slightly, and departed.

Lady Beccah curtsied, and the girls followed her lead. Their mistress sat on the nearest divan and motioned to Donella, who passed her the little wrapped boxes she had carried from her mistress's room. "I brought you presents from my estate in Kiwan."

Princess Sefira opened the box of sweets. "Ah, my favorite." She popped one in her mouth. She obviously enjoyed delicacies, as her plump figure was evidence.

Long, tapered fingers opened the second box. She smiled when she saw the fan, holding it up just below her eyes. She raised her eyebrow and blinked her long-lashed eyelids in a flirty manner. "Perfect for teasing all my suitors." Giving an example, she lightly rapped Lady Beccah's hand.

"I painted the scene myself." Lady Beccah puffed with pride.

Princess Sefira examined the fan's artwork. "Then it is more special."

Lady Beccah beamed. "I'm not sure whether I will give you a third gift or not. I am rather enjoying it myself." She casually took a date from a tray and ate it.

Donella had not carried in a third package. She wondered briefly if she had blundered. A glance at Jiana's frowning face reassured her that she hadn't forgot anything in the bustle to be presented to the princess.

"What is it?" the princess carelessly discarded the fan on the low table beside her.

Taking another date, Lady Beccah shook her head. "I cannot

spoil your birthday surprise. You will just have to wait."

Princess Sefira pouted momentarily. "Then entertain me with the latest news from Kiwan."

"Before I do, what do you think of my latest purchase?"

The princess glanced at her, puzzled. "Is that a new pearl necklace?"

Lady Beccah chuckled. Sweeping her arm toward Jiana and Donella standing to the side, she said, "Behold my new servants. Look at how well they contrast each other. Dark and light. One blond like the sun, the other brunette like the night."

The princess and their mistress discussed the girls' obvious points as if they weren't there. Of everything she had experienced, Donella found their conversation the most alien thing she witnessed since leaving home.

Donella shifted, uncomfortable at the humiliation.

Mulling over it the rest of the day, Donella finally gave vent to Jiana as they lay in their room that night.

"Doesn't anyone in Canteor value a person's abilities? Aren't all humans of equal value in the eyes of the Creator? Do they not believe slaves have souls, too?" Donella flounced onto her bed.

"In Valdeor, everyone believes freedom of all peoples as an absolute, God-given right. These rich women can only see what is before them. The greater contrast in the room was between the slim, young princess and the plump middle-aged woman. They have nothing in common but their haughty view of the rest of humanity." Donella banged her pillow into submission.

"Your ideas are foreign here." Jiana sighed. "We have first class citizens like our mistress and the princess, and second-class citizens like the merchants and physicians. You and I are in the bottom class as slaves, who are even below servants."

"It is wrong!"

"It's just the way it is here." Jiana shrugged.

Donella hunched her shoulder. "It doesn't mean I have to like it."

Having slept fitfully, Donella woke at the break of day. Dressing and slipping from the room, careful to not wake Jiana, Donella headed for the gardens.

The hairs on her skin lifted as she had a feeling of being watched. Gazing around, she saw above her a golden statue on the walls of the palace overlooking the city. Towering thirty feet tall, it was an idol of Panmin, the goat god. He had the head of a goat with curling horns. The torso was of a man with muscled arms. From the hips down he was again a goat with hairy, prancing legs that ended in cloven hooves. His evil eyes seemed to leer down at her.

Donella shuddered at the sight of it. She hurried past and into the perfectly manicured garden. A few birds pecking at the ground and trilling in the branches were her only companions.

The beautiful plants and rosy sky didn't bring her peace as she had hoped. Reaching the end of the garden, she sat beneath an apple tree and aimlessly pulled blades of grass.

Donella had convinced herself she could be happy in Canteor, working for a good mistress, as owners go. But sitting there in the light of day, she knew she had deluded herself. She would never be happy until she was home with people who thought as she did.

She longed for Odem and Guy, or even Gensard, to share her thoughts with. They would understand how she felt.

But she only had herself to blame. She knew, now, that she was meant to be a waykeeper, offering hospitality to wayfarers. Why had she spun a web of lies? What would happen when Jiana found out? Donella trembled at the thought.

Hope eluded her. She had clung to her faith in the One Who Fashioned All in spite of everything. But she didn't feel as if she could hope any longer. How could He forgive her?

Across the path from her was an enormous blooming bush.

Thick branches sprayed from the center. It looked as if it hadn't been pruned in years. Sitting in the farthest corner of the garden, away from the benches and fountains, it had been neglected.

At its base was a square-shaped rock. Encrusted with lichen, it still showed a slight swirl of some ancient carving.

Absently, Donella picked out the tracing with her sharp eyes.

A bolt of recognition like a lightning strike zipped through Donella's nerves as she thought she recognized the symbol.

Interlocking ovals!

Unmindful of her dress and the dew, as well as the branches scratching at her arms, she dove under the bush. She brushed off as much of the lichen as she could with a broken twig. No doubt lingered in her mind as she uncovered the trinity symbol. She dug around the stone, uncovering the uneven base. She absently brushed her dirty hands together.

Heart racing, she stared at the broken top of a waypost.

24 The Hermit

"I am searching for the Isle of Origin," Guy told the hermit, Ikonis, who leaned forward. "You see, I am from Valdeor. Reina Lauressa sent me and my friends to Canteor on a mission. But I failed them." Guy dropped his gaze. "I was in charge of getting us there safely, but we were separated." A pang of guilt assailed him.

"That is unfortunate." Ikonis lowered his chipped cup and leaned forward. "Go on." His sympathetic gaze loosened Guy's tongue.

Guy rubbed his hand across his eyes. "I washed up on the shore of Bidori where the inhabitants helped me. I made several friends there, who said they would travel with me on my quest to find the great shrine."

Ikonis gripped his empty mug in his hands, his head cocked to one side. "My, my. 'Tis not a good idea to disregard a mission from a princess."

Guy hung his hands between his knees. "I know. But she only asked me to deliver my friends to Canteor. I think they landed there."

"Then why are you filled with guilt?" Ikonis's good eye seemed to read Guy's soul.

The urge to confess everything grew inside Guy until it burst like a dam. "The separation was sudden. I dream every night that they are lost, calling out to me from the depths of the sea. But I can't reach them. I can't save them from drowning."

"But you didn't see them drown?"

"No. Lightning flashed, and I fell in the water." Guy stared into the past. "And I haven't found a trace of them on the islands."

"So, so. Your friends may be safe." Ikonis scratched his eyebrow. He gazed absently in his mug. Then he glanced up. "What should I tell him?" He stared over Guy's shoulder.

Guy resisted the urge to look behind him. He wasn't sure who the hermit spoke with. Probably himself. Being far from civilization, his manners were bound to be odd.

"Hmm." The hermit nodded, transferring his gaze back to Guy. "You must leave your friends' fate in the hands of the One Who Fashioned All and seek to do His will."

He gestured at Guy's left hand. "You have another mission to fulfill. Let go of your guilt. Only by doing so can you put your heart into the divine quest given to you."

Guy involuntarily glanced at his birthmark, faded, but still visible. He met Ikonis's gaze. A weight lifted from his shoulders at the hermit's words, and a calm settled over him. He had set out, after all, on the quest the Guardian gave him.

Ikonis put his hands on his knees. "I will guide you." He nodded. "I have waited many years for the chance to worship at the great shrine."

Guy blinked. "You know where it is?" His voice rose with excitement. *Finally, someone with the knowledge he needed!*

"Oh, yes. I tried to convert the islanders for many years. But Makba's cult was too strong. I wondered if I had any purpose since I could make no headway." His expression grew sad. "So I sailed to the east, past uninhabited islands to the farthest of them all. I was at my lowest point. Then the Guardian of Valdeor appeared to me."

His eyes distant, Ikonis's face showed the wonder he had felt. "He told me I was at the Isle of Origin but it was forbidden to go ashore. He said one day the One Who Fashioned All would require me to land there, but I was to live a life of penance until that time." Ikonis's eyes refocused on Guy. "So I settled on this solitary isle for the last twelve years. And now the Guardian has sent you to me."

"You haven't seen anyone for twelve years?" Guy couldn't imagine how lonely that would be.

"I live alone, but men have visited. Some come for curiosity. Some to rob me, though I have nothing of value. And some come for wisdom and guidance. A few have converted, thanks be to the Almighty."

Ikonis stood. He entered his dwelling and quickly placed a few things in the sack Guy had given him—a few dozen scrolls, a quill pen, and some provisions. He placed a cloak around his shoulders and motioned for Guy to lead the way.

In no time, they reached the dinghy and Enri rowed them to the *Diadem*.

The sailors stopped what they were doing to watch Pellas and Enri help the hermit aboard.

"My, my. I had forgotten the feeling of a ship's motion. Not fond of it. Not at all." The hermit hunched his shoulders as he took stock of his surroundings. He removed his hat, which exposed a bald spot, and rubbed his head. He was already turning green.

"You had better show me the map you mentioned, while I can still be of help."

Enri headed for the wheelhouse, Ikonis in tow, while Pellas and Barbu followed more slowly with Guy.

"Strange looking fellow," Barbu commented. Scooter the lizard stuck out it's tongue at the same time, making it seem as if he agreed.

"He has a good heart." Guy rubbed the back of his neck. "He guessed at my worry and put my fears to rest."

"You can't judge a man on first impressions." Pellas tapped his own breast. "After all, Guy took a chance on me, despite our previous encounter when I tried to kill him."

"Everyone deserves a second chance. Besides," Guy gave him a glance from the side of his eyes, "you saved my life, afterward."

Barbu swung around, facing Guy, walking backwards. "I saved your life, too, when you nearly drowned in the cave." His chest puffed out and his face was eager for praise.

Guy slapped his arm. "So you did, Barbu." He nodded at them. "I owe both of you."

After studying the map, Captain Anaru set sail for the distant end of the archipelago, the chain of islands, which strung out to the east.

Ikonis insisted on staying on the deck, saying it was the only way to overcome his seasickness. He took up residence on a coil of rope near Eliu. They soon formed a friendship, the odd hermit and the crippled beggar.

Maybe it wasn't so strange that they found a lot to talk about, Guy thought. They were both outcasts, used to solitary living.

One night, unable to sleep, Guy crept out of the stuffy cabin onto the deck. The sky was dark, not a cloud in sight, with bright stars in unfamiliar patterns. As he stood looking up, a falling star streaked across the sky and disappeared below the horizon.

A movement caught his eye, and he saw a figure shift at the prow. Ikonis.

Guy crossed the deck, coughing softly as he approached, so not to startle the man.

Half turning, Ikonis watched him draw near. Guy couldn't read his expression in the dark.

"A beautiful night." Guy leaned on the rail beside him.

"Do you know the constellations? No. Then I will point out

my favorite." Ikonis stretched out his arm. "The three bright stars in a triangle are the fin of the dolphin. See the stars arc below it. Have you ever watched the dolphins?"

"Yes, I've seen them following the ship at a distance."

"They are a symbol of joy. They jump in the air for the sheer pleasure of it. If only we humans could live that way."

They stood for a few minutes in companionable silence.

"Tell me about your mark. Have you always had it?" Ikonis's eyes sparkled in the starlight.

"Yes, I was born with it. My father was a waykeeper. He died when I was young. I didn't know of my abilities until Donella, a waykeeper, came along. She said she felt me through the portals. She was one of the friends who I was separated from." Guy paused, the familiar worry creeping over him. "Anyway, I learned to concentrate and use my power with my teacher, Usher. I eventually ended up at the palace in Mintala, having learned of the Canteor spies planning an attack. In the archives, I studied the portals. When I found I could open two at a time, Reina Lauressa used me to place forces in position for the coming invasion. And when she prepared to insert spies in Canteor, she thought of me."

Guy burned to ask a question. He clenched the rail. "Why does the Guardian want me to find the shrine? And why me? I am not more holy than the next person. In fact, I have many failings. I disobeyed the Guardian's direct order, and my friends suffer for it."

"You don't know that. If the One Who Fashioned All allowed your separation, he had his own purpose for your friends. Even now they are traveling the path he put them on. He draws good from all events."

"Even the bad ones?"

"Yes, yes. Even the bad ones."

Guy thought about this.

His stepmother worked him hard, even whipping him at

times for no reason. But now he was strong and wasn't afraid of hard work. Bandits had attacked him and taken his horse Seeker, but he had gained confidence when rescuing the stallion. Pirates had kidnapped him and pressed him into service. But now he spoke the Canteor language used on the islands. He had embarrassed himself opening more than one portal and causing havoc at the palace by doing so. But he ended up learning to control multiple portals. Pellas and Kadar had attacked him, so he sent them through a portal into a storm at sea. Yet, Pellas was his friend and ally now in that faraway place.

The light spray misted Guy's face. He tasted salt on his lips as he wet them. "Alright. I can understand the One Who Fashioned All has a purpose for me. Even when I didn't realize it, he shaped me." Guy ran a hand down his face. "But what is this shrine? Why is it so important?"

"Evil happened."

This was not what Guy expected to hear. He blinked, unsure he heard right.

"The Creator gave men free will." The breeze ruffled Ikonis's hair, his one eye intense on Guy. He leaned forward slightly, almost as if he willed Guy to understand.

"What does that mean?"

"He gave them a choice to choose him, to love him. Because he is goodness, he is love. But those that rejected him chose the opposite of goodness, the opposite of love."

"Evil."

"Yes. The One Who Fashioned All wishes us to be whole in mind, spirit, and body. So, he gave us the Waters of Regeneration. We can symbolically wash away the evil in our souls like we wash the dirt from our bodies. The shrine was built around a pool of healing waters. I have heard the blind see, the deaf hear, the lame walk again. But most of all, it has the power of healing souls. From fear. From hopelessness."

Guy gripped the rail, the calm night flowing over him. "Now I see. The pilgrims came to be healed. And they left with a greater faith."

"Yes. We live in uncertain times. Faro III and Queen Nerea are wicked rulers. Canteor seeks war with Valdeor. Hamleor lost the faith a long time ago. Restoring the pilgrimage route might change the course of events." For a hermit, Ikonis was very knowledgeable about current affairs. Maybe that's what he and Eliu discussed.

25 Reunited

Princess Sefira reminded Donella of a daffodil. This afternoon, she was dressed in golden yellow. Rings glittered on all her fingers. Her black hair was piled on top of her head in a crown of braids, several jasmine blooms tucked in. Instead of a crown, a square-cut diamond hung on a fine chain against her forehead.

Three girls, whose ages Donella guessed to be eighteen, sixteen, and twelve, surrounded the princess. Their marked resemblance to her made Donella sure they were her younger sisters.

Lady Beccah sat on a divan in the princess's sitting room, eating sugared strawberries. Several other ladies in waiting were in attendance. They were as drab as pigeons surrounding a peacock.

A slight breeze wafted the floor length curtains from the balcony door which stood open. The mid-summer heat was oppressive. The heady smell of incense combined with the heat made Donella lightheaded. She longed for fresh air.

The princess propped her chin in her hand. "Other than looking pretty, what can your slaves do to entertain us?"

Lady Beccah motioned Donella over with her pudgy hand. "I know you sing, but can you play an instrument? Soft music would suit us."

"Yes, my lady. I can play. But I don't have my zythrin, a stringed instrument."

Princess Sefira's eyes lit up. "Yes! That would be perfect." She snapped her fingers at her maid. "A kitara, Abelita."

The maid curtsied and left the room. Soon she returned with an oval shaped instrument with a long neck. It had five strings. It was larger than Donella's zythrin, and it was pitched lower. Donella tested out a few chords.

Sweat trickled down Donella's back, partly from the heat and partly from nervousness at playing an unfamiliar instrument in front of the women gathered. She plucked at the strings softly, trying different fingerings. After a while, feeling more confident, she played a simple child's tune. Needing more time to master the kitara, she played variations on the tune.

The assemblage soon lost interest in listening, exchanging gossip as she played. Her shoulder muscles relaxed as she realized she provided only background noise to their conversation.

The afternoon wound into early evening. Donella's fingers were sore with lack of practice before she was done. She was determined to learn the kitara. Music had always soothed her. She hadn't realized how much she missed playing.

"And what can your other slave do to entertain us?" The princess sipped a cup of citrus water.

Lady Beccah turned to Jiana, who blushed and fidgeted.

Donella mumbled under her breath, "Tell one of your tales." On their trip from Kiwan to Dabbori, Jiana proved herself a natural storyteller, entertaining Donella for hours.

When Jiana froze, she urged her with a poke of her elbow.

"I know simple folk tales. I don't know about politics or courtly intrigue." Jiana dropped her eyes and smoothed out her altered pink skirt. "I grew up in Tilmuk, which you would consider a backwater town." She gazed shyly at the princess. "I know a legend, though."

Nodding, Donella smiled encouragement.

The younger princesses clapped their hands. One cried out, "I love listening to storytellers at the fair." Another chimed in, "Do tell us a tale."

The encouragement seemed to give Jiana courage. She cleared her throat.

"Once upon a time there lived an elderly Canteor potentate. His wife and all his children died in a great plague. In order to have an heir, he demanded each town send the loveliest maiden for him to choose from. They were presented to him one by one. None took his fancy until the last girl, youngest of them all, caught his eye. On the occasion of their wedding, he ordered a great feast which lasted for a week. A year later, he was overjoyed when twin brothers were born by his beautiful young spouse."

Jiana lifted her eyes to Princess Sefira. "Not as beautiful as you, your highness."

Preening, she touched her throat where a large diamond dangled. "Go on."

"The young princes pranked everyone by imitating each other. They were very close until they came of age and their father grew ill. Then the younger grew jealous of the heir to the throne. When their father died, both sons claimed the throne. And since no one could tell them apart, they couldn't tell who was the eldest."

"Oh, no! Couldn't their own mother discern one from the other?" The youngest princess interrupted.

"No, for she predeceased her husband in death."

"How did they solve it?" Princess Sefira fluttered Lady Beccah's fan to cool her face.

"In ancient times, disputes were settled by tossing a tesco, a large gold coin with one side having a smiling lady luck stamped on it, and the other side having a frowning mister forfeit."

"Is that what a tesco is for?" the next to youngest princess asked before the others shushed her.

Jiana nodded. "Since neither brother would concede, the old king's adviser declared he would decide the succession on a toss of the coin. The brother who lost the toss gathered up his loyal followers and sailed with a fleet to foreign lands to establish his own kingdom." She lowered her voice, and the women leaned forward. "He was never heard of again."

A sad look settled on her face. "Then a curse fell upon Canteor. Crops failed. Starvation came. The plague returned and ravished the land. Parents sold their children into slavery for food. The king ordered merchant ships to become raiding pirates, stealing wealth from other nations. People began to worship Panmin, the goat god of wine and feasting. They offered blood sacrifices to him." She shuddered.

"Why was the land cursed?" the youngest princess asked when Jiana paused.

"The brother who won the toss admitted on his deathbed that he was the younger brother who had stolen his twin's birthright."

"At least he confessed before he died." Donella snorted.

"Isn't there anymore to the legend?" the eighteen-year-old princess asked when Jiana paused for effect.

"Actually, there is. The legend says that one day descendants of the firstborn shall return to Canteor. Brothers themselves, they shall return separately. Not recognizing the other, they shall engage in hand-to-hand battle. If one kills the other, the curse will continue. Only when they join forces, will they succeed in saving the kingdom. Then they will establish a time of peace, and culture will flourish."

Donella thought of the war Prince Pashmi wished to bring to Valdeor. She thought of the evil wrought by slavery.

Now would be a great time for the brothers to appear.

"It is too hot to eat." Princess Sefira lounged on her divan. "I know!" She sat up enough to call her maid over. "Abelita, tell Cook we will dine in the garden tonight." She turned to Lady Beccah and the other ladies in waiting. "A cool breeze will refresh us."

The younger princesses clapped and perked up.

Abelita hurried away.

The younger princesses drifted away, bickering about who would get to stay up late. The ladies in waiting tried to make peace.

At Princess Sefira's command, Donella beckoned to the tall guard who stood cross-armed outside the chambers. His bronzed torso under the maroon vest was all lean muscle. His chiseled face seemed cut from granite. His dark eyes twitched as she invited him in, but he showed no other sign of emotion.

Donella still felt there was something familiar about him. She wracked her memory but came up with no circumstance of their meeting before she came to the palace.

The princess tilted her head at the guard, a secret smile on her lips. "Andro, the ladies and I are having a picnic in the garden. Gather some men and see we aren't disturbed."

"As you wish, my princess."

The guard gave her a bow, but Donella thought she saw a spark of longing or desire in his eyes.

The princess smirked at him, holding his gaze longer than necessary. Something seemed to flare between them. Normally, Princess Sefira barely glanced at the slaves, but her eyes lingered on Andro's muscular form as he strode away to do her bidding.

She sighed and spoke privately with her aunt. "Andro is the greatest gladiator in Dabbori. When I saw him fight, I demanded my father give him to me to be my personal bodyguard. No one has ever bested him."

Lady Beccah narrowed her gaze, glancing from the princess to the departing gladiator's back. "Is that why you want the winner of the games to gain his freedom? Do you expect Andro to win?"

The princess licked her lips but didn't answer, inspecting an invisible piece of lint on her topaz-colored gauze sleeve.

"I see. You do have feelings for him." Lady Beccah fanned herself, perspiration along her brow. "He is handsome, even for a slave. But if he wins, you will lose him."

Princess Sefira put her nose in the air, ignoring the remarks. "Shall we have our picnic?" She stretched as she stood, like a cat awakening. She stalked from the room, her sisters and the ladies following.

Donella wondered at the overheard conversation as she and Jiana parted from Lady Beccah and went down the servant's staircase to the unbearably hot kitchen to eat with the other slaves.

Accepting the plate of stewed fish and tiny potatoes, she and her friend settled at the far end of the table where it was coolest. Abelita and the other slaves were wary of the girls. They weren't as friendly as Lady Beccah's slaves.

Biting the buttery new potatoes, Donella listened idly to their gossip.

"Did you see the size of that fighter? Why he must be six and a half feet tall. He towers over Andro by several inches." The female voice gushed with admiration.

Another slave girl giggled. "I thought you had a crush on Andro, but you sound enamored of this new wrestler."

With a sniff, the first girl answered, "I am not good enough for the likes of Andro. These days he is looking higher than the female slaves." The gossiping girls shared a look.

Andro's secret admiration for the princess and her silence on the subject had been noticed by the staff. Seemingly, their flirtation wasn't new. Donella was always surprised how gossip traveled as quick as lightning.

Flicking her hair, the second one asked, "So, does your new interest have a name?"

"I heard the slave owner call him Hazibal."

Donella choked. Jiana thumped her on the back, while all eyes swiveled her way. "Sorry," she choked out. Wiping her mouth with a napkin, she whispered to Jiana, "Let's get out of here."

They put their plates in the washing area and escaped to their room. Donella immediately opened the shutters as far as they would go to let in the evening breeze from the sea. Gazing east, the water sparkled in the lowering sun and pink tinged the clouds as she watched.

"What happened back there?" Jiana put her hands on her hips.

Turning to face her friend, Donella rocked on her toes. "Didn't you hear what they said?"

The stars were aligning for something big. She could feel it in her gut. First the waypost, now Hazibal.

"I wasn't paying attention."

"The girls were talking about a new wrestler who came to compete in the games. His name," she paused dramatically, "is Hazibal."

Jiana put her hand up to her face. "Could it be? It is a popular name."

"But he's taller than Andro, the princess's guard. And he's a *wrestler*. It's got to be our Hazibal."

The next morning, Donella woke up early. She was determined to find Hazibal. She readied herself quietly so as not to wake Jiana, but when she returned from relieving herself, wanting to grab her cloak, she found Jiana waiting.

"You are up to something. Whatever it is, I want to come." Jiana's normally docile expression was resolute. She put on her own cloak against the cool morning. "Where are we going?"

Donella gave her a nod. "Why, to the stadium barracks. That's where the contestants are."

As they left the palace, Donella grabbed Jiana's arm and guided her through the courtyard gates toward the town.

They walked down the hill. From this height, the streets spread out in a circular shape. The pink buildings were spread apart near the palace, then closer together farther from the palace.

At the start, they glimpsed cool fountains seen through the wrought iron gates leading into the patios. Palm trees offered shade while the scent of jasmine floated in the air.

As they neared the city center, the streets narrowed. Three-storied manors were replaced by streets of tottering buildings of cracked plaster. Cooking oil and frying fish replaced the pleasant smells of earlier.

"Are you sure you know the way?" Jiana moved closer as rougher inhabitants stared at them.

Donella pulled her friend out of the way of a wagon of kegs blocking the street. "Yes, I remember seeing it the day we arrived."

Soon they stood at the entrance to the great stadium which could seat forty thousand. Built into the hillside of a quarry, the tiered seats towered three stories high. In the open end of the quarry, stood elaborate wooden benches with coverings for the prince and nobles to watch the games. The royal crest of a scimitar on a black background was on display in the royal booth.

Donella's gaze was drawn to the sandy arena where men wrestled, while others practiced with wooden swords. She scanned the men, looking for the giant with the shaggy red beard.

Jiana suddenly clutched her arm. Pointing with a shaking finger, she gasped, "Gensard!"

Donella followed her gaze, her heart picking up its pace. *The prince? Here?*

Gensard was demonstrating his superb swordsmanship. Donella wasn't a good judge, but his opponent seemed on the defensive.

A waypost. Hazibal. Gensard.

Hope swelled in her breast. The One Who Fashioned All had a plan for them. She just had to figure out what it was.

Sweat dripped in Gensard's eyes. The clipped sound of wooden swords clashing filled his ears. Sand puffed as he and Jod, his opponent, moved in the intricate dance of slash and parry. The taste of it coated his mouth. His eyes strained, watching for clues for what his opponent would do next.

A hesitation on Jod's part gave Gensard an opening. He lunged for a hit to the neck. Score!

Gensard stepped back and wiped his dusty brow.

Where was the boy with the water pail? His throat was parched.

Lifting his eyes, he saw a vision. Blue eyes gazing at him, lips parted, and blond hair waving in the wind. Gensard rubbed his hand over his eyes and blinked. Jiana was still there, smiling at him now. Everything else dissolved away.

Without seeming to command them, his feet walked toward her. He had the strange feeling of coming home.

"You're here!" "Are you alright? Tell me you're not hurt!" Both Jiana and Gensard spoke simultaneously.

"I'm well, thank you."

Gensard felt a silly grin on his face at her blushing reply.

She glanced at the girl next to her. "We're well. We have a good mistress."

Only then did he register Donella under her hood standing at Jiana's side. Gladness that they were both safe swelled in his heart.

"I was so worried when Zaniah took you away to the slave block." His voice came out hoarse.

"But what happened to you?" Jiana looked pointedly at his slave collar.

Gensard involuntarily touched his chafed neck. "Lord Paitar bought me as one of his gladiators. I am here to win the competition." He winked and spread out his arms. "I've sized up the contestants and don't see anything to worry about." He smugly grinned.

Instead of smiling back, Jiana clutched her hands together. She shared a distressed look with Donella, who twirled a piece of her hair, a sure sign of worry.

"What? Do you know something?" He glanced between the girls.

"The champion gladiator lives in the palace." Concern flickered in Donella's eyes. "He is Princess Sefira's bodyguard. He is formidable."

"I've fought and beaten formidable foes before. You know that." Gensard couldn't understand her concern. She had been there at Laketown. She knew he saved Princess Lauressa from a horde of Canteor cutthroats.

Jiana touched his arm. He gazed down at her pale face, fear for him written in her expression. "No one has beaten Andro in a dozen years. I heard the ladies in waiting say it."

A tic pulsed in Gensard's jaw.

A dozen years was a long time in the life of a gladiator. Victory was not guaranteed, then. Gensard knew his strengths but could not afford to be cocky.

He didn't want Jiana upset, so he put his hand over hers on his arm. "No fear. Now that you have warned me, I will be careful. I started using a sword when I was seven years old, and my brother taught me. By the time he was eighteen, he was the unbeaten champion of Samarantha. I learned the tricks of the trade from him."

Jiana relaxed slightly. Stepping away, she cocked her head. "I didn't know you both had another brother." Puzzled, she glanced from one to the other. "I thought you were the son of a rug merchant. Why did you and your brother learn to fight?"

He had forgotten his lie. Stalling, Gensard didn't immediately answer. He glanced at Donella for help.

She took the hint. "Before Prince Alloryn defeated Warlord Feornson, and Reina Lauressa ascended the throne, roving marauders threatened our small town." She changed the subject. "But obviously, we didn't come looking for you, Gensard. We heard of a wrestler named Hazibal competing. Have you seen him?"

"Yes. Hazibal is here, too. I met him yesterday. Follow me." Gensard turned on his heel and led the girls toward the barracks. Just short of the stone building at the edge of the arena, several large men wrestled. Hazibal was noticeable by his height and red beard. His chest was bare, covered in sweat and grime streaks.

He had his arm around another's neck. With a twist of the shoulder, he brought his man down. Corded muscles stood out on his arms and back as he defeated the other.

Gaining his feet, his gaze landed on the three watchers. Five strides and he was at their side.

"My friends, it is good to see you!"

"And you!" Donella grasped his arm, a grin plastered across her face. Hazibal responded by picking her up in a bear hug. Donella turned bright red. Jiana put out her hand, and Hazibal hugged her, too. Then the giant slapped Gensard so hard on the back that he struggled to keep his feet.

Donella motioned them all to lean in. "It's getting late. Jiana and I must return to the palace. We'll come back and visit when we can. It's only four days before the princess's birthday. We need to make plans."

After agreeing to watch for the girl's return, Gensard whispered to Jiana, "I didn't mean what I said that day." Her puzzled expression soon became a blush as he continued. "I do care for you. And when I win the contest, I will take you far away from here."

Jiana shyly nodded, then hurried away with Donella. Gensard watched until they disappeared. Walking back to the practice area, his heart swelled with gratitude that he had found her again and she was well.

He would win the competition and find a way to take her back with him to Samarantha. And prince or not, he would take her as his wife. Even if it meant exile. Her approval of him meant more than his father's.

26 Secrets & Lies

As the day of the princess's birthday grew near, excitement was in the air. The cooks and bakers prepared for a large feast with measured pandemonium reigning in the kitchen. Seamstresses fitted the ladies in waiting with new gowns for the occasion. Nobles from all over Canteor traveled to the city from their country estates. Those who were not special guests staying in the palace threw open their mansions surrounding the palace. Slaves festooned the grand reception hall with colored silk drapes, palm trees in pots, and garlands of flowers. The smell of perfume was everywhere—on the guests, from the flowers, and incense wafting from the guest rooms.

When Lady Beccah was not attending the princess, she was visiting the homes of her newly arrived friends. Donella and Jiana hardly had a moment to themselves, at their mistress's beck and call at all hours.

"Jiana, where is my purple shawl? It matches my dress." Lady Beccah bestirred herself to open the wardrobe, and not finding it, went back to her vanity. "Donella, did you see my pearls? I wore them the night before last. I think I left them by my bed."

Donella scurried into her ladyship's bed chamber. Scarves, shawls, and shoes were scattered about as Lady Beccah had spent a long time deciding what to wear to the night's gala.

The bed was neatly made in contrast, although the finely woven coverlet was hard to see under the many articles of clothing. The table beside the bed was no better, covered in odds and ends. A couple of painted fans, done by her mistress, a piece of torn lace, a sash, a comb of pearls, and under it all, the pearl necklace Donella had been sent to find. She snatched it up, about to leave, when she saw a glint of gold under the bed.

Automatically, she picked it up to put it on the table. A gasp escaped her when she saw what it was—a simple gold band topped with a raised, flat circle. Etched on it was a design of three interlocked spirals. *A waykeeper's ring! Here in Dabbori!*

Donella's breath left her. Her hand tingled where the ring lay. First, she'd found the broken waypost. Now she held the ring to open it.

How did it come to be here? Lady Beccah had never worn anything so plain.

Donella slid it over her finger. A perfect fit. That didn't make any sense. Her fingers were much slenderer than her mistress.

"Have you found the pearls?" Lady Beccah's voice spoke behind her.

Donella's heart jumped into her throat.

Spinning around, Donella hid her left hand behind her back. She hoped her mistress wouldn't notice the blush staining her face. She held out her right hand, clutching the pearls, and offered them.

"You found them! They were a very expensive gift from my late husband." Her sentimental exclamation was ruined when she added, "No one at the gathering tonight will wear anything to touch them."

Donella sighed with relief when her ladyship sailed back into the sitting room, letting her lady's maid fasten them around her neck, at the same time praising Jiana for finding the missing shawl.

Donella slipped the ring off her finger and into her deep pocket. A twinge of guilt assailed her at stealing it. But, for all she knew, it was her own, given to Lady Beccah by Zaniah at the time of her purchase. It seemed more likely that Agomeisa had sold her ring a long time ago. But it did fit perfectly, so Donella took that as a sign it was hers.

She had no chance to visit the garden waypost with the ring. Her mistress embarked on a round of calls and parties that took all her time. But a plan brewed at the back of Donella's brain.

Two nights before the birthday feast, Donella brushed her hair before turning into bed. The shutters were open to the breeze. There was no moon, but the girls could see by the lamplight.

Donella had pondered the best way to approach the subject since finding the ring. Her stomach clenched at admitting her lies to her friend.

"Jiana, there's something I need to tell you." Donella paused, letting her hands fall into her lap. "You know, I'm not from here."

"Yes, you told me that you and your brother are from Valdeor." Jiana sat by the lamp, mending.

"Uh, yes." Donella wasn't going to explain the brother and sister lie. Let Gensard do it. It was his fabrication, after all.

"Our real reason for traveling here was to learn about Canteor's fleet. We heard Prince Pashmi was building one to attack our land."

"I thought you were rug merchants?" Jiana paused in sewing a tear in her gown's hem.

"That was our cover story." Donella bit her lip. It was harder to own up to her lies seeing Jiana's shocked expression. "We came to assess the threat of an invasion. You can see how that would be important."

Jiana dropped her sewing in her lap. "You're a spy?"

"Yes. But we didn't learn much." She searched Jiana's face, afraid to see condemnation. "I no longer wish the life of a spy. It seemed so romantic once." She longed to be a waykeeper again, sharing hospitality with strangers. Not only a safer life, but more satisfying.

Jiana hunched her shoulders. "It sounds dangerous to me. Always the fear of getting caught. Don't they hang spies?" She shuddered.

A quiver ran up Donella's spine. She hadn't thought out the consequences of getting caught in a land with different laws.

"There's more." Donella bit the tip of her finger. If she wanted to save Jiana, she had to explain what she could do. But it was hard to put into words. Would Jiana even believe her? Showing her would be best, Donella told herself.

Donella cleared her throat. "I have found a way to escape for all of us. But I can't go into my plans yet. Will you trust me, no matter what my plan is? I couldn't bear to leave behind my best friend."

"I'm your best friend?" Jiana's expression went from hesitant to puzzled to surprised. "You're like a sister to me," she whispered. She moved over and they hugged. "I trust you. I'll do whatever you say if you take me with you."

The next morning, before dawn, Jiana hurried after Donella along the streets to the stadium. Her heart thumped at every noise or movement. Or did it race at the thought of seeing Gensard again?

Their shoes tapped hollowly along the ever-narrower byways. The only inhabitants they saw were a few drunks or beggars asleep in doorways. A dog barked as they passed a dark alleyway.

The road ended in a large boulevard surrounding the stadium. A couple of figures detached from the shadows. Jiana bit down a scream. One was giant in size, and she knew it must be Hazibal. Her breathing evened out.

The other shadow stepped near her. She could just make out Gensard's serious face in the lightening sky.

"We don't have much time," Donella said. "Hazibal, I need you to retrieve something from the palace garden. Do you have a place to hide an object this big?" She motioned with her hands.

"What did you find?" Gensard demanded.

"A broken waypost. I think I can get us away from here." She flashed her hand at him.

His face went from skepticism to amazement. "You found a ring, too?"

Jiana didn't understand their excitement, and by Hazibal's frown, he didn't either.

"Yes! Don't you see? We can leave anytime!" Donella was bursting with hidden excitement, shown by her inability to stand still, and the enthusiasm in her voice.

"After the tournament." Gensard had a stubborn look to his jaw.

"What? Shouldn't we leave now?" Donella twisted a lock of her hair. A sure sign of worry.

"Did you find out the ship strength?"

"I—I haven't done much investigation."

"You're the spy. What have you been doing with your time?"

Jiana felt uncomfortable watching the siblings spat.

"Get what information you can at the palace," Gensard hissed. "We're out of time. Then tomorrow after the games, we'll disappear."

Gensard glanced over his shoulder. "We have to get back or we'll be missed. Take Hazibal with you. I'll cover for him."

Subdued, Donella nodded. She strode off, Hazibal following.

Jiana glanced once at Gensard.

"Just a moment. There's something you should know." Gensard looked uncomfortable. He rubbed the back of his neck and didn't meet her eyes.

She was reminded of Donella's similar words the previous evening. She put up her hand. "Donella already told me last night."

"What?" He looked startled, then ashamed, and finally relieved. "It doesn't make any difference. I swear. I still want you to accompany me to my home. My father will have to pick another to be his heir."

"His heir?" Jiana blinked. She couldn't imagine a rug merchant needing an heir.

"My father remarried when my mother died." He shrugged, as if it didn't matter, but his face was pinched. "He has several younger princes and princesses to choose from."

Jiana heard his words but didn't comprehend them. He put his warm hands on her cold shoulders. Time slowed as she stared up at him. He leaned toward her.

A bell clanged.

"I have to go. I'll see you tomorrow." He touched her hair, then was gone.

She stood stock still, feeling as if the earth had rocked beneath her. What had he been talking about?

Heir? Prince? Princess?

Jiana turned toward the road Donella and Hazibal had disappeared down. She ran away from the stadium and toward her friend. She had to find Donella and ask what Gensard meant.

Her feet faltered. Did that mean Donella was a princess?

Trembling, Jiana lost her footing and fell in the dark road. Several people stirred along the street. A man weaved toward her on unsteady feet. A housewife emerged from a doorway with a basket on her arm.

With a sob, Jiana pushed herself to her feet and ran toward the palace. She wanted desperately to be alone to think on what Gensard and Donella had told her.

They had lied to her about everything. Could she ever trust them again?

The rest of the day passed in a blur.

Andro, the princess's bodyguard met Jiana in the entryway. His height made her lean her head back. His stern jaw and cold eyes stared at her without warmth. Hazibal, although having several inches on Andro, was like a soft kitten compared to this bear of a man.

"Lady Beccah is asking for you. Were you on an errand for her?" His voice was like steel, hard and unforgiving. "She seemed unaware of your whereabouts."

Jiana's heart sped up. His intense eyes seemed to see through her. What could she say? She was sure he would see through her lie.

Abelita came at that moment, fabric draped over her arm. "There you are! Lady Beccah wants you to return this. It is the wrong color. She said you knew which fabric she ordered."

Jiana was grateful for the interruption. She took the fabric with a murmur of assent and hurried back out the door.

Andro frightened her. And yet he was familiar to her somehow. As she walked to her errand, she mulled where she could have met him before. Surely, she wouldn't forget such an imposing figure.

Returning an hour later with the correct fabric, she spent the rest of the morning entertaining the princesses, playing a simple strategy game with them. Their squabbling, along with her anxiety, gave her a headache.

Donella strummed the kitara as background music to Princess Sefira and her entourage's chatter. Donella had practiced whenever possible and was much improved.

The first chance to talk with her friend came when the princesses were having their final fitting of their gowns for the festivities, and Lady Beccah retired to her own chamber to rest.

Donella insisted they get some fresh air. But instead of going into the garden as usual, she mounted the steps along the wall leading up to the leering Panmin god statue. Jiana shivered when they passed beneath it. She found herself whispering, as if the god could hear her, "Why did you bring us here?"

Donella led her along the ramparts until the town and sea spread out beneath them in a sweeping vista. "I wanted to see the harbor, and this seemed the best place." She leaned on a crenelation. She grew quiet, gazing over the busy shipyard and fleet rocking in the waves. She seemed to forget Jiana was there.

Jiana's resentment grew. She thought Donella was her friend. Jiana had spilled out her shame to her, yet Donella had kept her own past a secret.

Jiana had wanted to confront her, yet the hurt in her chest blocked her words.

A stiff breeze buffeted Jiana, whipping her cloak and tangling her hair.

Finally, Donella focused on her. "I found something special in the garden the other day." She pointed the other direction. "I can't really explain it. It's better if I show you." She clasped her hands together. "I'll show it to you tomorrow. We'll sneak away during the games when everyone is focused on the gladiator fight. I have a plan. But you must trust me. When I tell you to take my hand, you can't hesitate. No matter what happens!" Her eyes pleaded with Jiana.

Shutters had fallen around Jiana's heart. Whenever she let someone come close, they hurt her. Not again.

"You lied to me. You and Gensard." Jiana crossed her arms in front of her. "How can I trust you?"

Donella had the grace to look ashamed. "I'm sorry about that. Really, I am. But we gave our word—"

"Gensard said your mother is dead and your father remarried," Jiana interrupted. She had to know what Gensard meant when he said he was the heir. Heir to where?

Blinking, Donella touched her ring and twirled it around her finger. "What did Gensard say to you?"

"Just that he has other siblings, princes and princesses, who his father could pick to be the heir. Why didn't you tell me you were a princess?"

Donella chuckled, as if she found it funny. "Me? A princess! I'm what's called a waykeeper." Her smile faded when Jiana maintained her stiff pose. "But never mind that."

Jiana's heart was pierced, and she didn't find it humorous at all.

"Gensard is not my brother." Donella lowered her eyes.

"What?" Jiana threw her mind back to the day they met. "He said he was. I distinctly remember it."

"Yes, well, I was as surprised as you when he said that." Donella's face grew somber, seemingly focused on the past. "I think he said it to protect me. If Sad-alah or Hazibal put their hands on me, they knew they would have to answer to him."

Jiana rubbed her hand across her face. She was having a hard time keeping track of the truth from the lies.

"I don't follow you. Please, start from the beginning." She leaned against the walkway crenelation.

Donella pulled her cloak tighter. "It all started when enemy scout ships landed in several Valdeor harbors last year. And although our ships and soldiers overcame them, Reina Lauressa feared Prince Pashmi was building an invasion fleet. She sent several of us on a spy mission to Canteor. We pretended to be rug merchants." Her expression grew sad. "But we got separated."

Donella paused and brushed stray hair from her eyes. "Prince Gensard and I ended up on the beach where you found us. Like I said, Gensard claimed me as his sister. But he's really the son of Prince Xander, the heir apparent of Samarantha, a kingdom within Valdeor. He is also their greatest swordsman. That is why the Reina sent him."

"But he can't care for me. A slave girl!" Jiana twisted her hands. "Is that part of his disguise?"

"What? No!" Donella took her hands in her own. "I've seen the way he looks at you. He does care. In fact, my nickname for him used to be Prince High and Mighty. Until he met you, he cared only for himself and his own advancement. He held me hostage, once, in order to get his own way." She squeezed Jiana's hands and let go. "I first noticed the change in him when he fixed your shoe." She shook her head. "You could've knocked me over with a feather."

A knot in Jiana's stomach eased. Donella's eyes shone with sincerity.

But a prince in love with her?

As if reading her thought, Donella continued. "You are good for him. Gentle. Compassionate." She smiled. "I think he likes being needed for himself. You're the first person who looked up to him, not knowing he is a prince."

Jiana hardly dared hope it could be true.

Suddenly, Donella nodded her head up and down, her face animated. "That's it! You didn't know his background and yet you fell for him, not his title." She smirked.

But she grew somber and crossed her arms, sighing. "Yet he is as much of a slave here as we are."

"That must have been hard on him." Jiana thought how galling it must be to a prince enslaved. If she was unhappy about being someone's possession, how much more so for someone used to servants waiting on him.

"I suppose he could have allowed himself to be ransomed. He itched to claim his title, I'm sure." Donella raised an eyebrow. "I must warn you, he can be very proud."

"That's understandable. I mean, he is a prince after all." Jiana recalled the humiliations he suffered on their journey. "He showed great restraint."

Donella's eyes twinkled. "I've seen the secret glances you send him when you think no one is looking."

A blush spread over Jiana's face. She had secretly watched Gensard.

Donella's eyes lost their teasing light. "Please, please say you forgive me! Say you are still my friend!"

Jiana swallowed. Donella had hurt her. But she couldn't lose her best friend. The lump in her throat prevented her from speaking, so she hugged Donella instead.

"Goodness!" Donella exclaimed, suddenly. "The shadows have shifted. It's late! We'd better get back before someone is sent to search for us!"

They hurried past the goat god statue and headed down the staircase.

Tomorrow, the princess's birthday celebration would start. Lady Beccah was sure to have many last-minute items for them to do.

But the rest of the day, Jiana hugged Donella's words to her heart. *You are good for Gensard. He really cares for you.* Maybe if they could escape to Valdeor, she would be valued for herself. Wasn't Donella always saying there were only free men and women in her country across the sea?

27 Isle of Origin

$\mathcal{A}$fter another week of sailing, Guy awoke to a strange feeling. It took him a moment to realize the ship rocked from side to side as if they were anchored. He hurriedly climbed the ladder. Guy was startled to see fog stretched across the horizon. No land was in sight. The ship was becalmed.

The crew hung around the wheelhouse, where Captain Anaru consulted with Ikonis.

As he walked toward the knot of men, he heard snippets of their conversation.

"Unnatural it is."

"We'd better turn back while we still can."

"To go any farther would be falling off the end of the world!"

Barbu detached himself from the crowd. The whites of his eyes huge in his brown face, he clutched at Guy. "Please tell Captain Anaru to turn back! I do not want to die!"

"It's okay. Ikonis knows the way." Guy noticed Scooter was missing. "Where is your chameleon?"

"Hiding. He knows something is wrong." Barbu seemed genuinely distressed.

"Let me talk to Ikonis. Have faith, my friend. We are nearing the end of the journey. I can feel a portal nearby. An island is out there."

Barbu's breathing calmed somewhat. Guy passed him over to Pellas, who stood nearby.

The men parted at Guy's approach. Ikonis and the captain glanced up from the maps laid out as he joined them.

"What happened?"

"The wind died down to nothing. We can break out the oars, but where do we head? According to the maps, there's nothing beyond this point." The captain gestured at the map.

"Yes, I heard the men saying we've reached the end of the world."

"That's their opinion, and mine too. I don't think they'll follow my orders to row into the fog and certain death. I'm afraid no bribe will entice them at this point."

Ikonis had remained silent. Now he looked Guy in the eye. Deep lines showed starkly on his face without his hat.

"This is the time for faith. If the captain permits, I will row the two of us past the fog to see what we can."

Guy swallowed and his hands began to sweat. He nodded up and down once. "I came this far. I will go the rest of the way, whatever comes."

A quarter of an hour later, the sailors stared at them solemnly as Ikonis rowed the dinghy with even strokes away from the *Diadem* and toward the fog bank. Barbu's apprehension was mirrored on Pellas' face as they stood at the prow.

Forty-five minutes later, the first tendrils of clouds reached out and swirled around them. Within moments, they were swallowed in the whiteness. The sound of the oars was muffled. Gentle waves lapped the dinghy.

Guy was unsure how Ikonis could tell they moved in the right direction.

His shoulder muscles were taut. He wiped his hands on his trousers for the dozenth time. His ears strained for the sound of a waterfall that would mean plunging from the earth into the unknown.

The wisps of mist grew thinner. A darkness appeared before them. It reconciled into a cliff towering above them.

The Isle of Origin!

Jubilation surged through Guy.

The cliff rose directly from the sea with no place to land.

Seeing Ikonis bent over the oars, Guy volunteered to take over.

Changing places, Ikonis guided Guy along the island's perimeter until a break appeared. Guy rowed into a sheltered inlet. They jumped out when they were close enough and dragged the dinghy to the beach.

Sweat dripped down Guy's back from exertion and earlier apprehension. He stood and gazed at the mysterious isle.

Strange trees had tall, thin trunks with branches reaching up to form a half dome. Guy had never seen trees like these with their umbrella-like tops.

"They are called dragon's blood trees because of their red sap," Ikonis told him.

The lush island smelled of exotic flowers. Life teemed everywhere. As they stepped ashore, strange cries and chatters echoed in the fog, which surrounded the island, forming a barrier.

Seeing movement from the corner of his eye, Guy swung around to see a chameleon scramble from under one of the dinghy's seats. The lost Scooter! The lizard made a chirp and headed into the forest.

"Hey!" Guy ran after it. Barbu would kill him if he lost his pet.

Scooter darted down a path that hadn't been visible from their position on the beach. By the time Guy caught up with the little lizard-like creature, he was deep in the woods. He coaxed Scooter onto his shoulder. The little claws tickled where the chameleon clutched him.

He spotted a monkey staring at him, then realized a group of them watched him from the trees, their bulbous eyes curious.

A crashing sound behind Guy made him swing around, blood ringing in his ears. It sounded like a large animal. He felt foolish when it was only Ikonis joining him.

Ikonis passed the supply bag to Guy, who shouldered it.

"It looks like the vegetation has overgrown the path. You can see where rocks once lined the trail."

Guy hadn't noticed, but now that Ikonis pointed it out, he saw rocks on either side of the open areas showing how once four people could have walked abreast.

"This looks like the main route. Let's follow it."

They continued walking. The parasol-shaped trees towered thirty feet above them, blocking the light. Birds of many colors fluttered from tree to tree with strange calls. The humidity made Guy's shirt stick to his back. Moist earth smells mingled with sweet flowers.

An hour later, they came to a cliff edge overlooking a valley with a river flowing through it. Across the chasm from them, a magnificent waterfall plunged into the river. A stone bridge led across the turbulent water to where a beautiful white structure arose. The walls seemed to shimmer in the sunlight. A twisting spiral of marble and glass topped the main turret. Airy and light, it looked like nothing man-made Guy had ever seen.

"The great shrine! Just as I saw it in a vision," Ikonis murmured beside him.

Excitement tingled through Guy's body as they zigzagged down the cliff path toward the bridge. The back of his left hand itched and he absently rubbed it.

The bridge which had seemed small from the top of the cliff proved to be wide enough for six men to walk abreast.

Scooter however took exception at it. He ran down Guy, scurried to a nearby tree, and rested on a branch out of reach. No coaxing would get him down. Guy had no choice but to leave him.

Crossing, Guy's heart thumped with anticipation. The waterfall roared deafeningly as they neared it, the spray wetting them.

On close inspection, the shrine walls were not marble, but some white substance embedded with tiny fragments of glass, causing it to glitter as the sunlight caught each one.

At the end of the bridge was a massive, arched doorway. Like the fortress at Sikarta, the door stretched two stories high, but this one had been carved with vines and leaves over the surface. Over the door was a triangular window with an expanded trinity design. It consisted of three interlocking circles picked out in all the colors of the rainbow. The very center matched the birthmark on the back of Guy's left hand. The Safe Haven emblem.

In the cool air from the waterfall, Guy shivered. What lay beyond?

Taking a deep breath to calm his nerves, Guy pushed on the door. With a loud groan, the door opened a few inches, then stuck. Guy was ready to put more muscle into it, when Ikonis spoke.

"The man size door is probably easier, you know."

Turning, he saw Ikonis at a smaller opening cut into the large doors. Guy's face flushed as Ikonis pulled on an iron ring he had missed, and a normal sized door opened.

A chill met them as they stepped inside. Guy was sure it was going to be dark and gloomy. Why hadn't he thought of bringing a torch? So he was surprised at the colored light streaming in by fifty-foot-high windows.

At his feet, the tiled entryway floor was the multi-colored interlocking trinity symbol again. It suddenly reminded him of Reina Lauressa's medallion. Each colored gem represented the seven virtues. The rainbow-colored tiles also consisted of seven colors, if you included white as a color.

Above him, the ceiling stretched up impossibly high. White pillars inside marched like the tree trunks of the forest. In the middle of the enormous room stood a raised marble dais.

Guy's footsteps echoed on the tile floor. An elusive sweet smell perfumed the air, relaxing his muscles. Then it was gone, like a ghostly presence.

He paused, glancing around. The floor had a layer of dust, but he didn't see any flowers.

"Guy, look at the windows!"

For the first time, Guy realized that pictures were depicted in the stained glass. Water was featured in all of them. Men and women and children on a path overlooking the shrine in the distance made Guy think of their first view of this place. The next image dealt with lines of people entering the shrine. Many leaned on crutches, or had bandages around their heads, or their arms in slings. Some were carried on pallets. Guy moved to the next scene where some figures dipped water from a pool while others received it on their inflicted body parts, such as ears and eyes and limbs.

The next window was divided into two parts. In the upper part, a paralytic had a pitcher of water poured over him by attendants. On the bottom, it seemed the same man stood beside his pallet, his hands raised in praise, a joyous look on his face.

Guy turned toward the dais. He approached it and slowly mounted the steps. He detected the sweet scent from before, even stronger now. The aroma originated here. At the top of the steps was the pool depicted in the stained glass. It measured twenty feet wide, surrounded by a thick white marble wall eighteen inches high. He expected to see murky water or debris floating in it. But the water was pure and clear and still. It looked too deep for a man to stand in.

At his feet, he noticed a silver pitcher. Glancing around the rim, he saw several similar pitchers.

Ikonis left his perusal of the glass windows. With a reverent expression he climbed the steps and stopped about five feet from Guy. He removed his ever-present hat, exposing his thinning hair. He took off his eye patch.

Guy winced when saw a scar and an empty socket in his lined face. Ikonis dipped his hands into the water and immediately applied it to his missing eye.

Guy held his breath, the hairs on his arms standing up.

When Ikonis dropped his hands, water streamed down his face and dripped at his feet. Ikonis opened his eyelid, which hadn't been there a moment ago.

"My sight! I can see!" Ikonis's whole face lit with wonder. He held out his hands and stared at them. He brought his finger toward his new eye and blinked. "I can see from my lost eye!" Two eyes gleaming, he dashed over to Guy. "I'm whole!" He grabbed Guy's shoulders and squeezed.

Guy expelled his breath in a gasp.

Ikonis was miraculously healed!

"You—you have two eyes. The missing one grew back!" Guy stood still with shock, examining Ikonis's face. The scar had disappeared, and his two brown eyes shone with joy.

"Bless the One Who Fashioned All for his mercy!" Ikonis's praise echoed around the room.

"We must return to the ship!" Ikonis stepped away and flung out his arms. "They must see this place."

Laughing and talking, Guy and Ikonis crossed the bridge. Reaching out for the lizard as they came to the dragon's blood tree he perched in, Guy coaxed the chameleon to jump onto his shoulder.

A sudden movement caught his eye. A figure which had been bent over beside a tree stump straightened.

Yarto! What was he doing here?

Catching sight of Guy and Ikonis, Yarto turned and ran away from them.

The cacophony of birdcalls ceased. A sudden silence descended on the forest. A wind ruffled the air like a presence passing through. A deep vibration thrummed in the quiet, causing the hair on Guy's arms to stand up.

Guy noticed the stump was actually a waypost at the bridge's end. How had he overlooked it? Mist pooled at its base.

In the opening portal, Guy glimpsed three figures. The dark visage of Londo/Lemmo, the malevolent eyes of Queen Nerea, and the pudgy face of Faro stared back at him.

No!

Heart stuttering, Guy sprinted to the waypost and laid his marked hand upon it.

The chameleon scurried away with a cry.

Glancing down, Guy saw Queen Nerea's pearl ring. Yarto must have put it there as a token leading to this portal.

Guy's mind spun. Yarto betrayed them? Why?

The aperture opened farther, as Guy wrestled to close the doorway between them. He tried to focus on the task at hand, pushing all other thoughts from his mind. He envisioned the trinity symbol as a lock and forbade entry to the shrine waypost.

Lemmo narrowed his eyes and bared his teeth, pushing at the barrier to enter. His lips moved, as if he were conjuring a spell.

If only Guy could take the ring from the shaman's finger. He had missed that clue at the fortress. The man calling himself Londo in Sikarta had the glint of a ring on his finger when Guy first encountered him. But when "Londo" pointed to the map, the ring was missing.

Now Guy was sure it was he watching them from the foliage when Yarto showed up asking for passage on the *Diadem*. How had Guy let himself be fooled?

And how was Yarto mixed up in this?

Guy forced his mind to focus. Time to ask questions later. Right now, he had to save the shrine.

Lemmo's will was strong, like a gale wind force pushing against Guy's mind. Guy didn't know how long he could withstand it.

He suddenly found himself floating in the between places. Along with his three enemies were a dozen soldiers coming toward Guy.

He opened another portal, this one to a mountain fastness in a remote region. He tried to push the enemies there.

But Lemmo's will resisted. His eyes burned with hate and determination.

"You cannot stop me, farm boy!" The ruby on his staff glowed, creating a bubble around the group.

Guy did not know how to fight such magic.

His mind extended and touched the many portals available, trying to send the wizard and the others to any location but where Guy was.

After several futile attempts, Guy began to fear he wasn't strong enough to expel the invaders.

He must win this battle of wills. The shrine could not fall into their hands!

Help me!

Energy crackled, like the buildup before lightning struck. Hairs rose along Guy's skin. The air beside him shimmered.

Guy's heart stuttered. He was unprepared to fight another foe.

A brilliant light exploded.

Guy squinted in the sudden illumination.

He became aware of the Guardian of Valdeor. The winged being on his left confronted the group.

"It is forbidden to bring war to the shrine!" The Guardian's voice boomed like a thunderclap. He raised his hand toward the invaders.

Lightning flashed. The ruby shattered. Another bolt. A tendril of it snaked out and struck Lemmo's ring. The man screamed as the ring dissolved into molten metal.

Vibrations like an earthquake rippled in every direction. Guy held himself in place with a thread of thought, connecting him to the waypost he entered by. But the invading group dispersed, flung as if by a giant hand. Guy opened doorways of the most desolate places and felt each of them ejected through a different portal.

Floating, Guy tried to force his heart back where it belonged.

The Guardian focused his resplendent gaze on Guy. His features shone like the sun, blurring the details. "You have done well. The High One has forgiven you your transgressions.

"Prepare the shrine for the pilgrims who will visit. Many miracles will convert the nations. But the Water of Regeneration will restore hearts and minds in the coming years, more than just bodies."

The light gained in intensity. Guy squeezed his eyes shut and turned his head away.

"What just happened?" Ikonis asked in a shaky voice.

Guy opened his eyes and found himself standing beside the waypost, the stone cool beneath his hand. Solid ground felt good beneath his feet. The forest around him was once again alive with fluttering birds and strange animal cries.

White-faced, Ikonis petted the chattering chameleon clinging to his shoulder.

"The enemies I made on my quest tried to enter through the portal." Guy rubbed his left hand over the top of his head. "The Guardian of Valdeor appeared and flung them through the portals to distant lands."

The comforting words of the Guardian replayed in his mind.

The deep sorrow for the loss of his friends flowed like the river over the waterfall, disappearing. Joy bubbled up like a spring in its place. "He said I was forgiven." A wide grin spread over his face. "And we must prepare the shrine for those who are coming."

Guy had little memory of their return trip. His amazement at the momentous events was too great.

The crew crowded around the dinghy when they arrived at the *Diadem*. Not until they hauled up the hermit was the miracle apparent to them. Most backed away. Some clutched their amulets in a superstitious motion. Their faces reflected shock, awe, and confusion.

"A miracle!" one sailor exclaimed with astonishment.

Eliu pushed to the front when he heard that. "Friend, what happened? Are you back from the dead?"

At their return, Barbu had rushed over to Guy, exclaiming at being reunited with his pet. But at these words he clutched his hands together, the whites of his eyes prominent. "Are you ghosts?" his voice trembled.

Ikonis snorted at the questions. "Nothing of the sort. We found the Isle of Origin and visited the great shrine. It is built around the pool of the Water of Regeneration. Beautiful glass windows depict miracles." Ikonis gently touched his eyelid. "I poured the water on my eye, and the healing water restored it!"

The sailors mulled this over, exclaiming with marvel.

"Do you think it can heal my crippled hands?" Eliu stretched forth his twisted hands.

A sailor motioned to a puckered line down his leg. "What about my scar?"

"Forget that, how about my deaf ear?" an older, thin man cried out.

Guy motioned the captain aside. "Do you think the crew will agree to sailing through the fog now?"

Captain Anaru lifted one eyebrow and a lopsided grin

touched his lips. "Aye. No fog will stop them."

And so they sailed through the mist and anchored in the inlet. Everyone wanted to see the Waters, so Captain Anaru decided not even to leave a skeleton crew. Ikonis and Guy led all the men through the woods and to the shrine.

Those who wished for healing followed Ikonis and Guy up the steps to the pool, while the rest clustered in a group and watched in wonderment. A reverent hush fell over them until the man with the leg scar yelped with amazement.

"Look! It's gone! My scar is gone!" He danced around.

The crew congratulated him and spoke in awed voices.

Then suddenly the healed man yanked off his amulet of Makba and dropped it at his feet. "I renounce the false sea god." And he showed his contempt by stomping on the shell.

After a momentary hush, Barbu nodded. "Makba and Varu not as powerful as this God." He pulled his prized sea monster teeth necklace over his head and threw it on the floor. Others removed their amulets and did the same.

As he poured water over the men using the silver pitcher, Guy could not help but think this was a repeat of the images on the stained glass. They were the first pilgrims in centuries.

When he was done, the back of his hand itched. Rubbing it, Guy glanced at it, absently. He expected to see a bug bite. Instead, he saw his birthmark had visibly darkened.

He didn't know if he had splashed a drop of water on it or being in this place had restored it. He was just glad that he was forgiven, and still the Gifted One.

And his guilt no longer pressed down on him unbearably. He knew the One Who Fashioned All protected and provided for his friends, just as He always had.

28 *Panmin Unmasked*

The day of Princess Sefira's twenty-first birthday dawned cloudless and perfect.

Nervous energy demanded Gensard release it. After his morning stretches, he ran up the stadium steps and surveyed the scene below.

The roadways were packed with merry makers headed to the stadium for the day's long Celebration Games. Carriages bearing nobles moved at a snail's pace, hemmed in by Dabbori's inhabitants and the visitors from distant cities and rural farms.

Women and men carried baskets of pastries, hawking their wares as they slowly moved through the crowds. Outside the stadium, brewers offered tankards of beer from kegs on the back of their wagons. Fruit vendors set up makeshift tables of crates and their voices competed with the others for customers. Stray dogs weaved through the area, searching for scraps, and the vendors chased them away.

At the end of the games, Prince Pashmi had proclaimed there would be a great feast for the masses. Armies of slaves had dug pits behind the arena, and the smell of roasting hipopo tantalized Gensard's nose. Every man, woman, and child would receive a slice of meat, a baked potato, and as much bread and cheese and fruit as they could eat.

The girls had informed him that for the invited nobility, the palace slaves readied a private banquet with a selection of meats, sides, and sweet concoctions set out on overflowing tables. Musicians and performers would entertain the honored guests as they ate and drank.

Afterwards, fireworks set off from barges in the harbor would end the celebration.

Gensard ran back down the stairs and around the arena, anticipation tingling along his nerves. Doza gave his men a fair amount of freedom. Lord Paitar's mark on his slave collar made sure Gensard would not escape very far.

When his stiff muscles felt loose, he joined the other competitors. He was outfitted like them. Wearing short robes to their knees covered by leather mail and wearing leather arm braces, each man held a leather shield. They would carry their weapon of choice when the fighting began.

The gladiator barracks hummed with nervous activity. Several fights almost broke out. Ishmi quelled a few with a crack of his whip.

Gensard had seen enough. He marched up to Ishmi who was in charge. "The men are wound up. Practice would calm their nerves."

The dark eyes regarded him blankly. The diagonal slashes on his cheeks stood out sharply in the early light.

Gensard persevered. "The wrestlers are up first, then the animal tamers, the knife-throwers and jugglers. The gladiator battles are last. The men have too many hours on their hands."

Ishmi's eyes twitched as another flare-up of tempers started. "You're quite opinionated for a slave." But he disappeared through the barrack door. In a few minutes, he returned with Doza.

"To the practice yard!" Doza commanded. He motioned Gensard over. "You are no ordinary slave. Ishmi normally ignores the men, yet since his brother's death, he has listened to you.

Why?"

Glancing at the giant's back as he ushered the men to the training area, Gensard wondered himself. "I told him I once killed one of his tribe in battle."

Doza's eyebrows rose. "They are a warrior tribe, fiercest in Canteor. Their leader won the Games at the time of Prince Pashmi's twenty-first celebration. The fight was so glorious, the prince promised their leader anything he asked. The wily man asked for himself and his people to be set free, never to have to fight in the ring again. The prince agreed and kept his word from that day to this."

A sliver of hope lodged in Gensard's chest as he contemplated Doza's words. "Pashmi keeps his word? He will free today's winner?"

"Oh, yes." Doza narrowed his eyes. "But Andro is likely to win. I've seen him win these past dozen years. His reputation is unbeatable."

"As is mine, back where I come from."

The grizzled warrior only raised an eyebrow, staring at him as if he sought the truth of Gensard's words. After a few seconds, he dismissed him with a wave of the hand. "I will be watching. If anyone has a chance, it is you."

Gensard went to calm his nerves in practice.

Hours later, the wrestlers oiled their chests, while the gladiators tended to their wounds gained during practice and rested as best as they could as their time in the ring approached.

Dabbori's gladiator master had ranked the men in the days preceding the festivities. The lesser fighters would compete in pairs. Each round of elimination would result in better swordsmen sent out. Once the preliminary fights finished, the twenty best men would compete in pairs. In that way, the top-level competitors, including Gensard, would be rested for the best show.

Although the day had stretched endlessly, Gensard was startled when the junior competitors retired to the quarters where the best warriors waited.

Doza urged the final contestants onto the field., "Fight for the glory of Lord Paitar and he will reward you." As they filed out, he gave Gensard a tight-lipped nod of encouragement.

At the door, Ishmi handed each man his sword or scimitar, his expression impassive. When Gensard reached for his own scimitar, which Agomeisa had given Lord Paitar as part of the sale, Ishmi met his eyes. "If you truly killed one of my kind, I expect you to win this contest. If you do not, I will know you are a lying dog, like the rest of the slaves."

Gensard would prove himself to both these men.

As he passed beneath the archway into the arena, a wall of sound and color blasted him from every side. The stadium was at capacity. Small specks of distant people even perched on the top of the quarry. Spectators cheered with a roar as the gladiator master announced the most anticipated event.

Gensard searched for the royal box. He desired a glimpse of Prince Pashmi and Princess Sefira. Having been confined to the stadium complex, he had not set eyes on them yet.

A pennant of a scimitar snapped in the wind over a canopied seating area. Large black men dressed in the costume of Ishmi's tribe stood behind the chairs set for the royals. Pashmi wore a golden turban, reminiscent of Gensard's own father. Royal purple robes flowed around him. He gestured to a young woman beside him, rings twinkling on his fingers. The princess at his side was gowned in maroon, with a gold scarf from neck to opposite waist. Her dark tresses were elaborately braided into two loops on each side of her head, the rest fluttering waist-length in the breeze. A single ruby of enormous size dangled against her forehead, sparkling as she moved.

She scanned the men, her gaze touching Gensard's for a second. Then she sat forward and grinned at something to his left.

Gensard brought his head around and stared at a tall, lean man swaggering into the ring from another opening. Taller than Gensard, he had wide shoulders. His chest was bare except for a maroon vest the color of Sefira's gown, showing off his sculpted muscles. He carried a wicked scimitar, wider than Gensard's. Where his face should be was a grotesque mask of the goat-god Panmin, its horns curved over his head. He crossed halfway across the field, then stopped.

If Gensard thought the crowd was loud before, now the cheers deafened him as they recognized their champion.

A frisson of fear crept over Gensard's spine. He knew in his gut that this man was his match.

Now seemed a good time to pray. Gensard hunted for words, but flowery, long praises wouldn't come. *Almighty Father, let me win this battle. Not for me, but for Jiana. And for your glory.*

As the crowd passed from cheering to stomping and setting the earth shaking, Gensard turned back and searched for Jiana in the nobility's stands. He saw her to the right and above Sefira's ladies in waiting. Her gaze connected with his, and she raised her hands to her mouth. He raised a fist of triumph in a show of confidence for her.

Panmin the warrior ascended a platform, seemingly set up for him on the sidelines. He sat on a chair overseeing the competition.

As the crowd subsided, the twenty men paired off as the gladiator master had instructed them.

Settling into a rhythm, Gensard delivered each blade stroke with precision. He wouldn't tire himself with fancy moves. His life, Jiana's life, as well as Donella's and Hazibal's, hung in the balance.

His scimitar seemed an extension of his arm, slashing, parrying, blocking. His brain was clear, every opening for a thrust noted and acted upon almost simultaneously. He'd never felt more in tune with his senses.

Gensard beat each man he faced in the elimination contest as Panmin brooded above them.

With a pierce through the ribs, the last man fell.

Blood-soaked sand stretched before his tired eyes. A figure moved in his peripheral vision. The swelling noise of the crowd penetrated Gensard's consciousness as they began to stamp their feet.

Wiping sweat from his eyes, Gensard breathed deeply. He wished for time to recuperate, but that was never a part of battle. A slave ran up with a skin of water. Gensard gulped it. Then he poured some on the top of his head to cool down, before passing the skin back.

The moment had come.

Bending quickly, Gensard picked up a handful of sand, rubbing it between his wet palms, improving his grip on his scimitar.

Time slowed to a crawl as Panmin approached.

Freedom or death.

Deciding that offense is the best defense, Gensard charged headlong at his opponent, sword swinging down in a vicious arc. Panmin blocked with his shield. Expecting that, Gensard was already following through with slash upward. Another block. Panmin came at him with an overhand thrust. But Gensard's shield was already moving to block.

Not able to easily see his challenger's eyes was a disadvantage, so Gensard backed away and circled. Panmin turned with him. When the sun was in his enemy's eyes, he planned to attack. But Panmin seemed to anticipate his move and attacked before they spun that far.

Watching the other's face for any telltale twitches, Gensard noticed a slight compression of lips before a sudden move.

Slash and parry. Back off and come together. They moved in a dance of death.

Panmin thrust from overhead, but at the last second, he slashed his blade at a sideways angle. Gensard blocked automatically. He recognized the feint. He had used that bluffing strategy himself many times to advantage. It had been his brother Leander's signature move. Puzzled, he hesitated for a fraction of time.

Panmin took advantage of the pause to strike the scimitar from his hand and knock Gensard to the ground. He countered by wrapping his legs around his opponent and bringing him down as well. Rolling on top of his attacker, Gensard pinned down Panmin's sword hand with both hands, wrestling the scimitar from him. During the struggle, he knocked off the goat god mask.

Gensard froze as he looked into familiar eyes. Time stopped. He was twelve years old again, fighting with his brother.

Leander's face was older, and he wore a short beard, but it was definitely him. His hands reached for Gensard's throat.

As his world rocked on its foundations, Gensard's body refused to work. His mouth dry, he croaked, "Leander? Is that you?"

Gensard's throat tightened under the pressure. Black dots danced before his eyes.

Leander's hands stilled. "Gensard?" His brother gazed searchingly at his face.

At his brother's recognition, it was as if Gensard was released from a spell. Gensard scrambled to his feet and held out a hand to help his brother up.

"You have no idea how much I've longed to see you!" he cried as Leander let him pull him to his feet. "Now we can join forces and escape!"

To Gensard's dismay, Leander wasn't wreathed in smiles. He

reached for his dropped scimitar. This stern-faced warrior was not the fun-loving brother Gensard knew, but a stranger.

The crowd, which had held its collective breath when they were down, whipped into a frenzy of cheering. "Andro! Andro!"

Gensard's heart stopped. "Leander. It's me." But he stooped and retrieved his scimitar, holding it at the ready. The Almighty Father knew he didn't want to fight his brother, but he would.

"Keep up the appearance," Leander hissed, circling slowly.

Sweat trickled down Gensard's back and his whole body tingled with anticipation. He needed to convince his brother to throw their lots in together. "We have surprise on our side. The guards won't expect us to turn on them."

Leander thrust at him, but without his full force behind the swing. Gensard countered.

He searched his brother's face for any sign of yielding. "My friend has the ability to transport us anywhere we want to go. They won't be able to follow."

"And where would I go? Home?" Leander's mouth twisted. "You forget, I am exiled. I have an honored place here."

"As what? A gladiator? The princess's bodyguard? I'm offering you freedom."

Leander thrust low then high. They had fought many times, so Gensard knew his brother's favorite fighting patterns. Gensard parried without thinking but didn't press back.

It dawned on him that Leander was driving him toward the tunnel leading out of the arena. Maybe his words were getting through.

"I don't need your help." Leander's face hardened. "If I win this fight, Prince Pashmi will free me. Then I will be free to marry the woman I love."

Leander kept pushing him back with every stroke, using more force. Gensard saved his energy, defending rather than pressing.

His heart was being ripped from his chest. *Please, please,*

Almighty Father, let me convince him. If he couldn't sway his brother by the time they were beside the tunnel, he would have to do his best to kill Leander. Not something Gensard wanted to do.

"The girl I love also watches in the stands. We can come back for your sweetheart. Come with us, Leander." Gensard panted with the effort to parry the hits coming faster and faster.

"How will you escape? The guards won't let you leave the arena alive."

Gensard didn't think he could trust Leander, but he had to get him on his side. "Through a portal."

Their blades locked. Leander's hard eyes were inches above him. His face was familiar and yet not. Gone was the mischievous prankster. In his place stood a hardened warrior with his brother's face.

"Don't you see? We were meant to meet again, here and now." Gensard gave it one last try. "The One Who Fashioned All brought us to this time and place. We can overcome the odds together!" he pleaded. Yet he braced himself for action, gripping the scimitar with both hands.

Doubt crossed Leander's expression. Breathing heavily, his gaze drilled into Gensard's very soul.

Gensard took advantage of the hesitation. He drew on his remaining strength and stomped on Leander's left instep as hard as he could. Pain and shock crossed his brother's face. In that instant, Gensard broke the lock with a twist of his wrists which sent his brother's scimitar flying. Quick as a whip, he touched his sword tip to his brother's throat.

A collective gasp came from the stands, followed by a deep silence as the people's hero stood defeated.

"You are the one who taught me to distract the enemy and strike." Gensard hardened his heart. "Are you with me, or do you die now?"

Confusion and anger crossed his brother's face in quick

succession. Finally, resignation won.

But Gensard remained tensed in case Leander tried to grab his sword or pull some sudden stunt.

"You turned out well, little brother." As Leander's lip curled slightly, Gensard thought he saw a flash of admiration in his eyes.

Leander put his hands in the air. "I'll take the guard on the right." And he winked.

The moment of truth. Did he trust his brother not to stab him in the back?

"May the Almighty Father guide our scimitars." Pulse hammering, Gensard stepped away.

"May it be so," Leander breathed before diving for his lost scimitar.

Gensard spun to the guard on the left, attacking him in one long leap, exploding with pent up emotion. The guard's eyes widened but he was too slow to defend himself. Gensard separated his head from his body. All the while he feared a blow from behind.

Hearing a grunt, Gensard swung in that direction. The second guard fell as Leander pulled his weapon from the man's belly.

"I hope your friend is ready, or this is going to be the shortest escape in history," Leander called over his shoulder as he sprinted toward the tunnel.

The crowd gasped and roared their disapproval as Gensard followed.

29 Escape

From the royal box, Donella's view was directly above the combatants.

Prince Pashmi sat below, all in purple silk wearing a gold turban decorated with a giant pearl. Princess Sefira, beside him, wore maroon and gold, her elbow-length sleeves slit open. Her slender arms showed off her myriad of gold bangles. She smelled of sandalwood and vanilla. Lady Beccah was directly in front of Donella in silver.

The crowd filled the arena with movement and sound.

Jiana sat with her, behind their mistress at the back of the royal box. Donella saw Gensard seek her friend in the crowd and salute her.

Tension filled the air between them every time Gensard fought an opponent. As he defeated each one, Donella found she could breathe again. She kept up a continual prayer as the games proceeded.

When the final competitor, Panmin, left his chair and approached Gensard, she heard Jiana's sharp intake of breath. Donella's own heart skipped a beat.

As the fight commenced, Jiana sat with her hands clenched as they watched Gensard attack the masked gladiator, who they knew was Andro. Every time the scimitars clashed, Jiana would squeak. Among all the cheers and cries, no one noticed.

When Andro knocked Gensard to the ground, Donella gasped and grabbed her friend's hand. Jiana was so pale, she feared she would pass out.

"Pray!" Donella murmured loud enough for only Jiana to hear. "O, please Almighty Father, give Gensard strength!"

"I have been praying!"

Donella sat forward on her seat as Gensard pulled his adversary down. She bit her thumb as they rolled on the ground. But when the prince revealed his adversary's face, something strange happened. The combatants froze for a long moment, then Gensard stood and pulled his opponent up.

"Why doesn't he strike?" Jiana voiced her own thoughts.

"What is he doing?!" The princess stood up in front of them, blocking their view, until her father gripped her hand and pulled her back into her seat. "Sefira, behave yourself. He might be your champion, but after all, he is only a slave. Handsome, I give you, but a slave, nonetheless."

The princess subsided, but Donella noted her hands clench on her chair's arm as the contest continued.

Panmin slowly circled Gensard. Gensard parried, guardedly. His lips moved continually, as if he were speaking.

Sure that the combat was nearing the finish, Donella tingled with anticipation.

She nudged Jiana. "Time to make our escape," she breathed in Jiana's ear.

Jiana's white face glanced from her to the fighters as they advanced ever closer to the tunnel leading from the arena.

"Gensard will make his move soon." Donella gently grasped Jiana and slid her across the bench toward the royal box's exit. The guard stationed there had moved forward for a better view. All eyes were riveted on the fight below.

Donella stood and inched toward the stairs leading into the

tunnels, dragging Jiana with her. The air was cool as they descended, their slippers making little sound on the stone stairs. Reaching a crossing which should've had a guard posted there, Donella took the passage which led to the gladiator's waiting area.

"Hurry!"

As they neared the room, a hulking figure stepped out of an alcove.

Sucking in air to scream, Donella recognized Hazibal at the last second. "You gave me a heart attack!"

"Sorry." Hazibal's eyes gleamed in the dim light. He held a bundle under his arm. "Are we ready?"

Donella nodded her head. "As ready as we can be. Unwrap it and stand by. Let's join Gensard."

Her pulse sounding loud in her ears, Donella watched Hazibal unwrap his bundle. She slipped the waykeeper ring from her pocket and donned it. They crossed the empty room and proceeded through the tunnel toward the light streaming in from the stadium.

The crowd suddenly roared above them in the stands. The sound echoed through the stone halls. Jiana threw her hands over her ears.

Donella and her friends stepped into the stadium.

She blinked in the sudden brightness and cacophony produced by forty-thousand throats.

Two guards lay dead near the tunnel entrance. Gensard reached for Jiana, pulling her behind him as other guards raced toward them across the sand.

As she reached for the broken waypost in Hazibal's hands, Donella was pushed from behind. Princess Sefira went past her and threw herself at Andro.

Mist gathered at Donella's feet.

A movement from inside the tunnel caught Donella's eye. Sad-alah stepped from the shadows, his two knives in his raised hands.

Donella's heart stopped. Time slowed.

In the rising mist, Hazibal raised his hands as if he would launch the object he held at Sad-alah.

"No!" she screamed.

She watched in horror as Sad-alah hurled his knives at Gensard and Andro.

Sefira jerked about at Donella's cry and threw herself in front of Andro. She fell against him with a groan, a dagger hilt protruding from her chest.

Paralyzed, Donella saw a red stain spread across Jiana's middle. Sad-alah had missed Gensard.

"Get us out of here! Now!" Gensard's panicked gaze went from Jiana's white face to Donella's shocked one. He grasped Jiana to his chest with one hand and grabbed Andro's arm with the other.

Donella snapped out of it.

Before the words finished leaving his mouth Donella's hand grasped Gensard and her ringed hand touched the stone.

The yelling crowd and arena dissolved into the mist.

Floating in the portal, tears gathered in Donella's eyes and streamed down her cheeks. She pushed aside the horror of the last few minutes and tried to focus on an endpoint. She barely sensed a waypost at a great distance. She had hoped that when the moment came, she would be able to perceive one that she could reach. The darkness and sparks of light surrounding her reminded her of the day she was separated from Guy. Fear gripped her stomach.

Inspiration struck. Guy! She would concentrate on her memories of him!

As soon as the thought came, she felt a strong pull of his

presence. She closed her eyes and fastened on it. Dizziness came in waves the longer she floated in the between place.

Opening her eyes as she felt herself draw nearer, she observed a glittering building forming in the mist. Gripping Gensard's arm tighter, she hit the ground hard. Quickly gaining her knees, she glanced around.

Gensard touched Jiana's cheek gently, calling her name. Jiana lay pale and unmoving, Sad-alah's dagger sticking out from her stomach. She was alive, her chest barely moving.

Beyond him, Andro held the lifeless body of Princess Sefira, the bloody knife discarded at his feet. His cheeks were streaked with tears and grime as he mindlessly rocked her. "My sweet! My love!"

Hazibal sat stunned, clutching the broken waypost top to his chest.

A rustle in the bushes around them caused Donella to unfreeze.

Guy appeared from a tangle of ferns. "Donella!"

Her heart leaped at the sight of him.

Taking in the scene, he strode over. "We must save them! Come on!" And with those words, he grabbed Donella's hand and helped her up. He pulled her after him as he ran across a bridge toward the magnificent edifice. The spray of a waterfall hit her with its cold touch, dissolving the unreality of it all.

If only he could bring them back to life!

Guy pushed open the doors, which were two stories tall. Cool air rushed out, scented with jasmine.

Donella entered the dim interior with trepidation. The ceiling stretched up impossibly high above her. Pillars like tree trunks led toward a raised dais in the middle of the structure. Fifty-foot-high windows let colored light in. Pictures were depicted in the stained glass.

But Donella could not take it in. Anxiety for her Jiana choked her, and her brain was fogged.

Guy dropped her hand and picked up a silver pitcher on the bottom of the dais. He walked up the white marble steps, leant down, and scooped something up.

Seeing her standing there, he called, "Grab the other pitcher!"

She obediently picked up a vessel like his and climbed the steps. At the top was a round pool filled with crystal clear water, smelling of jasmine.

"Where are we? What is this place?"

Guy flung out his free hand. "We are on the Isle of Origin, and this is the great shrine!"

She blinked and gazed around, unable to comprehend it. The legends were true!

Then reality intruded. "Oh, Guy. My friend Jiana is dying! And Princess Sefira of Canteor is already dead." A stone settled on her heart, squeezing it. More tears flowed. "I couldn't save them! If only I had acted quickly, this wouldn't have happened."

Guy held up his silver pitcher. "This is the Water of Regeneration. It can even bring the dead back to life." He smiled encouragingly.

His belief was infectious. Hope welled in her middle.

He motioned and she dipped the pitcher in the pool. Cool drops splashed her as she righted it, filled to the brim.

"Let's save them!" He quickly descended the steps and strode toward the doors, Donella on his heels.

They rushed over the bridge to the stricken girls.

Guy poured most of his water over the princess before Andro figured out what he meant to do.

Laying his love on the ground, he heaved himself up. "What do you think you are doing?" Andro gripped Guy by his throat. "She is the royal heir to Canteor. Show her dead body some respect!"

Guy, unable to answer, met Donella's eyes, pleading.

"Stop! Andro, look at her! The Water of Regeneration is working!" Donella stared at Sefira, unable to believe her eyes.

The princess moved. Her eyes fluttered opened. Her hand touched her chest where the dagger had been.

Andro, seeing it, let go of Guy. He fell to his knees beside her. "Sefira! You live!" Shock and confusion chased across his face.

Donella tore her gaze from the sight as she suddenly recalled Jiana. She rushed to where her friend lay.

"Remove the knife!" she urged Gensard, who stared in awe at Sefira brought to life. Guy had her sipping the leftover water in his pitcher.

Gensard turned his head and stared at Donella in bewilderment. He swallowed as he reached for the weapon. Pausing, he glanced from the knife in Jiana's midsection to Donella.

"The water! The water will save Jiana! Hurry!"

With a pained expression, Gensard put his hand on the dagger. Clenching his jaw, he yanked it out. Blood spurt over his hand. He paled and looked ready to be sick.

Nudging him out of her way, Donella bent and poured the whole pitcher over Jiana's wound. Donella held her breath.

Within moments, color returned to her friend's face. Her breathing became regular. She opened her eyes and looked from one to the other. She sat up and touched the wound site.

Joy exploded in Donella's heart. And by the expression on Gensard's face, he felt the same. He embraced Jiana and held her tightly. "Sweetheart! You're well now! Everything is going to be alright." He mouthed 'thank you' to Donella.

A touch on her arm and Donella found herself in an embrace.

"You have no idea how glad I am to see you." Guy picked her up and swung her around. "I was so afraid you died that day!"

"I feared you were dead, too." Donella blushed, out of breath, as he set her down. He was grinning from ear to ear, as was she.

She studied his face. He looked more mature. She thought he had grown an inch or two. His normally straw-like, blond hair curled in the humidity. But his smile lit up his familiar brown eyes.

Before they could say more, Andro approached with Sefira leaning on his arm. "I don't know who you are, but thank you. Both of you." His stern mask of indifference was gone. Gratitude shone from his eyes. His face softened as he looked down at Sefira. "You have saved the one who means the world to me."

The princess blushed. She bit her lip as she addressed Donella. "Andro says you brought us here. You saved my life. I don't know what to say."

"I didn't save you. The water did."

Donella introduced Guy, and then Gensard, as he and Jiana joined the group. The prince struck a conversation with Sefira and Andro.

"Is your limp healed, too?" Donella wanted to know.

"No. But it doesn't matter. My heart and spirit are whole." Jiana smiled, her eyes sliding to Gensard.

Donella noticed Hazibal sitting nearby and held out a hand to him.

He was seemingly still in shock, whether from the trip through the portal, or the miraculous cures, or both, Donella didn't know. He slowly stood to his full height, leaving the cloak and waypost on the ground.

Guy glanced up at the giant as he overshadowed the group and blinked. Then he glanced down. His face changed when he saw the chunk of stone inscribed with the interlocking ovals. He turned his head and stared at Donella. His eyebrows rose.

She shrugged. "No wayposts in Canteor, you told me."

He barked with laughter. "I should have known you'd find an unusual way to get here." He took her hand and spoke to the others. "Come and eat and I'll tell you all about this place."

Holding Guy's hand, Donella walked with him past the main

shrine entrance along the right wall, the other five following close behind. The building glittered in the sun from the tiny glass chips embedded in its walls. The whole structure seemed to shimmer.

They entered a side door into a huge kitchen. A fireplace big enough for five men to stand in dominated one wall. Iron hooks and rusted spits were plenty enough to feed an army. Twelve-foot prepping counters stretched on either side of it, with shelves above stacked with hundreds of plates and mugs visible behind thick cobwebs. Six trestle tables thirty feet long with scarred sitting benches filled the rest of the space.

Guy introduced Barbu and Pellas. "They have been my companions since I washed up on an island after our separation."

Enri and Eliu were cooking stew in a giant pot. A savory smell wafted from it.

"I traveled with them aboard the ship *Diadem*." He pointed out the crew who lingered over bowls of food at the far end of the kitchen. The sailors sent a few stares their way.

Enri waved the arrivals to a nearby table. "Sit. There's plenty to eat." When Donella and her group and Guy and his two, new friends were seated, Enri came over with bowls of hot meat and vegetable stew, as well as warm rolls.

"I cannot believe I'm really on the Isle of Origin. How did you find this place?" Donella could hardly wait to hear Guy's tale.

"A holy hermit guided me." Guy motioned at an older man sitting at the crew's table. He strolled over and joined them.

"This is Ikonis. Until a few days ago, he had only one eye." Guy grinned at their shocked expressions.

"Start at the beginning. What happened after we stepped through the portal near Tilmuk?" Donella tore a piece from her roll and put it in her mouth. Adventure always made her hungry.

"I saw our destination—a waypost on a sand dune. We were almost there when lightning flashed and Prince Gensard and Odem's hands were ripped from my grip."

Donella scanned the group of men for a familiar face. "Where is Odem? I don't see him."

Guy frowned. "What do you mean? I thought he was with you."

Donella stopped, her spoon halfway to her mouth. "I haven't seen him since that day." She had imagined all this time that Odem was accompanying Guy. Fear for the man who was like a father to her settled in her stomach. She put down her spoon, appetite gone.

"It's okay. He can take care of himself." Guy reached over and gave her hand a squeeze.

She relaxed, knowing the soldier wayfarer was more than capable of finishing Reina Lauressa's mission by himself. Odem was a master spy and tactician. Guy was right. She had no need to worry about Odem.

She dug into her stew, joining the others in enjoying it.

Guy sat back, hands over his stomach, watching them eat. "I ended up on an empty beach of an uninhabited island. Making a raft, I sailed to Bidori, where the islanders helped me," Guy continued.

"That's where Pellas and I offered to join Guy," Barbu interrupted.

"But I couldn't sense a waypost at either place. In fact, my birthmark faded."

"What caused that?" Donella stopped chewing.

Guy rubbed his hand over his face. "I thought it was because I disobeyed the Guardian of Valdeor."

"Who?" Andro interrupted.

"He is a winged being whom I saw several times in a vision. He's the messenger of the One Who Fashioned All. The Guardian gave me the quest to find the Isle of Origin and shrine."

Andro gave Guy a strange look.

"I too have seen him. He guided me here once long ago," Ikonis chimed in. "But I was not allowed to come ashore at that time. Not until Guy found me. Now I am rewarded with both of my eyes for doing the Almighty Father's will.".

Flashing a look at Gensard, Andro asked, "You journeyed with these wizards. Don't tell me you've seen this Guardian as well, little brother?"

Stillness followed his words.

"Brother?!" the three girl's voices cried simultaneously. Donella, Jiana, and Sefira looked in amazement from one brother to the other.

"I thought you looked familiar!" Donella was the first to recover.

"You said you are the royal heir of Samarantha," Jiana turned her head to Gensard, her brow furrowed. "But how can that be if Andro is older?"

"I am confused." Sefira paled and put her hand to her cheek. She stared at Andro. "My wits are befuddled with all that's happened today. Gensard is a prince wearing Lord Paitar's slave collar? You are a prince, as well?"

When Andro looked sheepish, she exclaimed, "All this time you kept it from me. Why didn't you tell me?"

"I'm a prince without a country. My father banished me for opposing him." Andro's jaw clenched and his eyes hardened.

Sefira glanced from Andro to Gensard, who didn't contradict him.

"How do I address you? What is your true name?"

"Andro is short for Leandro, your language's version of my name."

"Well, it doesn't matter to me if you are exiled. A prince is a prince." She tossed her head. "I can twist my father around my finger. He'll come around to our marriage." She winked at Leander, resembling a cat with a bowl of cream. "Especially when I return from the dead! He'll fall all over me and promise me anything."

Leander's face softened as he gazed at her. He took her hand in his.

"Why, you're the brothers in the legend!" Jiana nearly jumped from her seat.

They all turned to her in surprise.

"You know, the descendants of the true king of Canteor. The one who left when his twin brother stole his throne." She clapped in delight. "You are destined to bring peace to Canteor."

"I don't know about that—" Leander began in a wry voice.

Sefira shushed him. "Yes! It all fits! Jiana is right. Bringing me here and saving my life will change the course of our history."

"What legend?" Gensard glanced from one to the other. "Please, Jiana. Enlighten those of us who don't know."

Jiana retold the story of the twin brothers both claiming the Canteor throne.

Gensard frowned, then slowly nodded at the end of the story. "I thought it curious that the ancient Samarantha language was so similar to modern Canteor. Our esteemed ancestor settled that region of Valdeor."

"Of course!" Sefira snapped her fingers. "We must bring some of the miracle water with us when we return. If my people can see the effect on me and others, they will believe in this god of yours—"

"The One Who Fashioned All," supplied Ikonis.

"Or I will pound anyone who still worships Panmin." Hazibal slapped a giant fist on the table, making the crockery jump. He suddenly squinted at Leander. "Don't you wear his mask?"

The prince blanched. "No, I'm done with that. No need to pound me, friend."

Donella giggled. His mask and scimitar still lay in the arena, left behind when he picked up Sefira.

"Our nations will be at peace!" Donella spread her hands, a large smile blooming on her face. She suddenly saw what the finding of the shrine could mean. "Not only the citizens of Valdeor, but of Canteor will come here on pilgrimages. The war between our nations can be averted."

Guy cleared his throat. "I've been thinking over this same thing for days. That is what the Guardian had intended with the quest. It was more important than the mission Reina Lauressa sent us on."

He glanced around, solemnly. "Not only can this save Canteor, but the islands I visited on my journey here, Bidori and Cressava and others."

He looked at them each in turn, his eyes crinkling, confidence pouring from him. "We can defeat their false worship of the sea god Makba, too."

"Or I will clobber them." Hazibal got in the last word.

30 Pilgrims

*W*hen Sefira decided she was ready to return home, they filled several waterskins with the healing waters.

Donella touched the broken stone Leander held. They would return it to Canteor. Indicating she had the palace image in her mind, Guy put his hand on her shoulder. He helped her bring it into focus over the long distance. With promises of letting them know how everything turned out, Sefira and Leander were enveloped in the swirling fog and disappeared.

At a later time, Guy and his friends learned what happened when they reappeared in Dabbori.

Finding themselves in the garden, Leander hid the stone where Donella had said she found it.

Sefira led the way into the palace. In the dining room, the magnificent buffet was untouched. It had only been hours since her "death."

They paused at the doorway of the throne room. Prince Pashmi slumped on his throne, his face drawn and dejected. His magnificent outfit was wrinkled, and his turban sat slightly askew. A scattering of guests whispered in solemn groups. Two foreigners, by their dress, stood before him, only their backs visible.

Her slippers tapped on the tile floors as she approached her father, Andro trailing behind.

Glancing up at the sound of her approach, Pashmi blanched. He put out a hand with an upraised palm. "A wraith!"

"Fear not, Father! It is I, your daughter Sefira." She came closer.

The foreigners moved to the side, giving everyone a clear view of the princess.

"But I saw you die! Everyone here saw it!" Pashmi indicated the courtiers who looked on with fearful and shocked expressions. "Where is that witch who whisked you away?"

"She saved my life! She is no witch, but someone called a waykeeper." Sefira knelt before her father. She reached out a hand. "Touch me. See how real I am."

Pashmi extended a shaking hand and put it on his daughter's head. His expression was one of incredulity. He stroked her cheek and seemed satisfied. "How is it you are alive?"

"The slave girl Donella took me to the Isle of Origin. When the Water of Regeneration at the shrine of the One Who Fashioned All touched my death wound, it healed me."

When Pashmi stubbornly insisted that the wound must not have been as bad as it seemed, Sefira took matters into her own hands. Standing up, she commanded her father's guards to bring two crippled beggars from the city gates.

By the time they returned with the beggars dressed in tattered rags, the throne room was packed. Word had spread like wildfire through the palace and beyond that the princess was alive, and all came to see the truth for themselves.

As Sefira took one of the waterskins from Leander and walked over to the first beggar, the murmuring died down as the audience held its breath.

A crippled man had a deformed arm. Sefira whispered words of comfort and poured some of the water on the afflicted arm. Within minutes, the man waved his straight and perfectly formed arm for everyone to see.

A gasp went up. People exclaimed. An expectant hush came over the room when a guard led the next beggar to her.

He had what looked like white scales on his eyes. He shook and cried in fear as the guard dragged him and dropped him at Sefira's feet. Up close, his putrid smell had her holding her breath. He wriggled and turned his head away when she tilted his chin up.

Leander stepped forward and clasped the man's head in his hands. "Trust us. The princess wants to give you your sight back."

The blind man stilled at Leander's words.

Sefira gently dribbled water on the man's sightless eyes. He blinked several times. His scales fell away and his blue eyes peered up at her astounded. He slowly stood and his gaze roamed around the room. Wonder and joy lit his face.

"I can see again!" He turned back toward Sefira. "Blessed be the princess!"

One of the ladies in waiting fainted. A female servant cried out, "A miracle!" then burst into tears.

Prince Pashmi stared at Sefira in amazement. "You astonish me, daughter! But I believe your story now." He motioned to his guards. "Take this man away." He indicated Leander.

Three guards surrounded Leander.

"Why, what has he done?" Sefira cried.

"He slew a guard in the arena after he lost the competition. I decree he be put to death along with the knife-wielder who nearly killed you." Pashmi's face wore a mulish expression.

"I command you to stop!" Sefira put herself in front of Leander and eyed the guards, who hesitated. She glared at her father. "He was instrumental in saving me. He is secretly a

prince."

Prince Pashmi put a hand to his head as if a headache was coming on. *"Your bodyguard is a prince? I don't believe it!"*

One of the foreigners stepped closer. He had a short, pointed beard and sharp brown eyes. He wore a black robe edged with geometric designs and a magistrate's medallion around his neck. *"Actually, Your Benevolence, I recognize him. He is Prince Leander, the elder son of Prince Xander of Samarantha. I should know because I was sent by Prince Xander as an envoy to your court."*

A fresh wave of shock went around the room.

The second foreigner bowed and addressed them. He was middle-aged, lean and muscular, having an air of a warrior. *"I, too, will swear that he is Prince Leander. I am Commander Odem, sent by Reina Lauressa of Valdeor, Your Highnesses. I met the prince many years ago."*

A smile spread across Sefira's face at the incontrovertible truth. *"Ah, yes. You traveled with Donella and Guy. I will tell you where they are when we are done here."*

Pashmi adjusted his turban. *"Very well. You established he is a prince. But I will still arrest him for killing a guard."*

Sefira crossed her arms. *"You are lucky he doesn't claim your throne."*

Angry murmuring went around the room at her statement. Another woman in the crowd fainted at her words.

"What is this, daughter? I indulge you too much!" His face was suffused with color, and a vein throbbed at his temple.

Sefira knew she mustn't push him too far. She knelt back at her father's feet. *"Let me explain."*

When he nodded stiffly, she stood and addressed the room. *"You have all heard the legend of the twin brothers who both claimed the throne. Yes?"*

Most nodded.

"The younger brother stole the inheritance of the older by claiming to be him. The real king sailed away and was never heard from." Scanning the faces of those present she paused dramatically. *"Until today."* She threw out her arm toward Leander. *"Andro, who you know as the champion gladiator Panmin, fought gallantly. You saw, he was winning the contest. No one has ever beaten him. But today you saw a younger man rip off his mask and disarm him. Who was he?"*

The audience was spellbound. Even Sefira's father leaned forward in his seat.

"Leander, who you know as Andro, was the best swordsman in all of Samarantha until he left in exile. His brother Prince Gensard over time became his equal. That is who defeated Andro.

"Just like the legend says: One day descendants of the true king shall return to Canteor. Brothers themselves, they shall return separately. Not recognizing the other, they shall engage in hand-to-hand battle. If one kills the other, the curse will continue. Only when they join forces, will they succeed in saving the kingdom. Then Canteor will know a time of peace, and culture will flourish."

She smiled. *"Andro, Prince Leander, has broken the curse. Plague and starvation will be a thing of the past."*

Two days later, Guy and Donella were cleaning the dormitories attached to the shrine when Guy felt a pricking sensation run down his spine. He felt a vibration as the portal opened and closed, alerting him to the portal's use.

He stopped in mid-sweep with his broom. "We have a visitor."

Donella paused in washing the window, a streak of dirt across her forehead. "Someone came through the portal?" She put down her rag in a bucket of soapy water as he nodded and propped the broom against the wall.

Their steps quickened as they approached the waypost and saw Odem gazing about. Tall and fit, yet he seemed to have more gray in his temples in the months since they last saw him.

After Donella hugged him and Guy shook his hand, they led him to the kitchen which had become their meeting place.

Prince Gensard and Jiana were washing and drying the myriad of plates and bowls in anticipation of pilgrims flocking to the shrine. Hazibal had removed Gensard's slave collar with his blacksmithing skills. Gensard wiped his hands and greeted Odem with a warrior's clasp, then introduced Jiana.

They left their task and joined the other three around one of the refectory tables. Jiana offered Odem an ale.

"Princess Sefira sent you a message." Odem smiled at Jiana as she served him. "She said to tell you that she accepted you and Donella as birthday gifts from Lady Beccah."

Jiana's shy smile was replaced by consternation. Donella gasped.

Chuckling at the expression on their faces, he held up a hand, palm out. "But not to worry. She set you both free."

Odem then launched into Sefira's return, as he had witnessed it, and later as she had recited all the details of the tale to him.

"A born storyteller, Sefira convinced everyone that Leander and Gensard were the brothers in the legend." Odem sipped his mug of ale.

"Did Prince Pashmi agree to their marriage?" Donella asked.

Guy wondered the same.

"I think it is a foregone conclusion." Odem smirked. "She can be very persuasive."

Donella and Jiana exchanged glances and nodded in unison.

"This morning, before she sent me on my way, the princess had her father gather all the citizens in the stadium again. She showed herself alive and healed more cripples in front of the tens of thousands gathered there. She already has many converts to the true faith. Her last words to me were that she planned to have the golden statue of Panmin melted down and made into coins. She said they would use the money to buy the freedom of all the slaves in Canteor."

Jiana put her hand to her mouth, tears gathering in her eyes. Gensard covered her other hand. Guy was unused to the prince's display of compassion. He had changed the most in the previous months.

After a pause, Guy and Donella asked simultaneously, "What happened to you?"

Odem chuckled. "You two haven't changed much. Still curious." The smile lines around his eyes crinkled.

Enri approached the table where they sat. He put down another brimming mug of ale. "A man gets mighty thirsty talking." He winked and strolled away.

Donella blushed. "We haven't offered you anything to eat. What terrible manners for waykeepers, known for their hospitality."

"The ale will do me." Odem lifted the mug and drank. He sat back. "That day on the cliff, I stepped into space with the rest of you. I saw a distant shore, when suddenly a blast of wind knocked me back. I opened my eyes and found myself at the starting site. When I realized I was alone, I feared the rest of you had fallen over the cliff. But looking over the edge, I didn't see any broken bodies on the rocks below. Taking no chances, I climbed down the cliff and searched for any sign of the three of you.

"As the tide turned, I had no choice but to give up my search. I walked back to Tulken Harbor. Retrieving Seeker, I spent the next morning re-searching the tide pools. When I deemed it futile, I returned to the palace." Odem rubbed his hand over his face. "Of course, Reina Lauressa was upset by the news. But then she divulged your quest, Guy. She was sure the Guardian of Valdeor had intervened. She said he explicitly forbade you to use the wayposts for war. She claimed it was her fault you tried."

"It was my own fault." Guy grimaced. "I knew it was wrong, but I used the portal to jump us to Canteor anyway. As a punishment, my birthmark nearly faded away. I couldn't sense any wayposts." He swallowed, remembering the weight of guilt that had settled in his gut for weeks. "I feared you all were dead because of my sin."

They reassured him that they had known the risks at the time.

"But how did you end up at Dabbori, Odem?" Donella wanted to know.

"Lauressa abandoned the idea of spying. She decided on formal negotiations. She sent me to Samarantha to enlist Prince Xander's help. She knew the kingdoms were distantly related. She hoped that with the kinship connection we two envoys could broker peace with Prince Pashmi.

"So we set sail about a month ago. And you know the rest." He glanced around the group. "Now it's your turn. What happened to you that day?"

And they told him.

Captain Anaru and all the crew, except Eliu, departed the day after Odem's arrival. They emptied the ship of all the supplies they could spare and promised to bring more.

Barbu departed with them, pledging help from his father. "We are good friends, no? You come and visit Bidori before you go back to your land of hard rain?"

"Of course, Barbu. I wouldn't leave without saying goodbye." Guy slapped the younger teen on the shoulder, eliciting Barbu's gleaming grin.

Hazibal chose to go with him, declaring he had always wanted to see the world. Ikonis went with them to bear witness of the One Who Fashioned All to all the islands.

Enri admitted he was the next in line for chieftain. He said he would bring word of the miracles to his subjects in Sikarta.

His nephew Yarto hadn't been seen since the day of his betrayal.

"I can't believe Yarto would turn on us. I'm certain Faro III had his mother killed." Enri had been distressed since he learned of Yarto's actions.

Guy stood on the shore with Enri waiting for the dinghy to return and ferry the rest of the men back to the *Diadem*.

Enri rubbed the back of his neck. "You know, I never felt he was my sister's son. The real Yarto had a scar on his neck from falling out of a tree. I convinced myself it could have faded after a dozen years. And he didn't look like either of his parents."

"His timing was interesting. I mean, he waited until we were ready to leave to contact you." Guy didn't know how to comfort his friend. In his own mind he wasn't convinced that Yarto was fake. "I thought someone was watching us that day. I bet Lemmo put him up to it. I think his act about being Ikonis' follower was to reassure us that he was trustworthy. I think he was going to ask to come along on the trip until I guessed his identity. So Lemmo recruited someone above suspicion."

Enri nodded. "I think the young man calling himself Yarto was Faro's spy. I fear my real nephew is dead. I will overturn every stone in Sikarta to learn the truth."

"I wish you the best of luck with that." Guy shook his hand as the dinghy drew nigh and the passengers prepared to depart.

Eliu, now strong and hale, held back. He declared he had no family and nowhere else to go. "If it's alright with you, I would like stay and be the cook and caretaker."

Guy gladly agreed.

Odem reported to Reina Lauressa, traveling through the

portal with Guy's guidance. Guy laid out a series of jumps for Odem to follow. Guy told him to announce the day Guy determined the shrine would be ready. Odem returned a few days later with her good wishes and desire to see it for herself. And he let Guy know the waykeepers would be ready on the day appointed. Then he used the portal to return to Canteor as the Reina's envoy.

Within two weeks the *Diadem* returned with three more ships, one from Bidori, one from Cressava, and one from Sikarta. The crews unloaded enough supplies for an army. They brought not only dried goods like flour, sugar, caffeine beans, and dried jerky, but also chickens, goats, and pigs.

In another month, the shrine was ready for pilgrims. Guy, Donella, Gensard, Jiana, Pellas, and Eliu had worked hard readying the buildings for an influx of visitors.

Once they finished all the preparations, Pellas chose to build a hermitage in the hills overlooking the shrine. Near enough to be at hand, yet far enough away for peaceful meditation. He claimed he needed to atone for his past life and so embarked on a life of penance.

On a fine morning, the day of the first pilgrimage dawned. At the time he appointed, Guy gathered Donella from the chicken house and Odem, who had recently come from Canteor, and they went to the waypost.

Guy sensed his old mentor reaching out to him as he touched the portal. As the aperture widened in the mist, it was as if he saw his bald mentor at the end of a long hallway. Each portal between them was like a series of doors in a dark corridor lit by starlight.

Guy could feel the other waykeepers' presence—Evodia at the portal beyond Usher's, and Brodyn even farther back at Mintala itself.

Finding the closest portal between Usher and himself at Cressava, he directed Donella to it. When she stepped through and activated it, Guy reached out with his mind for the portal between

Donella and Usher. He dispatched Odem to hold Bidori's portal open. In this way, the waykeepers made a chain, unlocking the wayposts from the islands, across the sea, to the palace of the Reina.

Each opening vibrated to its own frequency, and as they connected, waves of power intersected exponentially. The vibrations washed through Guy, setting his teeth on edge.

He signaled to his friends to be ready. Instead of allowing Reina Lauressa and Prince Alloryn to be disoriented multiple times, he decided to pull them across the vast space in one leap.

As they came closer, Guy's head pounded with the effort and sweat poured down his brow. Maybe this wasn't such a good idea. He feared if he stopped trying, the royal couple would be lost in the between place. His strength ebbed as his legs turned to jelly.

"Drink," a soft voice said at his ear. He felt a mug pressed to his lips. He took a gulp of refreshing water.

A cold trickle worked itself down his throat and into his chest. Energy rippled from his center to his fingers and toes. He absorbed the crashing vibrations, harmonizing them until they pulsed as one.

Reina Lauressa and Prince Alloryn stepped through the mist.

Guy collapsed, his breath coming as if he had run a race. Jiana stood beside him, a mug in her hand.

"I feared you were dying, so pale as you were."

Guy realized she had given him the Water of Regeneration to drink.

The prince held up his wife, white-faced. "She's fainting." Prince Alloryn rocked unsteadily on his feet. Gensard was suddenly there, gripping the prince's arm to steady him.

Jiana moved to Lauressa and held up the mug to her mouth. After a sip, her color returned, and she straightened.

She put a hand to her forehead. "Gyfar, what happened?" Lauressa's soft eyes held his.

A blush climbed up his neck and spread over his face. "I tried to bring you through with one leap. I thought it would be less disorienting. I guess I made it worse." He rubbed a hand over his face.

Alloryn scowled. "I think it better that you bring the rest of the retinue through one portal at a time."

Guy nodded, sheepishly.

A smile spread across the Reina's face. "Just being here, I feel more energized than I have since the birth of the twins."

Guy blinked, then grinned. "Twins? Wait until Donella hears that."

"I gave you the Water of Regeneration to drink." Jiana blushed in the presence of the Reina's attention.

Prince Gensard introduced Jiana as his fiancée and guided the royal visitors to the shrine.

The other waykeepers remained in place to let a line of peasants and beggars, soldiers and priests follow the royal couple, jumping through a portal and resting between jumps. It took two days for them to arrive.

All the waykeepers came with the final group.

Standing under a giant dragon's blood tree, Guy and Donella watched the last of the procession of worshipers cross the bridge.

"How does it feel, now, to be the Gifted One? You accomplished more than you set out to do." Donella twirled a piece of her hair around her finger.

"You are gifted, too. Don't you know that by now?" Guy's smile faded as he gazed seriously into her bright, blue eyes. "The One Who Fashioned All gives each of us talents to use in His service. From what you told me, you overcame great difficulties reaching the Isle of Origin. Your actions saved many lives, maybe a whole nation. Whereas I betrayed my calling." Guy flattened his lips.

Donella touched his arm. "The Guardian said you were

forgiven." She stared at the shrine, pensively. "My own faith wavered several times. Only Jiana's belief in me kept me going." She lowered her eyes and ran a hand down her skirt, as if she were embarrassed. "I imagined myself a spy, but my true calling is helping others and practicing charity."

Suddenly, her dimples peeped out. "But I couldn't have jumped here at all if I hadn't felt your presence tugging at me."

He put his hand over hers, nodding. "We are both blessed."

And so began a long series of pilgrims coming to the newfound shrine of the Water of Regeneration. Peoples from Valdeor and Canteor, as well as Nyrmidion and the other isles, streamed through the portals.

They were healed physically and spiritually, and eagerly returned home and spread the tale to their families, friends, and villages.

Canteor and Valdeor avoided a war and the two countries made treaties.

The waykeepers were no longer a forgotten and mysterious order. Applicants clamored to be trained in the way. Usher's fledgling academy soon burst at the seams.

And the One Who Fashioned All was honored as He ought to be.

Acknowledgments

This book couldn't have happened without the following: my editors Jacinta Patterson and Margie Cichoke; formatter Michelle M. Bruhn; cover designer Emily Anne Hickman; my sister Sue Peek who suggested I write a novel; and my husband Tom who told me to keep writing as long as I have stories to tell. And thanks to my readers who asked for more stories about Valdeor.

Author Bio

Sandra Hanley spent her childhood making up stories and illustrating them. An avid reader, she has devoured about 3000 books in many genres. She taught elementary school for eight years, and middle school for five. Her students know her as Miss Millovitsch. She has traveled to Europe, Australia and New Zealand, as well as through most of our beautiful states. She lives in beautiful northern Idaho with her husband. Her hobbies are painting, crocheting, reading, writing and dreaming up imaginary worlds.

Be sure to sign up for her newsletter at www.sandralenahanley.com for upcoming stories in the Valdeor Chronicles.

If you enjoyed this story, please consider helping the author by rating it on Amazon and Goodreads.